AF264798

Married by Michaelmas

A TRADITIONAL REGENCY ROMANCE

Kate Westwood

Published by Kate Westwood
www.katewestwood.net

ISBN: 978-0-6450494-4-2

Disclaimer

This is a work of fiction. Names, characters, places, organisations,
events, and incidents are either products of the author's
imagination or used fictitiously.

Books by Kate Westwood

A Scandal at Delford

Beauty and the Beast of Thornleigh

A Bath Affair

The Value of an Anne Elliot

Woodston

Married by Michaelmas

KATE WESTWOOD

Acknowledgements

Thank you very much to Cathy Walker at Cathy's Covers for yet another great cover design, to Kim Lambert at Dreamstone Publishing for formatting (and also for saying she thought it was 'a cute story', which is high praise from a very prolific and experienced writer), and to Eleanor Morrison for doing my social media... because I'm basically useless at it. Thanks everyone.

Dedicated to L, from a big stupid goober who loves you more

than you will know xx...x

Table of Contents

"'Tis safest in matrimony to begin with a little aversion."

—Richard Brinsley Sheridan, *The Rivals*, (1775)

Prologue

14 June, 1809

'Dearest Papa and Mama,

It pains me dreadfully to think of the alarm which this letter must inspire, but I write to say that I am not bound for Town as I led you believe yesterday, but I am gone away for a time and I cannot say where, for I don't want to be followed and made to marry Hart. He is very kind and everything he ought to be, but I cannot marry him, and I shall not be made to. I know you would neither of you wish me unhappy and such a union would certainly mean decided unhappiness for me. I cannot bear telling him in person, but I have written to him briefly and broken off the engagement. As it was not due to be announced officially until next week, I am sure that breaking the engagement will not bring any disrepute to Waverly, and I pray with all my heart that the affair will be forgotten quickly and that Hart might forgive my seeming capriciousness.

I know Hart will try to come to Waverly and dissuade me, but I have made up my mind. Therefore, I have decided to remove to a place which I cannot for now reveal, and where I may await certain events which are now unfolding, and which will decide if my future will be prosperous or not. More detail I cannot give at this moment. I am vastly contrite at having mislead you, but I could not take the chance of going my aunt in Hansford-place, as Hart would only come to me there and I have not the heart to face him and rebuff him directly. I beg you will understand my predicament.

I don't mean, dear Papa and Mama, to make you anxious for me, although I know you will be, but rest assured that I feel myself quite safe, and I shall think of you every day until I can return home. You will never find a more grateful and dutiful daughter, and know that I shall be humbly obliged to rely upon the kindness of strangers to supply that affection which I shall miss sorely by absenting myself thus from all my friends at Waverly.

Be not angry with me, I implore you both! By and by I shall know how to act, and I shall return to you just as surely your devoted daughter as I have left,
Louisa

Edgar Waverly, Earl of Loxford, removed his eyeglass and allowed it to hang from his maroon silk waistcoat, while Button, a silky tan and white cocker spaniel, sat at his feet.

'Can you believe it, Tabitha? Our poor Louisa, gone away in a fright of marrying! Not gone to her aunt after all! But if she don't want Rotherham, she needn't have run off to make a point! Why did she agree to his proposal in the first place? She might have declined him when he asked her last week, and saved herself the trouble! I suppose it is nothing but a lover's tiff.'

He was sitting heavily upon the sofa next to his wife, his oozing bulk threatening to engulf its other occupant, and gazed absently into the air above him, as if the answer to his daughter's strange behaviour were to be found in the dust particles suspended in the shafts of morning light coming through the drawing room windows.

Lady Loxford, a thin, angular, sharp-featured woman with a severe hair style under a lace cap, was as opposite her husband in manner as appearance. 'Decline him? I should think not! I am vexed, quite vexed with Louisa! Silly, ungrateful girl! Going away in a fuss! Who does she propose to have if not Rotherham? And he as rich as Midas! It is exceedingly vexing!'

'Yes, my love, exceedingly so,' agreed her husband placidly.

'With Waverly so impoverished, it is unthinkable that she would turn down such an opportunity to do her duty to us, and to our family.' Lady Loxford sighed and fanned herself rapidly, for although early, the day was already warm. In a sudden suspicion, she added, 'But perhaps her objection is because they will be so uneven in rank? He is not her equal, and she is sensible of it. Quite rightly so, too! He should be very lucky to get her — he has not even a knighthood, himself!'

'Quite so, my dear,' replied her husband agreeably, 'although I hardly think Lou sensitive to such things — she has never mentioned the difference before, and they have been friends for many years, you know! There are no true divisions between friends, surely! But my love, do not forget Rotherham is uncommonly wealthy, and besides boasting Hartley Park and a good lineage, the man possesses a great degree of consequence. He is hardly below her, even though it is true he is not a peer. We live in modern times, my dear. These days money supplies anything wanting to mark a gentleman's place in the world. A landed gent with money will always be respectable, even if he has no title.'

'But that is why I am so vexed with her! Rotherham possesses an exceeding degree of gentility and raised circumstance — she could do a deal worse — and at her dangerously advancing age! — she cannot afford to be nice at four-and-twenty! To think, she could be mistress of Hartley Park and ten thousand a year! They would dine in the best circles! She would be the envy of a veritable score of those females who have tried and failed to catch Rotherham. *They* have cared little for his not being titled! Why should she? His father was a Baronet! What a pity Rotherham could not inherit the title with the money... but even so, he has the air of one!'

'True, my love, true,' Loxford said complacently. 'I dare say it cannot be his lower rank which impedes the match. But I wonder what her objection is, then?'

'So do I, my love, so do I!'

'Well, well, poor Rotherham! It will be a blow to his pride I daresay. I have always thought well of the fellow. He has been acquainted with this family for so many years and passed so much of his childhood here, that I cannot but feel his humiliation. We have always looked upon Rotherham as one of us, have we not, my dear?'

'But that is nothing to the point, Loxford. If she won't have him, it is a low blow to ourselves, and to Waverly.' Lady Loxford had begun to dab at her eyes with a piece of embroidered fine linen. 'She *must* take him, she simply *must*! Where are my salts? I consider us to be quite abused, my dear! After all we have done for her! Naughty, rebellious girl! Turing him down, and after you being so good to Rotherham, despite his lower rank — remember how you wrote *such* a condescending letter to him when he wrote for permission to ask for her hand? And now it is all for nothing!' She sobbed into her handkerchief. 'She was to have been married by Michaelmas! Her future settled with so much convenience to ourselves, and to Waverly! It will not do!'

'Yes — indeed, my dear. But we cannot put ourselves, and this house — as much as Waverly is in need of assistance — before our daughter's happiness. I hold it a great error of judgement indeed to cling to these old-fashioned ideas of selling one's daughters off for pecuniary advantage!'

'Selling one's daughters? Pray don't be ridiculous, Loxford. It is Louisa's duty to us to preserve Waverly! Would she have us living in so lowered a circumstance as to bring shame to the family?'

Loxford patted her arm. 'Waverly is not yet in such reduced circumstances, Tabby, that we must fear poverty! We must simply apply some small economies, which we shall hardly notice, I am sure.'

Lady Loxford sighed. 'We would not have to be even thinking of such dreadful things as economies, if Louisa had not run off like this!'

'Now, Tabby, don't upset yourself!' He handed her the missing salts and patted her arm kindly. 'I expect she will get over whatever little tiff they have had and come back to us soon enough.'

His lady received the vial, took out the stopper and inhaled desperately. Her eyes watered. 'What if she does not? I always intended them for each other, you know! I expected him to ask for her hand when she came out eight years ago. I have always held it was the interference of his mother which prevented him marrying her immediately — such a jealous woman! She wanted Rotherham all to herself! Well! She ought to be glad that her son has his sights set on such a prize as Lady Louisa Waverly, daughter of the Earl of Loxford,' she finished bitterly.

'I cannot agree my dear. You know Rotherham was always averse to marriage — not the marrying type, and in singular enjoyment of his freedom. Can't blame the fellow's mother! But I hear Lady Rotherham is in very ill health,' added Loxford, mildly reproving. 'We must not speak badly of her, my dear, in case we live to regret harsh words.'

'And now that he has finally asked her, Louisa has decided to be missish and give us all this trouble! Ungrateful indeed! I am vexed, Loxford, vexed!' Lady Loxford, still watery-eyed from the effects of the salts, dabbed at her cheeks again.

Her husband, more puzzled than vexed himself, could not enter into his wife's unfeeling tirade. But he said as placatingly as he could, 'I quite agree, my love, but it won't do to be too harsh on Louisa, for she has never given us a jot of trouble from the day she was born. But it *is* a devil of a pickle for poor Rotherham! A broken engagement is just the sort of thing to bring a man down! And they were such good chums! I can't imagine what has gotten into her!'

'Nothing that a good box around the ear wouldn't solve,' replied his wife with offended zeal. 'Foolish girl! To turn down Rotherham, just like that, after accepting him! She must think herself very fine indeed, quite beyond the reach of the richest man in the county, to cut him as she has done. If she thinks herself above him, I cannot imagine who she thinks good enough for her! Does she set her sights on the Prince of Wales? The King of France?'

'Now, Tabby, don't be ridiculous. Our Louisa is a dear, good girl, not one to do something without sufficient reason, and if she says she cannot marry Rotherham, then I suppose she cannot. You would not wish her unhappy to please us, now would you?'

Lady Loxford made a noise of annoyance with her tongue. 'I don't see how marrying him would make her anything *but* happy! She would live in comfort at Hartley Park, want for nothing, and have his babies to give her occupation. I wanted for nothing more when I was her age.'

'But Lou has always been her own person, my dear. She was never conventional, you know. Perhaps she does not want babies! She has her painting and drawing, and you know that will keep her content enough!'

'*Not want babies!* Well, I never! The things you come out with, Loxford! I am sure your brain is addled! *Not want babies!*'

Lord Loxford sighed. His wife was prone to a little hysteria now and again, and he wished, not for the first time, that she was more like Louisa — calm, rational and easily content. He said as reasonably as he could, 'Young people these days, my dear, don't always want to be year after year abed with child. My poor sister Helena died giving birth to her seventh, you know! It is not always a good thing to marry and produce as many children as one can before one is too worn out to enjoy life. And I don't say her running off is due to her not wanting children. Perhaps it is that she don't wish to marry at all! She will have a little fortune once we are both gone; Waverly may be in straights just now, but the entailment won't be a hardship for Louisa, even if she doesn't marry. Her endowments will be sufficient to keep her tolerably well. She could go to live at Hansford place with your sister and spend her days painting those nice little pictures of hers. Or perhaps John will ask her to stay on when he inherits. Mary will like the company.'

'Yes, but we need the money *now*, Loxford! If Louisa could only marry Rotherham, just think how much that will benefit Waverly! Why, two months in a row I have been obliged to prevent Jones from paying the wine and tea merchants, just so I can pay for my fabric order from London!'

'Perhaps if you did not order such expensive fabrics, my love,' suggested her husband reasonably, 'we might afford to pay the wine and tea merchants.'

'Pray, stop talking at once! Where *do* you get these ridiculous notions? You are quite sending me into a flutter, Loxford, and you know how I suffer with my nerves. I feel the need for a cordial — or perhaps a small glass of sherry. Yes, that will calm me a little. Beecham! Beecham! Come here at once and pour me a *very* small glass of madeira. No, not *that* glass, it looks dirty to me. The large one will have to do!'

Poor Beecham fumbled, poured, and presently gave the drink

to her mistress, and too soon the glass was empty. 'Another.' Lady Loxford waved her hand and turned back to her husband. 'And what shall we say to Rotherham when he receives her letter? He will come here to make enquiries!'

'We can tell him nothing more than what she has already written us. He will want to know where she might have gone, and that intelligence is known only to Louisa, it seems!'

'There are surely few places she could have gone to, for she has no friends in the country, with John and Mary presently abroad.'

'Perhaps she has gone to your brother at Penniston?'

'But that is so far, I think she would not attempt such a journey alone. Besides, Edmund is so befuddled and ancient now that I wager he would not recognise her if she did turn up at his door.'

'And yet, she is so very fond of her uncle that perhaps she would attempt it — but then it is quite a journey, and I also doubt she would attempt it alone. Even with a maid to accompany her. You know Smithers is no traveller — remember when she accompanied us to Bath last year? Quite done in, very ill from the rocking and bumping!'

'But where else could she go? My sister would write us at once if she had gone to Hansford-place. Perhaps she has gone there after all, and deceives us? I must write them at once! Foolish girl! To decline Rotherham, in a fit of scatterbrain, and run away! He must not find out that she has run off! Then he will give up and never try to win her back! No, my dear, think! We must tell him that she is taken by a fright of bashful modesty, and all she needs is a little time to come around. We shall say that she has gone to a friend and will soon return. That will give you time to discover where she is hiding and bring her home.'

Loxford, like his daughter, for all his placid and easy-going nature, had a strength of character which he found himself called upon to exercise on rare occasions. He summoned it now. 'Tabby,' he said in warning tones, 'do not think of it! I shall not force Louisa to marry anyone if she does not want to. Lord knows what Rotherham will do — if he has his heart set on marrying, and Lou won't oblige him after all, then he will have to find another bride, or his mother can. Lady Rotherham has the most comprehensive set of acquaintances in the whole county! She will find him someone else, that is all there is to it. Poor fellow will be dashed, but a man's heart mends more quickly than a woman's, you know. I suspect his pride will be the worst off. He will move on, and there will be an end to the whole affair.'

Lady Loxford was forlorn. 'Still, it seems a pity he should waste his money on a family who does not need it as we do. You simply *must* find Louisa and tell her she has a duty to marry Rotherham!'

'That is something which, even if I desired it, I could not do, my love, for I have simply no idea where she has gone. I shall write to Penniston, of course, and enquire there, and you may write to your sister in town, but I cannot see her going to either household.'

'Indeed! Penniston is too far; she would not travel such a distance, I dare say, and she has already declared her intention to avoid town! Perhaps she has gone to town after all and thinks she will conceal herself at Hansford-place? Well! Amelia shall certainly give her a stern lecture when she discovers what her niece has given up!'

'My dear, you may write your sister of course, but I doubt Lou has gone to town when she has already admitted fears of Rotherham's pursuit. Even if we find her, however, I shall not force her to marry Rotherham. There is nothing for it but we must wait and let the young people sort out the matter themselves.'

At Lord Loxford's feet, poor Button sighed and settled against his master's feet. He did not like it when his mistress was away, and he hoped she would not be long. Loxford was kind to him, but Louisa was the only one who would throw his sticks and feed him tidbits from the table. He sat up and scratched his ear with his paw then settled again, closing his eyes. There was nothing for it but to sleep much as he could until his mistress returned to Waverly!

When Rotherham jumped nimbly from his carriage outside the front door of Hartley Park, he was met in state by his aging valet and confidante, Wilkes. Wilkes had been in service at Hartley Park since Rotherham was in knee-breeches, and Rotherham had come to look upon the older man as a trusted confidante, as well as a loyal friend. Now this illustrious fellow had been watching for his master's arrival for some half an hour, and when he spied the carriage come through the gates, he slipped from the hall, closed the large front door behind him, and hastened with a surprising agility to meet his master as he alighted from the vehicle.

'Good morning, Sir.' The valet's expression was as dignified as ever, but there was an expression of abject sympathy upon his visage, which did not go unobserved by Rotherham.

'Good heavens, man,' he greeted Wilkes doubtfully, 'you do look glum! Never tell me my mother has taken a turn? I left her in pretty good form only twenty-four hours ago!'

'Worse, Sir,' intoned Wilkes mournfully. His silver whiskers shook as if in silent sympathy for his master. 'Lady Forster and her daughter have been here these last two hours. I thought you ought to know, so that you may take any necessary... evasive action, Sir.'

The ancient blue eyes watered, and Rotherham was hard pressed to know if this was due to Wilke's usual cataract problems, or to deep sympathy over the bad news he had just imparted.

'Ha! Is that so?' he asked in mild amusement. 'That fripperied-up daughter-dangler at it again, is she? Well, don't worry, Wilkes — my mother may be planning to leave this world but you know she has a backbone of steel and a hearty dislike for Lady Forster and her daughter. United, they may do much. Besides, once Miss Forster discovers I have already made an offer to Lady Louisa Waverly, I suspect they will the both of them give up the scheme. Poor Miss Forster will be so out of sorts that Lady Rotherham will be quite amused by it all. I only hope Lady Forster has not been taxing my mother's strength too much. She seems always to contrive to be here on some errand or other.'

He strode to the front door and Wilkes only just managed, by dint of a short burst of speed and a great deal of pride, to precede him in order to open it, much to the annoyance of Burns, the butler.

Having now regained his dignity, the valet held out his hands and took his master's coat and gloves. 'I believe it may the other way around, Sir,' he remarked, poker-faced. 'Your mother has had Lady Forster in the garden for over an hour, in the hot sun, cutting roses. I believe Lady Forster is quite done in,' he added in satisfied tones. 'Did you find the young lady at home, Sir?'

Being Rotherham's confidante, Wilkes had already been apprised of the letter his master had received yesterday from Lady Louisa Waverly. Rotherham had left strict instructions not to inform Lady Rotherham of the sudden news that his intended had up and fled the scene of her short-lived triumph, knowing his mother would be most upset at her favourite scheme going awry so quickly. But Rotherham knew he now had no choice but to inform his mother of the disappearance of Lady Louisa.

'No, I did not,' replied Rotherham, momentarily grave. 'Loxford was most puzzled, and declares his daughter has given them no intelligence of her whereabouts, nor a reason for her sudden change of mind. This is rather a blight on Mama's plans, however, Wilkes. I believe she will not take the news well. I hope she does not give in to Lady Forster and attempt to marry me off to Miss Jane Forster in lieu of Lady Louisa! I'd as soon marry the poker beside the drawing room fireplace!' he added dryly.

Wilkes withheld a dignified snicker, and merely let his eyes water in pleasure. 'Certainly, Sir. I cannot fault your taste. The lady is rather — stiff, Sir!'

'Stiff! She resembles a marble bust, man, with a heart of granite to match! She is much too bland and chilly to suit me! Give me a warm temper, and an argumentative tongue over a silent one! I'd rather have too much character than none at all!'

'Mr Reynolds might suit the lady better, Sir? Or Mr Lionel Edmonton, perhaps,' supplied Wilkes helpfully. He did not wish to see his master married to the likes of Miss Forster; it would auger very ill for his comfort at Hartley Park if such a mistress were ever to disturb its corridors with her chilly reserve and stony countenance. With such a one in charge of his comforts, which he had, he thought with some quite reasonable jealousy, earned by dint of a thousand services to a family whom he had long held in high regard, and a loyalty which the younger generation were apt to regard lightly, his final years of service would be miserable indeed.

Rotherham laughed. 'Reynolds, is it? That stuffed waistcoat who dined here last week? I collect they *would* suit each other! Well, don't worry yourself, Wilkes, I have no intention of marrying Miss Forster. Reynolds can have her, as far as I regard it, or Edmonton. Aye, the lady will be an interesting challenge for young Lionel's ardour, I collect. I cannot account for his taste, but it's true he's been casting his line for that fish for months — well, he can wed the granite maiden and bed her too; however, he'd better mind she don't break his tackle in the process!'

Wilkes restricted himself to a slight choking smirk, and murmured, 'Very good Sir. Shall I take you up?'

'Don't bother,' exclaimed Rotherham, halfway to the grand staircase already, 'I shall surprise the old ba— er, Lady Forster. Only do have some spruce beer sent up, there's a good chap; I despise taking tea after ten o'clock as you know!' He was bounding up the stairs in his gleaming black Hessians before Wilkes could put forth his usual sallies regarding the evils of spruce beer over the most English of traditions.

At the drawing room door, Rotherham paused. Voices issued from within.

'...concern over my happiness at this time is gratifying, Sylvia. I can tell you that if I live to see him suitably married, I shall be satisfied,' said one voice, quite firmly. 'However, you know Hart has his own ideas on matrimony, or he has had, until my illness. However, I fancy I may soon be the most content of mothers.'

There was satisfaction in his mother's tone, and Rotherham, outside the door, regretted that he must soon enough break the news of his fiancé's untoward escape. But another voice now replied to the first.

'Rotherham has always been averse to the female sex, it is true; but he *must* do his duty now, Lady Rotherham, and to fulfil what will be, perhaps, a mother's final wish — and we all hope that is not the case, my dear friend! — but as to that, I daresay he is dutiful enough to see you with an heir before your health deteriorates further.'

There was pregnant silence as the two females each manoeuvred around the matter which was unspoken. Lady Forster had not been idle in making a great deal of fuss over Lady Rotherham, now that it was public knowledge than she sought a wife for her son, and her visits to her 'dear, dear friend', with her eligible daughter in tow, had increased with the deterioration of Lady Rotherham's health.

Rotherham, outside the door, let out a little snort of derision. He was under no misapprehensions that the lady was dangling her daughter for all she was worth, not realizing that Lady Rotherham had already privately declared her wishes to her son — that he should offer for Lady Louisa Waverly — and two days previously had congratulated him on his winning suit.

Rotherham, having no other candidate in mind, and no particular desire to marry, other than to grant his mother's dying wish, had conceded that if he was to do his duty finally and produce an heir, he might do worse than Lou. She had always been Lady Rotherham's choice for him, and he was not the kind of man to dismiss a mother's fondest wishes. Sensible of his duty to his one remaining parent, he had duly offered, Louisa had accepted, and Lady Rotherham had been made a most happy creature indeed, although she had only reluctantly conceded to keep the engagement quiet for a few days, which had been Louisa's only proviso. But Lady Forster, not privy to this new development of a runaway fiancé, was still trying with the most admirable effort, for her daughter.

No word from the cold Miss Jane Forster yet, but behind the door, Rotherham could almost hear the young lady's mind clicking and whirring as various cogs and wheels worked themselves into position as she sat quietly while her mama manoeuvred and contrived on her behalf.

But Lady Forster was continuing to fish for information. 'I daresay you have *some* idea who might be the lady of choice? Miss Abigail Sanderson, perhaps? Or... Lady Louisa Waverly? She and your son have always been great friends...? Of course, Loxford is of excellent stock but mighty poor, I heard, and besides that Lady Louisa is no oil painting — not as pretty as Jane, of course — I have always held that a handsome man had better not to marry an inferior woman, for he will always be judged wanting taste, however much attachment may have driven him to it. Do you suppose your son *much* attached to Lady Louisa?'

'I can hardly say,' replied the other voice, and Rotherham, listening at the door, was not sure if his mother was provoked or amused or both.

Lady Forster, however, did not appear to notice and was continuing. 'But I daresay Rotherham has as much taste as will make him the envy of society, for with his looks and his position he may procure only the prettiest of wives as befits the Rotherham family. Do not you think it his wisest course, Lady Rotherham?'

With the notion of giving his mother the satisfaction of not having to respond to this most archaeological line of questioning, Rotherham adjusted his cravat, planted a most innocent look on his face, and opened the door.

The three women sat before the windows, a tray of tea and refreshments before them on a low table. All turned their heads at his arrival, and his mother, reclining upon a couch dressed in a very fine loose gown of pale pink spotted muslin, upon spying him, exclaimed, 'Hart! I thought you gone away until dinner time! Lady Forster and her daughter are come to sit with me, as you see!'

Lady Forster joined her welcome. 'Yes, do come and sit beside dear Jane, Mr Rotherham, for I am sure she is tired of the conversation of two silly old ladies by now!'

He almost laughed as he bent to bow politely to the visitors. Lady Forster always amused him with her frothy creations, all lace and ruffle and silly caps, whereas Miss Jane Forster's manner of dress bore a strong resemblance to her character, in that both were insubstantial enough to be seen through immediately. She did not disappoint him now, for she had on the finest sheer muslin dress, through which, in the right lighting, her admirable figure could be seen to advantage.

Above this, a deep neckline showed two round, white mounds very enticingly. She was tolerably handsome, he owned as he bowed in her direction, and at little more than one-and-twenty, a perfect prospect for marriage, if he had been so inclined. But her eyes held too much of hardness to be called pretty. She was, he thought, quite a creature, if one had a fancy for alabaster and ice.

'Lady Forster, Miss Forster, how do you do?' He bent to kiss his mother on the cheek, then to Lady Forster's not quite concealed irritation, sat himself comfortably beside Lady Rotherham on the chaise. 'Wilkes tells me you were cutting roses in the garden this morning, Mama. You must not overdo things, you know.' He patted her hand. 'You look a little peaked.'

Now Miss Forster, suddenly jolted into animation in the presence of her mother's favourite prospect for her, interjected composedly, 'We were cutting roses for Lady Rotherham, and since she was resting in the shade, I don't suppose any harm was done. We wondered where you had gone, Mr Rotherham. Your mother seems not to know anything about it but told us you had gone off very suddenly yesterday.'

Three pairs of enquiring eyes fixed him pointedly, but he was unmoved. 'Indeed, I did not tell Mama where I was going, which was the very reason she could not tell you,' he supplied amiably.

Lady Forster gave him a strained laugh. 'Aren't you the coy one, then, Mr Rotherham! But a gentleman's business is his own, I suppose. Lord, you needn't tell *us* why you go rushing about here and there, is that not so Jane? I suppose it is some important business or other. You men always have *something* important to do, it seems! But I do hope you will pity your dear mother and stop teasing her with your secrets!'

'Indeed, I do pity her, Lady Forster,' he replied cheerfully, 'for she has the most wayward son and no daughters to keep her company when I am not home. How kind of you to call in, however!'

Now the spruce beer was brought in and he partook of it standing in the corner by the windows, while the ladies finished their tea. Every now and then Lady Forster directed some little comment to him, to which he was civil enough to make a brief reply, but as soon as his glass was a second time emptied, he replaced it on the tray and said, 'Mama, I only called in to see how you were, and regret that I am called away again shortly. I shall be home for dinner, however, and we shall have a very cosy evening together.'

He left the two Forster females looking after him, wistfully, he fancied, and when he came in later for dinner, was gratified to find his mother alone. He joined her in her own room, where the servant had set a table for two. His mother, usually finding herself in a weakened state by the end of the day, sat among pillows and half reclined for her meal. When they were finished, he waited for coffee to be brought. Now he was able to break the news to her of Louisa's letter, and the reason for his subsequent hurried departure for Waverly.

When he finished his brief explanation, Lady Rotherham sighed heavily. 'My son, I shall not live much longer than perhaps a few months, and if I live that long, it is only to see you happily married, and a prospective heir to Hartley Park likely to bless these halls. You know I have set my sights on Louisa Waverly for you; I would be very much disappointed if you do not bring her home to me here. You know I have intended you to have her for some time.' She paused, then said thoughtfully, 'Lady Louisa is, I concede, a singular sort of girl, with her penchant for painting as if all the world depended on it, not to mention her rather spoiled upbringing. Her father's fault — give a horse its head and you spoil it! But for all that, she's as unaffected and sensible a girl as I have met with; certainly she is of as good a breeding as would befit your position, and any heir of yours would be no disgrace to Hartley Park.'

'Yes Mama, but if Lou will not have me, what would you have me do? She's as good as disappeared, whether in a fright of me particularly, or of matrimony in general, I have no notion. But I cannot force her to marry me.'

Lady Rotherham sighed. 'If you had chosen to marry someone else before now, or had shown the slightest interest in any female of good birth, that would be a different thing indeed; but you have been as averse to the idea of matrimony as any confirmed bachelor could be, and that is why I must assert what little authority I have now, and beg you, give me an heir, or at least the promise of an heir, before my time runs out.' Lady Rotherham was not prone to fits of emotion, and she did not give him one now. She spoke with firmness, rather than with any overblown sensibility. 'If Louisa Waverly has truly rejected you, then choose another female — I shall not make any more dictates as to whom — so long as she is fit to be mother to the heir of Hartley Park.'

Rotherham took her hand. 'Mama, I know Lou is your choice for me, but if she cannot be found, or won't marry me even after I find her, then I have no choice but to disappoint you — as much as it gives me pain to say it. You know I have never found anyone who I wish to spend my whole life with, and unless that person is still waiting in my future, I cannot guarantee that I will marry at all.'

Lady Rotherham fell back onto her cushions and closed her eyes. Rotherham noted the paleness of her complexion and rung the bell for the servant and requested that her laudanum be brought in with some hot water. When it had been brought in and the girl gone away again, his mother sat up, aided by Rotherham's strong arms, and took her draught.

Lying back down, she sighed.

'Then you will not fulfill the last wish of a dying woman?'

Her tone was not bitter, but all the same Rotherham felt the sting of guilt which occasionally struck him when he remembered his situation. 'Mama, Lady Louisa Waverly is the closest I have come to being content with the notion of tying myself to another person for the rest of my life. It might have worked, since we are such good friends to begin with. But I cannot force her to marry me, and I will not.' He squeezed her hand. 'But I *will* undertake to find Lou, and see if I cannot fathom her sudden refusal. I own I am in some anxiety for her, since we are good friends, even if we are not after all destined for each other.'

'Then that is all I can ask,' sighed Lady Rotherham. 'You must judge between your duties to Hartley and myself, and your own calling. If not Louisa, then perhaps you can find someone agreeable to suit your overnice taste after all. So long as you do not bring me someone of inferior birth or common descent, nor anyone as ridiculous as that Mrs Forster's climbing daughter, whom we both know possesses not an ounce of real character in her soul, and knows you so little that she thinks wearing flimsy gowns is the means to Hartley Rotherham's heart and purse!'

Rotherham could hardly make a reply to this assessment which would be fit for his mother's tender ears, but he was grateful that she had not tried to get him to make up to the marble-hearted Miss Forster. He would as soon marry a dragon-tongued wash-woman than to marry Jane Forster!

He would try to find Louisa, but even if he was to discover her whereabouts, he held little hope of changing her mind, for although Louisa Waverly was quiet by nature, he had always known her to be a person of the staunchest character when it was necessary! But as for replacing Louisa with another — well, he would vouchsafe to say it was the most unlikely event, for if he had reached the ripe age of eight-and-thirty without meeting one single female whom he felt he could shackle himself to, it was unlikely that he would stumble across someone in the next few months!

The carriage bounced and jiggled and wove its long-suffering way along the rather stony road which led into the village of Longstoke, in Derbyshire. Its occupants, a pretty, ebony-haired female of around seventeen years, and a slightly older woman in a dull brown patterned travelling cloak, jolted along as long-sufferingly as did their vehicle. The younger of the pair was dressed in a stylish rose silk gown and pretty silver-grey travelling cloak. The other female, dressed in a plain bonnet of the same hue as her faded brown cloak, was as humbly clothed as the other woman was not, although the lady could not be called unhandsome with her burnished chestnut hair, pert nose and liquid brown eyes. At any rate, both of them were equally silent and had been for some time, each taking full charge of the window closest to them to inspect the countryside into which they had ventured.

Presently, the young woman remarked inelegantly, 'I am so excessively fagged! Are we never to arrive? Johns must bait the horses very soon, and I must bait with them or I shall not be able to move out of this carriage for weariness!'

'I believe we must be coming upon Longstoke just now, Alice dear. A little further and we shall arrive at the inn and order up a good dinner. And pray don't say you are "fagged", my love. It is such a vulgar expression.' The older woman's tone, while gentle, was that which belongs to a female much used to admonishing the young. That tone was not lost on its recipient.

'Yes, Miss Spinner.' Miss Alice Featherstone shifted in her seat and fidgeted a little with her bonnet, which was laid upon her lap. 'You are certain we are breaking our journey at the George? I am in a little anxiety about it — I would not like there to be any mistake?'

'Why should you be in anxiety about such a trifling detail? — but yes, I believe it is the George where we are to overnight. Why on earth would it matter?'

'Oh,' replied Miss Featherstone quickly, 'only that I believe it is the only inn fit for ladies — I believe the other one here, the Bull, is quite shockingly incommodious and you know how I dislike being squeezed in as we were last night!'

'It was not as bad as all that,' laughed Miss Spinner. 'I thought the Crown was altogether not so bad — it was cosy and clean!'

'Cosy, you call it! That is a new way to say 'cramped', I collect! Now I do hope they have a private parlour at the posting house. I so detest a public parlour! And I would very much like a room to myself tonight, if it is not offensive to you; I am old enough to fetch for myself you know!'

Miss Spinner looked her doubt. 'Your father—'

'Pshaw!' remarked Miss Featherstone with eloquence.

Miss Spinner merely smiled placidly and returned her gaze back to the view from her window.

Her charge, observing her governess's implacable immovability, added goadingly, 'Papa thinks I am still a child!' She was finally rewarded with a reaction.

'Quite. But nevertheless, I have been commissioned with delivering you safely to your aunt's, and I take my duty seriously.' Miss Spinner was composed, for she was used to the ways of her charge.

Alice, fulminating quietly, eyed her foe sideways, and said nothing else. But the little rose-bud lips firmed. She directed her glance back to the scenes which were now passing rapidly from countryside to cottages and from there to shops, people and carriages going in the opposite direction, and quite soon they were slackening their pace and entering a busy courtyard in which boys and men bustled, gentlefolk stepped up and down, into and out of carriages, and horses were being led to and from carriage traces.

To leave the hot, airless vehicle and breathe in cool fresh air was the object of both women and they were only a moment in eagerly stepping from the carriage and exercising their liberties by stretching and walking a few steps. Several hat boxes and trunks were being removed from the carriage behind them. The post-boy who had taken up their hat boxes, however, was clumsy enough to trip over and the only one of Miss Spinner's modest bonnets which she could in all truth call 'best' was inadvertently tipped out onto the ground. The lad had picked himself up and begun to stammer his apologies but at this moment, just as both Miss Spinner and the lad had reached down to pick up the bonnet, they had leapt back in alarm, for right in the middle of the bonnet's dull beige cambric-and-straw centre had appeared a horse's hoof, stomping firmly on the hat. Just as suddenly, the hoof released its straw prisoner, and moved a few steps onwards.

'Whoa there, Fitz! What have you done, boy?' This was the masculine comment which came somewhere from the air above the two women.

Miss Spinner in the meantime had not been able to prevent herself crying out in surprise, and even Miss Featherstone had exclaimed brightly, 'Oh, goodness me!'

The offending steed had now stepped sideways, much to the clever handling of its rider, and the two women raised their eyes upward in time to observe a dark-haired gentleman in a fine, blue long-tailed riding jacket, shining black hessians, and tall dark hat dismount his ride and step over to them.

'My profuse apologies, ladies. I had not seen the bonnet there. I am very much afraid it is ruined! And it is all my own fault.' He bent to retrieve the dirty scrap as they looked on speechlessly. Dusting it off, he exclaimed in a low tone, 'Shocking ill manners me of me I am afraid. Not at all looking where I was going. And Fitz usually never treats ladies in such a way. I don't know what got into him. We are both as contrite as could be!' He removed his hat and gave them a polite bow. 'Hartley Rotherham, at your service!'

The smile which he directed at Miss Spinner had the effect of rendering her momentarily inarticulate, but Alice had boldly stepped forward and taken the bonnet which Miss Spinner had not had the wherewithal to accept. 'I am sure we can get my governess another, Sir. One bonnet is the same as the next, when they are all brown-coloured and hardly trimmed at all!' she said wisely. 'Unless it was a very favourite bonnet, Miss Spinner? But I collect it cannot have been for I have hardly seen you in it all summer excepting at church!'

Miss Spinner had by now commanded her nerves again and said composedly, 'It is nothing, Sir. As my charge has explained, one brown bonnet is as the next and it is not a particular favourite of mine. It is fortunate, Sir, that my entire year's wages were not wasted on the purchase of it, or I would be sorrier even than you are!'

'Fortunate indeed!' laughed he. 'But, even so, it was perhaps one of your better ones? I perceive the quality of the fabric is not poor. Then the loss of it would be hard, indeed — even more so to a governess for whom income must always be considered when ordering a new hat.'

'It *was* my best bonnet,' she conceded with a slight smile, 'but is not the word 'best' quite objective? Had Miss Featherstone's 'best' bonnet fallen to the same fate, I collect it would have been a worse tragedy!'

Now the gentleman laughed, and said in easy tones, 'Yes, I see that it would have! Miss Featherstone's bonnet is very fine indeed. But I am glad to find that the words 'best' and 'favourite' in this case are not interchangeable, or I would not have easily forgiven myself. Still, I am dreadfully sorry to have squashed your 'best' bonnet, Miss... Miss Spinner? I will undertake to recompense you for my thoughtless ways, if you will allow me to pay for the damage.' He had already begun to pull out his pocket-book and extract from its leather depths notes enough to buy several bonnets.

Miss Spinner shook her head in alarm and waved his money away. 'Indeed, it really is nothing,' she replied, colouring a little. 'The bonnet was the gift of an acquaintance and therein lay its modest value. And although it was my best Sunday bonnet, I can hardly in truth claim that it had any more value than a few ha'pennies. I have now the perfect opportunity to replace it with a much better one than before, at no great expense to myself I assure you.'

Alice, who had been unashamedly listening in now cried, 'Oh yes, do buy another, but nothing more in brown, I beg you! The most detestable colour for a female, I think! Don't you agree, Sir?' She turned beseeching eyes upon the gentleman.

'Certainly,' he agreed obligingly. 'A most detestable colour indeed!'

'Only think, Sir,' continued Alice artlessly, 'that Miss Spinner only has three bonnets and all of them in various shades of brown!

It was a blessing in disguise to have that wretched, ugly old thing ruined! Oh, I don't mean to say it was so dreadfully ugly, Miss Spinner, but now you might have a pretty, charming bonnet for Sundays! Would not you prefer it above all things?'

'Yes,' echoed the gentleman, smiling with Alice, 'would you not like a new, pretty bonnet? Perhaps you might even please Miss Featherstone and go so far as to look for something in emerald-green, or coquelicot; I hear coquelicot is all the rage in town this season!'

His eye twinkled and she knew he was laughing at her. She set her lips in a firm line and addressed her young companion. 'Although I cannot profess to set the same store by fashion as you do, Alice dear, it seems providence has supplied the opportunity for change.' She turned to the gentleman. 'But I shall not need to accept your money, Sir; I am quite able to manage the purchase of a new bonnet myself. I am not quite in as dire circumstances as Miss Featherstone would have you believe. Thank you all the same,' she bristled primly.

The gentleman laughed. 'I can see that you are quite an independent female, Miss Spinner. I honour your pride. I would not think of offending you, and therefore I shall not offer again. But I perceive your object, and it is quite wicked of you.'

Miss Spinner was all astonishment. 'I assure you, Sir, that there is no ulterior motive, simply a wish to see to the purchase of my own bonnet!'

'No, no, I see it clearly! I was the means of ruining your hat, and now you see an opportunity to put me solely in your power by having me beholden to you! Well, it is not very Christian of you, but I must bear the burden as well as I can. I shall, for the rest of my life, be at your service. Again, my profuse apologies to give so much trouble, and Fitz here is very sorry, too.' His horse whinnied at this moment, giving all the appearance that the two were perfectly united in a scheme to give as much embarrassment to Miss Spinner as possible!

She did not know whether to be vexed or amused. She repressed a smile and said more sternly than she wanted to, 'Neither you nor your horse need consider yourself in my service; indeed, I shall have quite forgotten the incident by the time I go to bed! But I see you were just leaving. We must not detain you. Good day, Sir. I thank you for your concern. Come Alice, we must order dinner and unpack. Good day, Sir!'

She led Alice away, who was looking backward after the gentleman, who in turn was still standing where they had left him, watching them retreat.

'Hartley Rotherham,' Alice mused aloud. 'Isn't he the one who...?' But Miss Spinner had already disappeared into the depths of the tavern and she followed hastily. Soon they were too busy ordering dinner and setting about getting a room to think any more on the ruined bonnet and the gentleman who had ridden his horse right over it without stopping!

It was soon ascertained to Alice's satisfaction that not only were they to be provided a private parlour, procured with the addition of a little encouragement from the sum of money Sir George, her employer, had entrusted Miss Spinner with on their departure, but they were to have separate rooms after all!

'How terribly unfortunate that the only room they had left was fit only for one person!' Alice said happily as they sat down in the little parlour to await their meal. 'But it is likely for the best! I do not mean to say that I dislike sharing a room, Miss Spinner, but I slept so ill last night that I am sure to keep you awake with my snoring tonight and you know what a light sleeper you are! I would not like to be inconsiderate!'

'You are all consideration and sacrifice, my dear,' replied Miss Spinner with laugh. 'Oh, yes, I am fortunate indeed! I shall have a whole dressing room closet, all to myself!'

Alice was not as thoughtless as not to suffer some guilt at this remark. 'Well, I collect it is rather a small room, but that cot looked quite cosy, and you always say you do not mind a small quarters. But if you wish to exchange, I daresay I can bear it—' She trailed off, in some alarm of an unexpected acquiescence, but all was well.

'No, I am quite content, dear.' Miss Spinner shook her head. 'I will not exchange rooms with you. After all, your father's money is to be used ultimately for your own comfort, I am sure, rather than mine. I shall be quite well off, I think. But I do take my duty seriously, and only once I have you safe and sound at Cromford with your aunt, shall I truly be content.'

Alice did not say anything to this, and Miss Spinner ventured with some sensitivity, 'I hope, my dear, that you do not think too often of Mr Deed? Charles is a good lad, but you know you cannot hope that your father will sanction a union. You are so young — perhaps another gentleman may, in time, catch your eye—'

'Pray stop, do! I do not wish to talk on it, it will only vex me. It is not my fault that my father and Sir Alan are enemies! It is hardly fair to make Charles and I suffer because our fathers are at war! But I see that you agree with Papa. I care not, for I *will* — I *shall*—' she stumbled, reddened and then said more placidly, 'I mean, I know Charles and I are meant for each other!'

'It is not that I *perfectly* agree with Sir George,' corrected Miss Spinner carefully, 'but you are too young to disobey him, and if you really intend to marry Charles, you will have to wait until you come into your majority. Then, I suppose, you will be able to marry whomsoever you choose, or even no one at all!'

Alice uttered a shockingly inelegant remark under her breath, to which Miss Spinner feigned deafness, and the topic was passed over in favour of the scenery they had enjoyed. The peaks district was at its very best, in all its autumnal splendour, but although Miss Spinner thought Alice had made a very creditable job of appearing captivated during the journey, she had seen that the girl had been quite distracted by her thoughts all day. A good dinner would put her charge into a better mood, she thought.

Dinner had been ordered for five o'clock sharp. 'A pease-soup, a spare rib of beef, a dish of potatoes and a pudding, and some cheese and bread, and we shall have a dish of tea at seven o' clock. Plain fare, but fortifying. I think we shall do very well. Even if my poor bonnet has not,' added Miss Spinner ruefully, picking up the soiled hat once again and tugging at it.

'I don't know why you would not take the money from that gentleman, Miss Spinner. You could have had enough to buy a perfectly pretty Sunday bonnet, and another to replace that dull old thing you wore today!'

'I can hardly be so frivolous as to shop for new bonnets, my dear, when I can never be certain of my future. If my wages are to stop, then I shall want every penny I have to keep me going until I find a new position.'

'But you still have Anne to teach, while I am gone to my aunt. Won't you return to Lewisham as soon as I am gone — I mean, when I get to Cromford?'

'Of course,' was the calm reply. 'But Anne will turn eighteen in two years and then I must find a new position, you know.'

'I am sorry that you have no fortune, Miss Spinner,' said a suddenly conscience-stricken Alice. 'I think that it is excessively hard to be a woman, although I do like *some* parts of it, like pretty gowns and having gentlemen argue over who is to have the first dance with me,' she added ingenuously. 'But it does seem so unfair that we women have no control over where we go and what we do and whom we are to marry, even if we are rich! Although it is worse for a woman who is poor and has no family to keep her. Like you!'

Miss Spinner sighed. 'And yet, that is my lot in life. You must be thankful that you and Anne have a fortune, for without it you would be far worse off.'

'Were you — were you never asked to marry? Do you suppose that you will be a governess all your life?'

'I am not so old,' laughed Miss Spinner with good humour, 'that I have given up the thought of marrying, but at the age of four-and-twenty, the odds, I confess, are not in my favour. Therefore, I must be very wise and store up all my pennies in case they must feed me when I am no longer able to teach.'

'I am so glad I have a fortune then!' cried Alice, 'for I am excessively sure I should hate to be a governess and have to teach children all day! I would for a kingdom rather be married and rich than single and poor!'

'Then pity the lot of a governess, and remember when you are married and have a governess to teach your own children, to treat her as well as you can, for a governess's part in happiness is as certain as her income is guaranteed!'

Dinner was brought in and the two women ate well for they were both famished. After the plates had been removed and the waiting girl had gone away, they retired to the little parlour again. Miss Spinner brought out her sewing, and Alice her book. Glancing restlessly at the little clock on the mantel every few minutes, Alice finally lowered her book and sighed, 'How slowly time passes when there is nothing to do!'

'Have you not Mrs Edgeworth's novel to read?'

'Yes, but I cannot attend it at all — but now in fact, I have just remembered, I was going to mention something interesting to you, Miss Spinner.' She snapped her book shut. 'Do you recall that gentleman who rode over your bonnet today, who called himself Rotherham? Hartley Rotherham?'

'Was that his name? Oh yes, I think it was. But what is it you wish to tell me?'

'Why, only that I believe I have heard the name before.'

Miss Spinner cast her an enquiring glance. 'I see — and did you hear good, or bad, of him?'

'I recollect the name was mentioned by my brother only a few weeks ago, when he was home from Oxford — I recalled the name because it is so unusual. It seems Rotherham's seat is Hartley Park, a very sizable estate in the West Midlands, and he is quite rich. There was some to-do with a woman; there was an engagement, I think, but he broke it off — or she did, I cannot recall which — and she ran away in a fright of him and has not been heard of since! Stephen only heard of it because one of his school chums knows the family — at any rate, it was all very tragic and shocking. Do you suppose she *really* was running away from him? Mr Rotherham didn't seem to me a bit like a tyrant or anything so dreadful!'

'You know very well, my dear, that gossip is inclined to stretch the truth and is usually biased to the side of the teller,' reminded Miss Spinner sensibly. 'In this case, it is not very likely that the poor creature, if she has really disappeared, could be running *from* her lover. Perhaps they quarrelled and parted and she has gone to nurse her wounded heart with a relative? One ought not to jump to conclusions, and besides, the gentleman we met today may not even be the one of whom your brother spoke.'

Alice shrugged a dainty shoulder and took up her book again, but the tea things were brought in and as soon as they had taken a cup, Alice pleaded the head-ache and asked if she might retire early.

Miss Spinner cast her a speculative glance and said, 'Why yes, if you are unwell, by all means. You do look a little peaky. Take care to ask the maid to fetch you some lavender water, dear, and ask her to call you at eight sharp, for we leave at ten o'clock, straight after breakfast.'

'Very well,' replied Alice, unusually compliant, a slight blush overspreading her cheeks. 'Good night, then, Miss Spinner. Good night!' She swept open the door, casting a quick look backwards and giving Miss Spinner a rare, sweet smile before closing the door behind her rustling silk skirts.

Alone, the governess put down her sewing and pulled thoughtfully at her upper lip with her fingers, a habit of many years when she was engaged in deep reflection.

Miss Camilla Spinner had taken the post of governess to the daughters of Sir George Featherstone some five years earlier, when she had been forced to leave the home of her youth and seek her meagre fortune in the world. Her father, having passed on debts after his death when she was nineteen, had left her with no choice but to work for a living. They had lived in a quiet, unpretentious manner when her father was alive, living off his small income, and by clever management lived as well as they needed and were able to maintain two servants. Even so the debts had mounted, and just as Camilla had suggested that she take in some kind of sewing work, her papa had gone and died, and left her alone in the world.

She had paid her father's debts with the tiny store of coins she had managed to accumulate, but having no other family, she knew that she must fend for herself. It was not an enviable situation, yet being a sensible woman, she rejoiced frequently in the gifts bestowed upon her at birth — a rational mind and a willingness to undertake hard work. These had served her well in the past five years as she learned to live even more humbly and frugally on the wages of a governess than they had when her father was alive.

Tolerably well-looking, but possessing nothing in the way of consequence or connections, she had been grateful to have immediately found a position in the service of a well-to-do family, and had found at Lewisham Hall a place to call home. It was not *truly* home, with the warmth of family connections, but the real affections of the two amiable girls more than made up for the coldness of Sir George and Lady Featherstone. But at almost eighteen years, Alice was all but grown up and would no longer need her now that she was going to live at Cromford with her paternal aunt.

The circumstances which entailed this move were interesting to Camilla. The most headstrong of the two girls, Alice had for some time been harbouring a *tendre* for Charles Deed, the son of Sir Alan Deed,

Sir George's sworn enemy. The two families, although inhabiting the same corner of the world, took all pains to avoid the other at dances, dinners and picnics, and the two men, on the rare occasions they came face to face in town, would each walk on the other side of the street in open disgust of the other. The war had been declared over a sour land deal; one had cheated the other, or so it had been claimed, and the fact that almost twenty years had passed with sons and daughters born on both sides and parents lost, had done nothing to cure the animosity which the two patriarchs had allowed to spring up and rule them for two decades. So when Alice had taken a fancy to the young Charles Deed, and he to her, a union had been vehemently and unanimously denied them by both patriarchs, and the young people had been obliged to give up the scheme.

Alice had been unhappy for some weeks, and then, when she had been caught writing to young Charles, her father had immediately arranged for her to be removed from Shropshire entirely and go to his sister at Cromford indefinitely. Miss Spinner had been charged with her safe delivery, and she took her duty quite seriously, for not only would she have been mortified if the girl had not arrived in one piece, but her continued employment at Lewisham Hall depended on carrying out the important task successfully.

The governess pitied the girl, for while she herself did not have first-hand knowledge of what it was like to be in love, she felt that it was very unfortunate luck indeed that the two familial heads were so at war that a union could not be allowed to perhaps bring about some much looked for peace between the two great families. Nevertheless, she hoped that with a change of scene, young Alice might after a time come to mend her broken heart and find a more suitable young man upon whom she could endow her affections and fortune.

Putting away her sewing since the light was too dull to see properly, Camilla sighed and took up her candle. After calling the maid and ordering breakfast for nine o'clock, she went upstairs to the little closet which adjoined her charge's room, undressed and lay down in her under things. Moments later she was asleep, and it was not until the maid knocked on the door at half past seven that she stirred again.

Alice Featherstone, being the middle child of three, had learned quickly that nothing came easily in life. Her older brother Stephen, being the oldest and a boy, was, she thought, disgustingly favoured over his sisters. And Anne, her younger sister, being the youngest, always had more than her share of affection and attention from their father and mother. A middle child, she had come to learn, must demand, cajole, and even take forcibly, what it needed for survival and happiness.

Therefore, when escape from the confines of a stifling life at Lewisham Hall had beckoned in the form of young Charles Deed, she had seized the opportunity and fallen in love with him immediately. In turn, he had obligingly returned her affections, and quickly they had declared themselves deeply attached.

Of course she knew there would be opposition on both sides, but she had not accounted for the pig-headed stubbornness of the two papas, whom she thought would back down once they both realized there was nothing for it but to concede to a union. But both fathers had vowed themselves immovable in the face of such a true and abiding constancy of affection, and love was forced in turn to concede to parental tyranny.

'You shall not make a mockery of this family,' was the stern, sonorous echo in the long corridors of Lewisham Hall. 'You shall not make a mockery of me, and of the Featherstone pride, by forming a union with that man's son! Deed is a fool and a base-born toad-eater! Damn devilish fool! You shan't look upon any son of a Deed, my girl, make no mistake!'

And in the halls of Franley were to be heard strains of, 'No son of a Deed will unite with a Featherstone filly, Charles, and that's an end of it, boy! Look to another lass, I tell ye. Nothing'll give ye so much trouble as a Featherstone, mark my words!'

But when Alice had been caught writing notes and sending them between the estates, it had not been a day before she had been informed of her father's plan to send her into Derbyshire indefinitely. She had gone straight to Charles, leaving the house under cover of an early morning walk.

Charles had immediately given up the idea of their marrying in the face of a physical removal of his beloved, but Alice, head-strong, wilful Alice, was not going to lose her prize so quickly. 'I shall not give you up for a kingdom, and if father thinks himself equal to a war with your father, he shall also have one with me! We *shall* wed, Charles, I tell you! We must run away, that is all there is to it!'

'But father will make life very difficult, Allie, if we go against the wishes of both families. Where would we live, and what would we do for money, if we ran away? I don't take hold of my fortune until I am twenty-one. Should we not wait another year, until I am my own man entirely?'

'Do you love me, Charles? Do you *truly* love me?'

'Of course I do! If I can't have you, you know, I shall never marry! That will teach Father, when he can look to no heir at all to carry on the family name!'

'Then if you love me, run away with me to Gretna; we can manage it very well if we just plan carefully. I am not afraid of Papa, if you are not afraid of Sir Alan!'

'No, indeed I am not afraid of him,' cried Charles in some doubt of his own proclamation, but unwilling to be found less stern a character than Alice. 'I shall then! I shall run away with you, and we will come home as soon as it is done and there will be nothing they can do. Father will be forced to accept it.'

'Yes, but we must be careful, Charles. Perhaps we ought to go and live with one of my relatives for a time, so they can get used to the idea? Aunt Agatha is such a dear to me, she is never cross at all! And she thinks Papa quite stern to me, and she is not at all nice as to how things are done or about running away. She would be on our side, I am convinced!'

'Well,' ventured Charles doubtfully, 'I suppose that is a rather good scheme, if we can be sure of her being quite a good chap about not telling and that sort of thing. Is she wealthy? I have some allowance money about me, but nothing to live on for more than a month.'

'Oh pshaw!' remarked Alice disdainfully. 'That is nothing to the point! Aunt Aggie is dreadfully rich and will feed us both, and it will only take a month or two of lying low, and then we can write our parents and let them know where we are. I think Charles, that I ought to be with child, once we tell them — that will make it impossible for them to deny us!'

Poor Charles blushed a little. 'Why, y-yes,' he stuttered, red-faced. 'That would do the trick alright! Capital idea!'

'Then we can return to your father and go to live in the old parsonage, or take a house nearby or something. I am sure your father will allow it once he sees there is nothing else he can do.'

'But Gretna is really very far, perhaps a week's journey!'

'That does not signify, Charles, for we shall have a carriage at our disposal. You'll bring one to fetch me. We will both have our allowances to pay for posting inns and so on. We shall have to pretend all along to be a married couple, you know! Will it not be such an adventure?'

'I only hope,' submitted Charles mournfully, 'that we are not discovered and chased, and apprehended. Then we will have ruined our only chance to be together.'

'No we won't, silly! Only think! Even if they apprehend us, it will be too late, for we will have been together in a carriage without a chaperone. They will have to consider us married, they will have no choice!'

'Oh, I see! Of course.' He blushed again. 'But Allie, are you sure you want to do it this way, rather than have a proper wedding and breakfast and everything? Won't you feel — well, *wrong*?'

'This is the only way, Charles, or they will try to remove you from me for ever and I couldn't bear it!' she replied earnestly. 'Now, I know what must be done! I shall play along with this scheme to go to Aunt Martha, whom I detest — she smells *awful*, Charles, you cannot imagine, even though I once gave her a gift of remarkably strong pomade! — and on the way, since it is only Miss Spinner who is to accompany me, I am certain I can make my escape. Then all I must do is arrange to meet you at a nearby inn, or some place. You can hire a carriage and say you are gone to visit an old school chum or some such thing, and we can drive to Gretna without being caught!'

'How will you manage to get to me?'

'I shall find a way!'

'But will not your governess alert your father at once?'

'Oh no, for she cannot return to Lewisham without me or Papa will dismiss her and she cannot afford to risk losing her employment. She is very poor, you know,' Alice added with sympathy, 'and if it weren't for her position, she would very likely have to go to a poor-house. She will try to find me before she gives up and admits I am gone. I think we may buy quite a few days before it is known that I am gone at all!'

'Well, I suppose it is quite a good scheme, then, if you are sure Miss Spinner won't tell. You will have to tell her you are gone away somewhere else, so she does not follow us to Gretna!'

'I will tell her I am gone to Aunt Martha direct, and that I am quite alright. I am sure it matters little which Aunt I am to live with, so long as she thinks I am safely in the care of one of them. She can go home with no ill conscience and tell them I am safely delivered to my aunt — only she will not say which one — and when all is found out about our marriage, it will be too late for anything to be done.' She laughed. 'Do you not think it a very good plan, Charles dear?'

'Certainly, I do — you are very clever to think of it all — but is it entirely wise, to give up your father's favour, to disobey so completely? Do you not fear his anger? Father will be very angry indeed with *me*, you know — not that it signifies,' he hastily added, seeing her stern countenance, 'for I shall have everything I want in life, Allie, if you can be my wife!'

'Then you will say yes, Charles? You will meet me at an inn and take me away?'

He reached for her and gave her a little kiss on the rose-bud lips which were so firm. 'You have convinced me of the plan, and I shall do my part and meet you and take you away, just as you have desired! If you are not afraid, Allie, how can *I* be?'

When Camilla Spinner heard the knock on her door the next morning, she stirred sleepily and then leaped up from her bed in haste. 'Yes, yes, thank you, I am awake!' she called out, and she splashed her face with water from the ewer. Putting on her tired old brown travelling dress once more, she was just reaching for her serviceable nankeen half-boots when the knocking came again on her door. 'I am ever so sorry Miss, but the young lady ain't in her room. Was I not to wake her up, then?'

She at once went to the door and opened it to the maid. 'What do you mean she is not in her room?'

'Just that, if you please, Miss — the bed has been slept in, but Miss Featherstone is gone and her trunks too. Do you suppose she woke early and has gone for a walk, or gone downstairs to wait?'

'I can hardly say, at this moment at least,' replied Camilla, her mouth set in a firm line. 'Will you make some enquiries downstairs and see if anyone has seen her? I must finish dressing.'

With the maid gone off to investigate, she sat upon her cot bed and sighed. It was not as if the thought had not occurred to her that Alice might not be deterred from the fate her father had dictated so easily, but she had not thought the girl capable of disappearing under her nose! But perhaps she had only gone for a walk, or to look at the horses in the stables. She completed her toilet and snatching up her bonnet, she left her trunk for the boy to take down and made her way downstairs.

She was met half-way down the stairs by the maid coming to find her. The girl was red-faced and apologetic. 'It is very bad, Miss, very bad indeed. The young lady was seen this morning, very early, Miss. She ordered her trunks to be brought down and the carriage made ready at five o'clock sharp, and no-one thought to ask anything of it. I believe she has taken the carriage, and gone away more than two hours ago, Miss! But she left this for you, it seems.' The girl held out a folded paper.

Camilla took it and opened it out. It was very brief.

> *'Dear Miss Spinner,*
> *Pray don't be alarmed, but I have made up my mind to go on to Aunt Martha by myself. I did not care for company, although I do not particularly object to your own. Only I wished to have some time alone, to think on my great loss and what a naughty girl I have been. I am quite contrite, you know! I see now Papa was quite right to send me away.*
> *Cromford is only a day's journey and I shall send the carriage back tomorrow for you to return to Lewisham, so if you wait at the inn there, by and by you can return home and say you delivered me safely to Aunt Martha. I beg you will not tell Papa I went alone, but just say I am safely with my aunt. All is well, dear Miss Spinner, and rest assured I shall be quite able to get to my aunt's by myself.*
> *I wish you well and safe for as long as possible at Lewisham. Pray don't let Anne go into my room and touch my things, as she always breaks them!*
> *Your affectionate*
> *Alice Fstn.'*

Camilla, for all her sinking heart, was not in any way astonished. Indeed, she was not taken in at all by the words before her. Alice had always been headstrong and her governess had known the young woman long enough to be rendered suspicious when the girl was all sudden compliance and sweetness. This entire scheme of sending Alice off to her aunt's had gone far too smoothly for her governess's comfort.

It reeked of red herrings! The unusual fidgeting and air of distraction yesterday, the anxiety about where they were to overnight, the insistence on separate rooms — it was all the proof she would have needed, had Camilla had the foresight to recognise it yesterday.

She calmly sat at the breakfast table, sipped her hot tea, and grimly deliberated her future. There was no question of simply returning to Lewisham, for she could not be untruthful and hide the disappearance of Sir George's daughter, even though she had a pretty strong idea, if not where Alice had gone, at least to *whom* she had gone. If Alice was with Charles, as she suspected, then she was not in any grave danger other than the loss of her reputation, if they did not marry.

Charles Deed, she reflected, was a good sort of boy, certainly not one to take advantage of a young lady, and Camilla, while she was not entirely convinced that he harboured any enduring regard for Alice, did not think him callous. That having been said, she was disinclined to think that the couple would simply go to ground without marrying. If Charles's intention was to marry Alice, they had only one option, and that was to seek a hasty marriage where parental permission was waived and banns need not be read. Therefore, it was a simple enough conclusion that the pair were in all probability headed for Scotland this very minute.

Knowing she could not return to Lewisham Hall without having made some effort to search for Alice, Camilla made her decision. She had not the leisure to await the carriage which Alice may or may not return to Longstoke tomorrow. There was no time to be lost. She must hire a new carriage and post boys to take her to Gretna. She would have to use some of her own meagre savings but it could not be helped, for the small sum Sir George had provided her was not enough to get her to Gretna and would only have been sufficient to see her back to Lewisham. Gretna was a good seven days' journey at least, and there was the additional expense of overnighting at decent posting inns, but she could not think of returning to Lewisham without having made an attempt to recover the girl.

Camilla sighed again. She could not really blame Alice for having taken this course of action, for in most cases a young lady of marriageable age, who received a proposal from a family of tolerable circumstance and fortune, would never find herself being forced to give up the connection. It was a father's duty to marry his daughters well, and here was a match which was entirely suitable, with nothing to advise against it except a stubborn father's pride. The match would have removed Alice from a rather stifling life at Lewisham, under the heavy-handed guardianship of a man whose patriarchal ideas seemed almost to have emerged from the time of Noah! She did not suppose the two young people so *very* much in the throes of a true and lasting passionate regard, but many harmonious marriages had been built on less, and if the young people were suffering from a case of calf love, brought on by youth and a desire to rebel, she did not think even then that it was an inauspicious way to begin married life. To elope to Gretna, however, was a circumstance which would haunt them both, and make it very difficult to ingratiate themselves into their families' affections once they returned.

No, she would make haste after them, and hope that her employer would not see fit to dismiss her if she was to return to Shropshire empty-handed! She pushed away her tea and, fixing her familiar brown every-day bonnet to her head with little regard for style, left the little parlour and went to order a new carriage.

The landlord could not accommodate her, however. Now that Miss Featherstone was no longer her companion, the man looked her up and down as if his establishment was too good for the likes of a mere governess. 'If it's a carriage you are wanting, I have none,' he told her abruptly. 'I have only one other carriage left, which has just been hired by a Gentleman of *Quality*, Miss. Perhaps you can try the coaching inn at Hadlow, or the post coach? But there is not one carriage in my stables unbespoken at this time, I am terrible sorry, Miss.'

Camilla, usually unflappable, paled. 'The post coach? But I cannot be expected — you are certain there is nothing? Nothing at all? I would be happy to pay double, if I must, to secure it.'

The innkeeper had now embarked on an outpouring of insincere explanations and excuses, but she saw how it was and had begun to cast around for other means to get to Gretna, or at least part of the way. She thanked the innkeeper, ordered her trunks brought down, and went outside to the courtyard. Looking about, she had some idea of begging the mercy of one of the ladies that she had seen arriving yesterday, that she might be allowed to travel with them to Hadlow and see if anything in the way of a hired carriage could be gotten there. However, due to the earliness of hour there were few souls about, and only two carriages to be seen.

One of these was a pretty box carriage, but it was already being entered by two very well-dressed ladies, and a dark-haired gentleman, their numerous trunks and hat-boxes filling the remaining spaces, and Camilla sighed. There would be no room for herself, even if she did beg a ride!

The other carriage was empty, and apart from a liveried coachman with a wide hat tightening the traces, no one seemed about to claim it. Nevertheless, she approached it hopefully. It was a very fine black and gold post-chaise with a pretty team of match-greys attached to it, which were stamping impatiently in the morning air. Two postillions were attending to some luggage in the rear.

Not able to see anyone about to enter the carriage, Camilla stepped forward and went toward the vehicle to see if one of the post-boys might inform her as to whom the carriage belonged. As she did so, she heard a sound behind her, and issuing from the dim hallway into the morning air stepped the gentleman who had ridden over her Sunday bonnet the day before!

She could not help her astonishment. 'Why, I thought you had gone away!' she blurted rudely. 'I mean, I supposed you were departing, not arriving.'

'Good morning! Are you leaving? I am just leaving myself, you know,' he said cheerfully, bowing to her. 'I was arriving yesterday, and I am going today. It is often the way at posting-houses, you know.' His eyes were laughing at her.

Camilla set her face in its sternest 'governess' mode, and said coolly, 'I see. I do beg your pardon, only I was surprised. I thought you were come by horse-back? Surely you are not departing by carriage?'

'Indeed, it is the truth, I confess! Fitz was tired out coming this far, and I had my man take him back this morning after I secured this very nice little post-chaise. I now continue my journey, as you see, in more comfort.'

'I see!' She was vexed. Of all the people to have taken her carriage, it had to be the insufferable buffoon who had ridden over her bonnet! 'I had intended to hire the very carriage. It was the last one. But I suppose it does not signify, now. Good day, Sir.'

She stepped smartly back toward the inn door, her pride carrying her fully erect as his eyes bored into her back. But seconds later, she felt his hand on her arm and she swung around to face him.

'Now, I know I ruined your best bonnet,' he smiled impishly, 'so you have all the reason in the world to detest me, but tell me, why is it you wished to hire a new carriage when you arrived in a perfectly good one yesterday?'

'Because,' she snapped impatiently, 'my charge has run away to get married in Gretna, or I think she has, at any rate, and she has taken her father's carriage with her. I was to have taken her all the way to Cromford, to her aunt, then returned in it. Now I am obliged to find another form of transport!'

'And what do you mean to do then?' asked the gentleman, curiously.

'Why, I must go after her, of course! If I return to Lewisham now, and tell them she has run away, I shall be dismissed at once! I must try to recover her, if I can, before she is missed!'

'Ah! Then I see that there is only one course of action, if you will permit me to give you my advice. You must take my carriage, and go to Gretna. Happen you may chance to find her upon the road, if you are lucky enough.'

Camilla was speechless for a moment. 'You mean — I may have the carriage?'

'Yes, certainly. It is at your disposal. I am, as I said yesterday, in your power since I ruined your bonnet, and therefore I am at your service.'

How annoying, she thought, to be obliged to accept an offer from this gentleman, to whom she did not wish to be indebted. But knowing her circumstance meant that she had little choice but to accept, she said, 'Then I must thank you with all my heart, Sir. You cannot know how much this relieves me. I was certain there was nothing more to do but return to Lewisham without Miss Featherstone and risk my employment.'

'The pleasure is mine, Miss Spinner. I am glad I can be of some use. Do order your things to be put up in the back and I shall speak with the lads.'

In a few moments, the trunks were placed in the back and she was being helped up into the vehicle by Rotherham himself. Then, as she was embarking on a speech of gratitude and wishing him a good day, he, too, was climbing inside the carriage and seating himself beside her.

Her mouth dropped open. 'What in heaven's name do you suppose you are doing, Sir!'

Rotherham looked his surprise that she should ask. 'I am going with you! Did you — you didn't think I was *giving* you my carriage to yourself? What an amusing thought!' To Camilla's disbelief, he actually smiled broadly!

'This is no laughing matter, Mr Rotherham! Obviously, I cannot travel alone in a closed carriage with you! Look, that gentleman in the carriage there is already staring at us!'

Rotherham raised his eyes lazily to note the party inside the carriage who seemed to be staring at them. But their carriage was already rolling off and Rotherham shrugged.

'Quite so, Miss Spinner, but you seem to me to be in rather a predicament. There is, after all, only one carriage, as you say. But if I simply give over my carriage to you, I would be obliged to wait for another and who can say how long I must wait for that fortunate event? It so happens that my own business is as urgent as yours.'

Camilla's mouth dropped open, until she remembered to close it again. 'But — I have no chaperone — it is quite unseemly — you cannot—'

He laughed easily. 'My dear Miss Spinner, since I have had the privilege of riding over your best bonnet, and then depriving you of your carriage, I believe we might consider ourselves on terms intimate enough to share a vehicle, without either one of us fearing for our reputations. I shall behave as a perfect gentleman, if you will do the same.'

'But—'

'I am making my way to same part of this country as you are obliged to travel to, and it seems quite foolish for two rational adults, of mature years, to be fretting upon a principle, when there is no time to be lost for either of us.'

Camilla was quite astonished. Share a carriage! With a gentleman not her father or brother! What would her Papa have advised, if he were still alive? Then she recollected Alice's gossip from the previous evening, that Rotherham had been jilted and the girl had run away in a fright of him, and she wondered if it was safe even to consider sharing a carriage with the man. He didn't *look* dangerous, she thought, eyeing him with narrowed eyes, and had a general appearance of affability and frankness. She pulled thoughtfully at her upper lip, considering the likelihood of repenting her decision. He returned her gaze with the hint of a repressed smile, as if he knew just what she was thinking and found it amusing.

Well, there was no other way she could see, and after moment's deliberation of the risk to her reputation, Camilla decided that she had no choice but to take her chances on being murdered in her sleep, on the grounds that to lose her employment would be a worse, and more likely fate. She reluctantly conceded. 'Very well then, as I am in no position to be able to argue the point, I must accept your offer to share the carriage. I shall rely upon your *appearance* of gentlemanliness to reassure me that there will be no behaviour you might come to regret!'

Rotherham feigned offence. 'I might ask the same of you, Miss Spinner! I have my own reputation to protect, you know!' But he chuckled as her mouth opened to make a cutting reply. 'I will not stray from my word, for besides being quite proud of having an honest character, I own that am disinclined to have my trunks thrown from the carriage. Ha! Now I can see I have vexed you. I am so intimidated by your stern glare, that I shall not dare to stray from my seat here!'

'I am rejoiced to hear it,' she remarked dryly. She wondered if she was about to make the worst decision of her life, but the urgency of her scheme to discover Alice before they reached Gretna pressed upon her thoughts and she set her mouth in a prim line. 'I find myself at your mercy, Sir. It seems I am in a predicament, and I must now embark on a course of action I hope I do not live to regret!'

'Well then, let us make the best of an unfortunate situation and see if we cannot overtake your charge on the road. As for us travelling together, I would think it would be safer for you to have the protection of a man, than travel alone. I believe it is all for the best.' With these words, he knocked smartly upon the roof of the vehicle, and the carriage rolled forward obediently as the greys trotted out of the courtyard and onto the road.

Six

Alice, in a great anxiety, but trying to act with the most nonchalance, had rolled out of that same courtyard only five hours before her governess. Having given strict directions to the coachman to take her directly to the Bull, she had ignored his doubtful looks, and silently challenged him to override her instructions. Having a headstrong daughter of his own, the old fellow did not dare question the young lady travelling alone, but sighed and whipped up his horses. Minutes later, Alice was pulling into the courtyard of a posting inn of decidedly lower standards than that she had left, but she was not deterred. She looked around eagerly for Charles.

They had secretly agreed that he would remove from Franley the day before she and Miss Spinner were to leave Lewisham so as not to arouse suspicion, and that he would drive his carriage direct to Longstoke, where he would await Alice's arrival. They had arranged that Alice would somehow give Miss Spinner the slip, and that she would meet him very early in the morning at the Bull. Charles was to have his carriage made ready and all that was to be done was transfer her trunks to his carriage and they would be off.

Now, she could see at once that not only was there no carriage waiting ready, but there was no Charles waiting for her either. She waited for the postillion to hand her from the carriage and she stepped into the courtyard, narrowly avoiding a pile of dung. She wrinkled her diminutive nose in distaste.

'Are you Miss Featherstone, Miss?' A young maid was coming out to meet her.

'Yes,' she replied in some relief, 'I am she.' Charles must be inside the inn, she thought.

'I have a note for you, Miss.'

Alice, with a sinking heart, took the note and opened it up.

> *'Dear Miss Featherstone,*
>
> *I have been obliged by my father to inform you that all must be over between us. I regret that I am not able to give myself the pleasure of meeting you at Longstoke, and I trust you will have a good journey with your governess and reach Cromford safe and sound. You must abandon your scheme of going north to your Aunt Agatha, as it cannot prosper. I have taken the liberty of sending this note on to the Bull at Longstoke and commissioned the innkeeper there to hand this to you when you arrive.*
>
> *Allie, I am so very sorry, but Father says I must not continue with this scheme, or he will disinherit me, and then I will have nothing to live on, for I have no career to fall back on and no talent for anything, and you would not like me very much if I was poor—why, you would have to keep me! A man has his pride, you know! I pray you will forgive me and in time see that this was the only possible course of action.*
>
> *I am always, and most sincerely, your humble servant*
>
> *Charles Deed.'*
>
> *PS I have convinced Papa to tell nobody of this, so that you can go on to your Aunt's and no one will ever know of our mad little scheme. You always were so much braver than me, Allie.*
>
> *Goodbye!*

Alice stood in place for some moments, her little heart thumping away inside the chest that suddenly felt too small for it. Then she rallied. 'Beast! Beastly, awful, despicable Charles!'

'I'm sorry Miss? May I do anything for you? You look awful white, Miss!' The maid who had brought the note was waiting.

'No, I am quite well, I thank you. I shall continue on. Only if someone comes looking for a young lady, will you make sure to tell them I am gone on to my Aunt Martha, at Cromford. They might wonder if I am safe, you see, but it is only a few hours from here and I shall be perfectly fine to travel alone for a few miles.' She smiled determinedly at the young woman.

'Certainly, Miss, if you are sure you are quite well.'

'Perfectly, I assure you. Driver, carry on, please!' She climbed back into the carriage, settled against the cushions and once the vehicle was at a safe distance from the village, she indulged in a few silent tears, presently wiped her red nose, then rapped on the roof to stop the horses.

The coachman came to the window. 'Miss?'

'I have changed my mind,' she said imperiously. 'Take me to the nearest posting house north of this place, if you please. In the direction of Yorkshire, mind!'

'Why Yorkshire, that is a long way off!'

Alice immediately held out two silver coins, which the old fellow looked at dubiously. 'Are you very sure Miss?'

But seeing the look upon her countenance, he thought better of argument and took up the coins. 'Of course, Miss. Yes, Miss.' Having a headstrong daughter of his own and therefore used to the whims of young ladies, he took the new direction in stride and an hour later they were coming to a halt in a smart courtyard, where the bustle of morning departures covered the arrival of a lone carriage with one young, unattended lady.

'Take my trunk and boxes off, if you please. Then take the carriage back to Longstoke and see that Miss Camilla Spinner is informed of its arrival. Here are two more shillings — will that do to pay you, do you think?'

The old fellow gave her a broad smile and did as bid, happy with the young lady's generosity.

Alice watched her things into the inn, and mentally calculating the sum of money she had remaining in her purse, followed them inside, satisfied she could afford to spend a day or two thinking of what to do next. Of one thing she was certain — she would never return to Lewisham unless she was married to Charles!

But alas, inside she met with ill luck — there were no rooms to bespeak, not even a dressing room with a cot. Alice, for all her determination and strong will, was close to losing her composure. Her carriage would be gone by now, and here she was, stranded in the middle of nowhere! But being largely of a practical bent and a vigorous appetite, she very practically decided to order refreshments. This would give her time to take stock of the situation and to devise a new scheme.

She was shown into a small public parlour, and there, trying to be as inconspicuous as possible, she took a seat at the table in the corner to await her breakfast. Several other travellers shared the large room, some sitting at tables, some sitting upon a few sofas strategically placed before the fire. Most of these were gentlemen, accompanied by their wives, and none of these noticed the little dark-haired female who sat quietly at the table in the corner, her pretty bonnet not yet removed from her head. Nor did anyone notice when after a moment, she lay her head on her arms and was suspiciously silent for some time, moving every now and then to sniff gently and dab at her eyes with a very wrinkled handkerchief. Anyone close by her might have heard her remark archly through her tears, 'Scoundrel!' and 'How could he be such a weakling, such a — a — decided coward!'

Finally, after a long wait, her meal was brought in and she sat up, nose rather pink, and proceeded to consume a good deal of the kippers and eggs and toast, and a quantity of the hot tea. By now, she had attracted the attention of a few of the gentlemen who were single and therefore at liberty to openly notice a very pretty young woman travelling alone. However, it was not a gentleman who finally approached her, but another lady.

Alice looked up in surprise as the young woman came up to her table. This female appeared to be around five or six-and-twenty, was dressed in a well-made blue and cream striped gown and matching spencer, and had on some pretty cream gloves with a monogram Alice could not make out. Her face was not particularly handsome, but her hair was a lovely burnished-gold colour, and her blue eyes kindly.

'I do beg your pardon, but I could not help but notice — are you all alone here? Might I be of assistance?'

Alice thought quickly. 'I can hardly say — I am alone — just now, that is — but I am meeting my — my brother here, in an hour or so — but I thank you for your kind enquiry.'

The other lady made a little moue with her mouth. 'It's only that, well, I saw you were very unhappy, just a little while ago, and I wondered if you were in any sort of trouble. I am sorry for mentioning it, but you looked quite forlorn!'

Alice, whose usually boundless pride had nearly been used up, mustered the last of it and said very firmly, 'I assure you, I am meeting my brother here. In fact, he ought to be along very soon now to collect me. We travel to Yorkshire, to — to Innesfalls. To visit my aunt.'

'I see,' said the other woman, regarding her kindly, 'Then I don't wonder that you are unhappy at the prospect of such a journey, it is quite a distance — at least five days, I collect.'

'Oh yes,' replied Alice eagerly, 'it was the thought of being squeezed into a horrid small carriage for five days which is the reason I was crying a little. But I dare say I shall be alright.' She gave the other woman a brave smile.

'Well, that is quite a coincidence that you are for Yorkshire, for it happens that I am headed north myself,' explained the other woman. 'My maid took sick getting here and now she is abed to recover. I shall have to send her back home, for she is ill-suited to carriage travel. So I have been obliged to ask the innkeeper here to procure another woman to accompany me; it does make such an odd appearance when females travel alone, don't you think? Not that I mind for myself, but there are proper ways of doing things, are not there?'

'Most surely!' exclaimed Alice, a sudden idea grasping hold. 'And did you find someone to go with you in the carriage?'

'Why, no,' the other woman repined. 'I have had such ill luck, that I cannot find anyone who will make the journey with me, since I must travel several days. I will very likely have to travel alone. But that will be no hardship, for I am excessively fond of books and have two excellent novels with me. Do you like reading, Miss — Miss?'

Alice's great intellect had processed this intelligence at a speed which would rival some of the great thinkers of Britain, and she had already decided at once how she intended to take advantage of the good luck which had been offered to her. She smiled at the stranger.

'Miss Spinner, Miss Camilla Spinner. How do you do?' She bobbed her head politely. 'Yes, I do like reading, sometimes, only I do like dancing and being in company so much more!' She smiled charmingly at the other woman.

'It is a pleasure to make your acquaintance, Miss Spinner. I am Louisa Wa — Fortesque.'

Alice had decided it was time to execute her plan, and she placed her hand on the older woman's arm. 'May I confess a secret, Miss Fortesque?' she asked tremulously. 'I must tell somebody, and you seem so kind.'

'Certainly!' was the reply. 'I hope it is nothing too dreadful!'

'Oh yes, it is very dreadful indeed, only I have not been entirely honest about my circumstances. You see, when you asked me if I was in some sort of trouble, you were not wrong. May I seek your advice even though we are only just acquainted?'

'Why, if I can help you at all, Miss Spinner, you must tell me how! I guessed all was not well when I saw you unhappy just now.'

Alice sighed. 'I am afraid I did not tell you the truth. I am not really meeting my brother here — I have no brother. I am excessively sorry to be untruthful, but I am in such a predicament, I don't know how to act!'

'Poor child! Do let me help you!' Miss Fortesque was all compassion. She pulled forward a chair.

Alice, jubilant to have the woman on her side with so little effort, said earnestly, 'Pray, do sit beside me so I can speak more quietly. There, I hope you are comfortable enough in that hard chair. Well, then, you see I have gotten myself into such a bother, Miss Fortesque, that I hardly know what to do.' She leaned forward. 'In truth, I am a governess, and I am running away from my former employer, who — who acted very forward with me, *very* forward indeed, and I had no choice but to leave his employ. I am going to my aunt — I was truthful about *that* part, you know — but the devil of it is that my aunt lives very far away, at Innesfalls in Yorkshire, and I tried to get another carriage, but now I am stranded here, for there is no carriage to be had for miles!'

'A governess!' murmured the lady in some astonishment. 'You look full young to be a governess!'

'Oh,' replied Alice calmly, 'I am almost one-and-twenty, which is full young to be sure, but my father died and I had no choice but to go into service. It is quite tragic, I assure you!'

Louisa hid a smile. 'And now you are obliged to leave your employer's house? I can see that you are in a predicament indeed! It is a wonder that you made it this far. From whence did you come, may I enquire?'

'Oh, from Shropshire,' replied Alice ingenuously. 'I was in service with a large family there — I was in charge of the two elder girls,' she added grandly. 'They are a very fine family, especially the eldest girl — but I dare say you will not have heard of them, so I shall not bother to mention their name, but I am very anxious that I should get on to my aunt's, Miss Fortesque, and from there I may be able to find a new position.'

Miss Fortesque chewed her lip and eyed Alice for a moment. Then she said very kindly, 'It seems we may be able to help each other, Miss Spinner. I require a female to accompany me north in my own carriage, and you require a means to get to your aunt's. It so happens that I am bound for Penniston, which is not so very far from Innesfalls, I collect. Well, as near as a very slight deviation in my route as will not excessively disrupt my own plans. I think the solution to both our problems might easily by solved.' She smiled at Alice. 'You must accompany me, and I shall ensure you are taken wherever it is you wish to be taken.'

Alice smiled the most charming smile back at her. '*Would* you carry me in your own vehicle? I would be ever so grateful, if you might not be inconvenienced by having a passenger... it is so very kind of you I can hardly thank you enough!'

'There is no need for thanks, but if you can engage me in interesting conversation I shall be very grateful myself.'

'Oh, I shall!' replied Alice, her eyes bright. 'You cannot imagine how indebted I shall be to you! When shall we set off then — this morning?'

'Certainly, if you are ready. I shall call the postillions and have your own trunks added to mine.'

The carriage was made ready, and quite soon, Alice found herself sharing a pretty little coach drawn by a pair of fresh-baited horses. Hat boxes and other small items piled on the seat opposite meant that Alice was obliged to sit beside her new friend, but as Miss

Fortesque was disposed to talk with great animation on the most interesting topics, and Alice was disposed to be distracted from her recent loss, both females were quite satisfied with the arrangement. Very soon they were on more intimate footing, becoming "Louisa" and "Alice" to each other quickly. As the little towns passed, and the scenery grew more and more hilly as they progressed, the conversation slackened, and the two women subsided into quiet companionable silence, each lost in their thoughts, and both careful to conceal from the other their real motives for removing north.

The carriage bumped and jolted, and Camilla was suddenly roused from the light slumber into which she had fallen. They had been travelling for much of the day and she was becoming hungry and thirsty. Little in the way of conversation had taken place in the first hours of their journey. Camilla had now and then thought of asking her companion the nature of the business which took him several hundred miles from his own home. She wondered if it had anything to do with the young woman to whom he was supposed to have been engaged. Had she truly run off in a fright of him? It seemed to her a far-fetched story, given the so far impeccable manners and character of her travelling companion. He did not seem the type of male who was frightening to a lady; he seemed to be as good-natured as any other man, and after all, if Camilla had truly thought herself in danger from Rotherham, she would not have agreed to share a carriage with him. Perhaps the rumours were merely that. At any rate, she would not ask. If he was in pursuit of the lady in question, he may soon reveal his object in travelling north.

After having established that Miss Spinner was quite comfortable, Rotherham had said little except to ascertain the likely roads which Alice and her young man might have been obliged to take on their journey ahead of them, and the likelihood of their final destination being Gretna. To this, Camilla had replied that she supposed the couple was either headed to Gretna, or perhaps to an aunt of whom Alice was very fond, who lived in Yorkshire.

'I can only surmise, but I believe they would have gone direct to Gretna to marry, and perhaps they might have decided to go on to Yorkshire, since they must know how unwelcome in either of their father's houses they would be after such an act of disobedience.'

Rotherham had promised to keep an eye peeled for a carriage with the Featherstone crest, but he did not hold much hope, he said, of discovering them upon the road. They would be more likely to find the errant couple stopped at an inn or posting house when they were forced to change horses. They would have to enquire at each posting inn, to see if such a carriage had passed through the town.

Sitting up now from her slumber, she caught Rotherham's eye scrutinizing her rather closely and she blushed a little. Was he laughing at her dowdy gown and bonnet, or perhaps he was reconsidering his offer to travel with a mere governess, when it was quite obvious he was a Person of Quality. It was impossible to know what he was thinking, and she surely was not going to ask him! To disguise her self-consciousness, she asked coolly, 'Do you have about you a pocket watch, Sir? Surely we must be soon stopping for a meal and to change horses?'

Rotherham obligingly dipped his hand into his waistcoat and brought forth an elegant gold pocket-watch. He snapped the face open smoothly. 'It is just gone the third hour, Miss Spinner,' he informed her pleasantly, 'and I think, from memory, that we shall soon arrive in a small town called Bottomvale, where I hear there is an excellent inn which serves the finest ale in the country. We shall overnight there.'

Camilla eyed him suspiciously. 'I hope,' she stated primly, 'that you are not given to being in your cups, Mr Rotherham! I need not remind you—'

But Rotherham had already begun to chuckle. '—that I am travelling with a female of the utmost propriety and the highest reputation. I am not given to drinking, Miss Spinner, and have never been found in my cups, although I confess I like a good ale from time to time. But as to your propriety and reputation, I shall do nothing to spoil either, I assure you.' He paused. 'Speaking of such things, while you were sleeping, I took the opportunity to think on our situation, and I wonder, would it not be prudent to imply that we are a married couple, so as not to incur any untoward remarks regarding your reputation? Of course, you shall have your own chamber, and I shall not abuse the privilege of being thought of as your husband, but I think it may be the best course to preserve your reputation,' he finished gallantly.

Pretend to be married! Camilla frowned and tugged absently at her upper lip with her fingers. Here was a new predicament, entirely! If the inn were given two different names, or was allowed to come to their own conclusions, it may well be surmised that she was woman of easy virtue, a barque of frailty, a light-skirts! It was unthinkable that such a conclusion could be made. If Alice could not be discovered and made to return, she would be faced with finding a new position. She must at all costs retain her reputation to secure a new post if needed. But on the other hand, to be calling Rotherham her husband! Which of the two were the greater evil?

'Could we not pretend to be brother and sister?'

'I had considered it, but I am too well known in the country. It is widely known that I have no relatives, and if someone were to recognise me, surely your reputation would be ruined in the first moment. I believe my suggestion is the only one which will safeguard you.'

She sighed. 'I suppose you are correct, and I must submit to circumstances and allow myself to be thought of as married. But, Sir, you forget the wide gulf between us — you are very obviously a man of rank and circumstance, and I am very obviously not your equal. My clothing and style of dress is hardly of the quality which would make it easy to pass me off as your wife. It will make a very odd appearance and may stir up suspicion.'

'Oh, that is nothing to the point, Miss Spinner. I would not worry myself about such things,' he said lightly. 'No one will notice us if we do not draw attention.'

'Then do nothing to draw attention, Sir, and we shall both protect our reputations!'

'Certainly,' he said meekly. 'I shall not think of being overfamiliar unless circumstance warrants my acting your husband to protect your reputation.'

Camilla cast him a suspicious look but seeing as he appeared perfectly serious, and it was difficult to tell if the glint in his eyes was a sign he was laughing at her or just the particular way the light was striking them, she decided to give him the benefit of doubt.

A degree of intimacy had now seemed to spring up between them which Camilla attributed to the circumstance of spending many hours inside a closed carriage with him. Taking advantage of this intimacy to finally vent her curiosity, she now ventured to enquire as to Rotherham's business in the north. 'I can hardly believe that in taking me so much my own way, you do not somehow venture off the road your own business requires you to take. After all, you cannot be going to Gretna, can you?'

Rotherham's face clouded a moment and Camilla at once regretted her enquiry. 'If my asking was at all impertinent, I am sorry. Do forgive me! Only I was concerned that your own business might be interrupted, or worse, prevented, by your obliging to take me as far as Scotland.'

He shook his head. 'I am not offended by the question. My business takes me — I hardly know — I think to a small town in Yorkshire. So you see, I was quite truthful before when I told you I had business in the same direction.'

Curiosity, and some regard for her own safety, made her brazen. 'I heard — that is, Miss Featherstone told me — that she had heard something of you from her brother, who spoke of a broken engagement — that the young lady in question has run away in a fright.'

Rotherham laughed but there was a hint of bitterness in his tone. 'Oh, so the gossip-mill has been working overtime, has it? Are you afraid you have put your life in my hands, Miss Spinner? What lady would run from her future husband, except one in fear for her life?'

'Not at all! — I never meant! — it is quite natural for me to enquire since I am to travel several days with you!' Camilla's cheeks were pink.

He relented. 'You colour quite fetchingly, you know, Miss Spinner! But I can certainly assure you that the rumours you have heard were quite true — but only in part, I must add. You needn't worry that I am going to murder you in your sleep, or worse. The lady whom I am pursuing was indeed engaged to me, and it was she who broke off the engagement. That, I am obliged to confess, is the power of a lady. We men have the power of asking, but a lady has more power, for she can say no, or change her mind. A man must suffer to be jilted and abused from time to time, I fear, and there is nothing to be done.' He shrugged hopelessly.

Blushing still more from his observation on her appearance, she replied 'Then why do you pursue the lady, if she has jilted you? Surely she has made up her mind! Do you have hopes of persuading her to change her answer?'

'She was fickle enough to accept my proposal then decline it in the same week,' he replied with a smile, 'but I don't say I go after her to change her mind — a man has his pride you know! I simply desire to ensure an old friend, for she is that much at least, is well, and is not made too unhappy by my proposal or by her declining of it. And perhaps I wish to understand her sudden change of heart. She broke our engagement without giving a reason, and you may call me a curious man.'

Camilla was astonished. 'How strange!' she mused. 'A female might do a lot worse than to be proposed to by a man of consequence and good appearance such as yourself—' she stopped short, cheeks pink again. 'I mean, Sir, that any female without a great fortune at her disposal, would be glad to make a match of the consequence which you would naturally supply. It is not very usual, is it, for the woman to break the engagement in those circumstances? But perhaps the young lady is capricious and does not know her own mind? There are those females who play with a man's affections and care not where they break hearts.'

'Lady Louisa Waverly is hardly such as you describe, Miss Spinner, for I have known her all my life, and we have always been very good friends indeed. While I do not understand her first accepting then declining my offer, I must respectfully abide by her decision, and I cannot allow any calumnies to be cast against her otherwise impeccable character.'

'I see.' Camilla's fingers pulled absently at her upper lip for a moment, then asked 'So you think you may find the lady in Yorkshire? Do you have a good reason to suspect she has gone there?'

'I am not at all certain, but Louisa has connections there.'

Camilla was silent for a moment, then said thoughtfully, 'I have never been in love myself, but I cannot imagine that to be jilted would be very nice at all. I am very sorry for you indeed, Sir. I hope that you do no suffer too much. Perhaps this Lady Louisa will change her mind, after all.'

He laughed. 'Oh, my heart is quite intact, Miss Spinner; pray do not think me heart broken. But Lady Louisa and I were, I once thought, very good friends, and it pains me to think that she felt so unable to speak openly to me about her wishes, that she accepted, then rejected my proposal. If my advances were so disgusting to her, our friendship and our history ought to have been enough to make her tolerably easy in rejecting me from the beginning.'

'Then you were not in love with Lady Louisa?' asked Camilla in some astonishment. 'I suppose there have been many unions based upon worse things than friendship — but then having no experience of the married state myself and known so few people who have, that I am ignorant of such things.' She laughed at herself. 'The only marriage I ever knew firsthand was that of my parents which was a happy one, but my parents loved each other very well, as I recollect.'

'There is nothing wrong with being a romantic, Miss Spinner. I may not be a great romantic myself, but I hear it is all the rage these days with young people like yourself!'

'Young! You mock me, Mr Rotherham! I am almost five-and-twenty. That is not exactly young by most people's standards.' She laughed. 'But do tell me, if you are not a great romantic yourself, and you were not in love with your Lady Louisa, what motivated you to enter the marriage state at all?'

'Why indeed?' Rotherham gave an odd sigh and turned his gaze to the window for a moment to survey the countryside which rolled past them. The sun was lowering toward the west and had begun to cast a golden light over the trees and fields. 'My mother is unwell. She has not been in the best of health for some time, and now that she feels quite keenly her quickly diminishing strength, she has requested that I marry.'

'Oh! I see. I'm sorry to hear of it.'

'So you see, I marry to please Mama, for I would be quite happy to remain single for my life. Who could deny one's mother her final wishes but the most hard-hearted of sons? I am very fond of Mama, despite her tendency to authoritarianism, and I wish her to depart this world as content as she can be. An heir to Hartley Park in the foreseeable future would go a long way to making that happen.'

'I see. But have you never thought of marriage before this? No young ladies have caught your eye in the years which have passed from your youth until now?'

'My married acquaintances might say I have been fortunate to escape the marriage state, Miss Spinner,' he said in amusement. 'Do not they say that courtship and marriage are like paying for a month of honey with a life of vinegar?'

Bristling for her sex, Camilla set her lips in a prim line. 'Do not they also say that "many a good hanging prevents a bad marriage"? Perhaps the woman in question has done you a service by preserving your life!'

'Ah, the lady has a fine wit hidden behind a pretty face! Do not they also say that "fools are like husbands are to herrings, as the husband is the bigger"?'

Camilla managed a grim smile. What an odious gentleman! Little wonder the poor lady fled rather than marry someone with such an attitude to matrimony! Really, she could not blame this Lady Louisa for running! She replied coolly, 'I really could not say, Sir, but you appear so averse to the institution of marriage that I cannot guess at your motive for attempting to enter it with the lady, whom I shall from now on refer to as the *fortunate* Lady Louisa!'

'Ouch! That is a sting, indeed! However, I concede that you would be quite right to say so,' he laughed, 'at least, it appears that "fortunate Lady Louisa" thought herself so too, when she repented her hasty decision to cast her lot in with mine!'

Rotherham had attempted humour, but Camilla was still eyeing him sternly. 'Well, the lady has certainly escaped in the nick of time, then!' was her prim reply. 'But if you are so averse to marriage, why on earth did you choose Lady Louisa to be your bride, other than that she was the only woman you could think of who would agree to have you?'

'Ouch! That is thrice now! It is a very good thing I am not marrying *you*, Miss Spinner, or I would suffer cruelly from that sharp tongue of yours on a daily basis, I am certain!'

Unable to stop the creep of pink up her neck, she said vehemently, 'What a ridiculous thing to suppose, Mr Rotherham. I hope you do not take advantage of my agreeing to *appear* married. I should be very quick to find myself another carriage if so.'

His eyes were amused, but he said very civilly, 'Of course. I will help you find a new one at once, if you desire it. And a new "husband" to chauffeur you, as well!'

She was cornered like a rabbit by hounds and she knew it. There were no other carriages, and certainly none which she could afford. She met his eyes directly. 'Did anyone tell you, Sir, that you are quite as vexing as any a gentleman I have known! But I see that a pretty set of clothes and an appearance of good breeding are all that is needed these days to be thought a gentleman!'

'Ah, touché, Miss Spinner, and there you have it, you have found me out entirely! Little wonder I cannot get a woman to marry me! You must teach me how to correct the error of my ways!'

Camilla saw that he was taking his amusement at her expense. She tried for a change of topic. 'I own it is perhaps a creditable thing to follow your mother's wishes, if she is indeed soon to leave this world... and now I understand your character better, I can see why you have so few brides from which to choose,' she added primly. 'Did you have any reason to believe the young lady would agree to your proposal?'

He was obviously at the whim of his mother and above all things, she despised persons with no backbone. Little wonder Lady Louisa had felt herself insulted. To be asked to marry, without there being some kind of mutual attachment, was abhorrent to Camilla's personal ethics. She knew that men entered into marriage sometimes for pecuniary advantages, and that was bad enough but to chance making someone else unhappy, simply to please one's parent! Her disapproval, she hoped, was apparent.

'I believed so,' he replied affably, ignoring her tone. 'We had spent much of our childhood together at Waverly, her home, after my father died. Her father, Lord Loxford, was a friend of my own father and after he departed this world, Loxford ensured I was invited frequently, whenever I was not at school in Oxford. Louisa and I spent much of our childhood together, and I suspect Lady Loxford had hopes we would marry many years ago.'

'Why ever did you not?'

'I don't think Lou ever thought of me as anything but a friend, and I certainly never saw her as a future wife. I think we both thought ourselves too much brother and sister for anything of that nature to be considered. Besides, at that time, my mother was content to have me single, as she had me at her command far more than if I had married. But now that she is in ill health, the doctors think she may not have more than a year left. And after all I must provide Hartley Park with an heir after I am gone, for I have no brothers to inherit. Mama is in constant state of anxiety that Hartley will pass to our obnoxious cousin, Lionel Abercrombie. Mama has an innate distrust of the Scottish even though we cannot hide our Scottish forbears,' he laughed. 'So I asked Lou, thinking that she might quite like to get away from Waverly and come and live at Hartley Park with me. She said yes, almost immediately, but a few days afterward I received a very short, very kind note, thanking me for my generous proposal, and the honour it did herself, but that she had decided to decline my offer of marriage. I drove over at once to Waverly, to see if Loxford knew anything of the business, but he only said that she had gone, and they did not know where. Feeling as if I had caused my dear friend some kind of suffering, I decided to see if I could discover where she had gone to hide, and at the very least, apologise for causing her distress with my proposal.'

'In my experience,' commented Camilla sensibly after a moment, 'if a lady intends to hide from an unwanted suitor she will make a very good job of it, unless she *intends* to be found. Some ladies play these little games to increase the ardour of their lovers, but from what you say, it seems that this Lady Louisa is determined not to be found.'

'Perhaps,' replied Rotherham with slight smile. 'She is certainly not the kind of female to toy with a man's feelings, but I shall not rest until I have called at Penniston, the seat of her mother's brother. He is, by Louisa's own account an elderly, rather singular old fellow, but given that he is rather a favourite with her, and that she has few other relatives or friends that I would think she could go to, I suspect old Stacey would be her first choice.'

Within the half hour Rotherham's carriage had reached Bottomvale, and the two occupants were stepping neatly into the courtyard at the King's Arms. Here, carriages of all types seethed and swelled the courtyard, and many beasts came and went as their riders entered and exited their lodgings. A few people noted the entry of the pretty carriage into the inn's yard, and one rider on horseback stared as Rotherham handed Camilla from the carriage, but the pair were occupied in seeing their trunks from the vehicles, and neither noticed the young man staring as he sat astride his horse.

Rotherham took charge at once, to Camilla's embarrassment introducing themselves as Mr and Mrs Rotherham, and very soon they were being shown to a set of rooms which, while small and over-furnished, seemed tolerably comfortable. Trying not to blush as the maid referred to her as 'Ma'am,' Camilla dismissed the girl as soon as her things were brought up, and she looked about her room curiously. She was instantly satisfied herself that her own chamber, which adjoined Rotherham's, was securely locked against unwelcome intruders, her travelling companion included!

They met on the stairs at an appointed time and went down to the dining room for their meal. This comprised of a haunch of over-cooked beef, slices of cold ham, fresh bread and cheeses, and dishes of vegetables which were severally placed about the meats. The pudding had been left along with the dinner, and the pink blancmange made for a strange appearance surrounded as it was by potatoes in gravy, and peas-in-the-pod.

When the maid had poured wine and served them both, Rotherham sent her away and the two hungry travellers tucked in. For some minutes, a strangely companionable silence pervaded the room as they both satisfied their appetites, although Camilla helped herself to a deal less of the fare than did Rotherham who seemed to have hollow limbs.

'I have,' he said in between mouthfuls of beef and ham, 'enquired as to a carriage such as you have described to me, but no one matching your description has stopped here in the last day. We shall ask again at the next posting inn.'

Camilla was disappointed. 'Oh! I had hoped that they were not much ahead of us. Perhaps the next inn might have news, since they must stop and change horses, unless they do not overnight but drive all night!'

'That is one thing which I have also feared,' replied Rotherham, 'but it is unlikely, for while a young man might have the stamina and the disregard for his own comfort to withstand such a gruelling journey, a female requires those little comforts she can expect on a long tedious journey. Although your Miss Featherstone seemed a girl with a remarkable spirit, she will still likely not withstand a long journey without stopping overnight.'

Camilla, admitting the sense of this was appeased, and they continued their meal in silence.

Finally, Rotherham put aside his plate and regarded his dining companion. Camilla in turn, being less on her guard against impropriety now that she had had a day to consider his character as *probably* trustworthy, returned the gaze without embarrassment.

He was a rather well-looking gentleman although she doubted that he had ever been called handsome. He appeared to be around eight or nine-and-thirty, with dark thick hair which sprung back from a commanding forehead. His eyes were darkish brown, and his nose was a little too large, with a slight curve which drew the eye. But it was his clothes which gave an observer the idea of consequence. They were of quality and good fit, and he seemed to be as easy in the wearing of them as he was in his manner generally. But there was an impish charm to his smile, and a glint in his eye that Camilla admitted could be quite taking, if a female were of the disposition to notice such things. She herself, having given up the thought of a man's ever liking her enough to think romantic thoughts, spent little time assessing the men she came into contact with, their being almost always married and very dull, or single and too old, even for her! She had not thought of marriage since she had been forced to earn her bread, and the irony of her posing as Hartley Rotherham's wife now amused her so much that she could not help a smile.

'And what is it about my appearance that amuses you so, Miss — Camilla?' He corrected himself in time, as the maid had come in to remove their dishes.

The use of her first name gave her a start. She glanced guiltily at the busy maid. 'I — I was only thinking how odd a situation in which I find myself,' she relied carefully. 'But it is my own doing for I ought to have realised Alice was planning something. Her going off to her aunt's house so readily, with so little argument, ought to have alerted me. I feel quite ashamed of my ignorance!'

'I have to say I admire her spirit,' remarked Rotherham seriously. 'She must be either very silly or very brave to have taken on such an adventure! But try not to make yourself anxious over it. I am certain that we will discover the carriage on the way to Gretna, or at least hear news of the couple. They will be easy to find, as a young couple travelling north through this country alone in a fine carriage will be sure to make for speculation. It will not be the first time a couple have made for Gretna in a hurry!'

'True,' replied Camilla thoughtfully. 'Following the road to Gretna is my only chance of finding them before it is too late. I am only grateful that we are in the summer season, and the roads are quite passable. I hear that in winter some travellers may be snowed in at posting inns for weeks, waiting for a thaw!'

The maid, having cleared away their dishes, left the room with promises of coffee and tea shortly and Rotherham watched her gone before he continued. 'Well, we shall be on our way tomorrow in good time, only I wish to see to a small matter before we leave town, so I shall order breakfast for ten, and expect to be on the road again by eleven.'

'Oh!' cried Camilla, 'I do hope we won't lose too much time. I do not mean to inconvenience you, and I am very grateful for the carriage, but I cannot afford to lose any time, for if they marry before I can get to them, Sir George will dismiss me at once!'

'My business here will not take more than an hour or two,' promised he, 'and I shall return to join you before we leave. A fresh team going at a brisk pace will not set us behind your errant pair by very many hours. But I wonder if you will satisfy my curiosity, Miss Spinner, and tell me how came you to be a governess?'

'Why, the usual way, I suspect!' Camilla was not sure if she ought to be affronted by his impertinence, or charmed by his interest in her. 'Why do you ask?'

'You don't really look the governess type.' He assessed her shrewdly, his head tilted to one side. 'I never had one personally from which to judge, since I was educated at school, but having read enough novels in my youth, I judge from the descriptions they give of governesses in general that you are much too pretty to be one. I'll save you the trouble of blushing, for I was about to add, you are only pretty when you do not frown! And you have an air about you which does not at all fit with the governesses I have read about in books!'

'How should a governess appear, then, in your opinion?' she replied haughtily, trying in vain not to colour at being called pretty by a man of his consequence. 'I suppose you subscribe to that unspoken understanding that all of society seems to agree with, that a governess must be tolerably educated but otherwise very dull, wear very modest gowns, appear comparatively poor and humble, and try not to stand out. As far as I can tell, I have fulfilled those requirements; my brown cambric gown and bonnet are simple and dull, and you have seen my trunks are scuffed and worn, as are my boots, Sir.' Her eyes challenged him a little.

'I see I have injured your pride again,' said Rotherham ruefully, laughing a little at the look on his companion's face. 'Now that you have your most severe frown on your countenance, I can see quite clearly that I was wrong, you look every part the governess! How foolish of me not to see it earlier!'

'You make sport of me,' said Camilla disapprovingly.

'I am sorry, most sincerely,' replied Rotherham, trying for a look of contrite humility, the smile on his face undoing all his best efforts.

'Sincerity! I can hardly believe it... you are a male, Sir and that circumstance therefore precludes sincerity from the time of infancy, I collect! I observe how you smile as you apologise!'

'While I must own a certain amount of insincerity is the nature of men, Miss Spinner, I cannot allow you to claim all the virtue for your own sex. Show me a party of ladies at an assembly, and I shall show you the very heart of insincerity!'

'How so, what do you mean, Sir?' She was not sure if she ought to laugh or be vexed for her sex.

'Only observe how a party of ladies will all eagerly hand out the most overblown compliments to each other, none of which they really mean, then return to their drawing rooms and laugh behind their fans at the dress and manners of those women they complimented to their faces! You cannot deny it is so! Therefore, I hold women are by nature more ready to be insincere than men.'

Smiling, she shook her head. 'You can hardly expect me to enter into your criticism of my sex, Sir! Besides that, I have little experience of parties of ladies since my profession means I am rarely in company or at assemblies. Therefore, I can only assume that you mean to mock me again!'

'Then allow me to apologise for my impertinence, and tell me how came you to the governess trade. I rather think it is not a vocation which a woman wishes to make a career of unless she has no other choice. You have the air of a woman of education and not insignificant birth.'

She eyed him, and deciding he was not merely asking to embarrass her, she relented. 'Our family was never of great means, Mr Rotherham, but we descended from a good family with a seat in Kent. The land was lost two generations ago. I cannot say what circumstances brought the family into poverty over time. But Papa was, I believe, the youngest son of a gentleman, educated to a tolerable level, and eventually he had a good business in the apothecary trade with a good many clients.

'When Mama passed away I was still quite young, and I helped Papa a little in making up the various concoctions and poultices that he sold. We lived very happily, and quite well for a time, with servants to help out at home and little to be made anxious about. Papa's business was so secure that I was even sent away to a good school to be educated. When I finished my schooling and returned, it was to find business had fallen off rather badly. We had to let the servants go, and we were obliged to practise a greater economy than ever before. Then Papa died suddenly from a seizure of the heart, and I was obliged to pay off his debts with our small savings. I had no means to support me, no connections and no family. I had little option but to go out as a governess.'

She hoped he was not going to ply her with the kind of pity she had come to expect from others, but there was no pity in his tone, only a matter-of-fact curiosity. 'I see. And you are currently in the employ of the Featherstones, and feel your employment is most precarious if you do not find Miss Alice and return her to her father, or safely deliver her to her aunt. It is a dire situation indeed.'

She studied his face to be sure he could not be mocking her in any way, but his interest in her position seemed quite genuine. 'Yes,' she replied, 'it is, for if I am dismissed, which I may well be, I certainly won't be given a character, and woman with no character is not likely to secure employment anywhere else. You see how I must find Alice, if I can.'

'Quite,' replied Rotherham decisively. 'I have great hopes of it, in fact.'

She hesitated, then ventured, 'But this puts me in mind of another problem, Mr Rotherham. I must pay my way. To that end, here are enough shillings to cover my room and meals for tonight and tomorrow night and perhaps the next, if we don't stay in so very grand a manner and eat frugally.'

Under cover of the table, she had emptied the little she had left from the money Sir George had supplied her onto her lap and counted out four shillings. There were four left. Plus the little store she had in her possession in her trunk, made ten shillings altogether. That would have to suffice for the few nights left, to get her home, and to purchase anything she needed until she could return to Lewisham. And if by great fortune she came across Alice and her beau, Charles Deed, she would beg more from Alice, who had a good allowance, to enable them both to return home in safety.

Rotherham had other ideas, however. Having watched her count out the shillings surreptitiously under the table in some amusement, he gave her a sideways look when she held out her hand. 'Besides having no wish to "eat frugally" as you put it, I will take it as the highest insult if you insist on payment. Money is nothing to me for I have plenty of it, and besides, had I travelled onward alone I would have incurred almost the same cost. You must keep your meagre supply of shillings, for you have a much higher purpose to which to put them.'

His mouth twitched upwards and Camilla was bemused and a little irritated. 'I do beg your pardon?'

'You must reserve something for a new Sunday bonnet, of course!' replied Rotherham, laughing. 'Or had you forgotten I ruined your other one? You would not take my money, so my not taking yours is a return of the favour!'

'I — I — Oh!' spluttered a discomposed Camilla, her cheeks pink. 'But—!'

'You will not allow me to recompense you for the ruined bonnet, therefore my taking you north must suffice as payment. No, I shall not allow the course of justice to be perverted. I did after all declare myself at your service on account of the mishap! You cannot argue with such logic and reason, I collect, or I will be obliged to think you the most unreasonable female I have encountered! Now will you take some tea or coffee? Here is the girl just come in.'

The serving maid had now brought in the tea things and a pot of coffee for Rotherham. She poured tea for a still pink-cheeked Camilla, and left the coffee for Rotherham to serve himself.

Camilla knew when she had been outfoxed. When the door had once again closed behind the girl, she bit her lip in vexation. 'Very well, then, I must accept your kind offer, I suppose, although I am certain the price of new bonnet will be but a fraction of the cost to transport me into Scotland! But when if we can find Alice and I can return her home, I shall ensure Sir George will repay you everything spent on my keep.'

'Won't that be rather difficult, if you wish to protect your reputation? You will not be able to tell Featherstone you travelled unaccompanied in a carriage with a man, and pretended to be his wife! I think you had better conceal *that* gem!' he added in amusement.

'You seem to find this situation quite diverting,' replied Camilla reprovingly. 'I shall have to tell untruths, and I have a great aversion to dishonesty,' she added primly.

'Before you make yourself anxious over it, let us ascertain if the girl can be discovered first,' he suggested sensibly. 'Now, finish your tea, there's a good girl, and don't keep giving me those governessy looks of yours, for I am quite put off my coffee by them!'

Lady Louisa Waverly watched the sleeping figure beside her rock gently with the motion of the carriage and sighed. A slight snoring sound emitted regularly from the pink rosebud lips of her travelling companion made her smile. The girl was exhausted, that much Louisa could ascertain! Of course, she strongly suspected that the girl who claimed to be a Miss Camilla Spinner was not a governess, being far too young and far too well-dressed for such a claim to hold water, and as for the other parts of her story, Louisa could not tell. But she had detected about the girl an air of desperation and she had admired the spine it must have taken for this unprotected female to take a course of action which was clearly leading her away from home and everything she ought to value as dear. If poor Camilla was indeed running from an oppressive home life, Louisa herself could understand it. She was doing the very same thing herself, and it had required the same amount of courage!

It was not as if Waverly was a dreadful place to live. She had her dear little Button, who was as loyal and true to her as any friend could ever be! But Louisa herself, while knowing herself valued dearly by her father, had not found the warmth and affection she would have wished from her other parent. And if marrying and leaving Waverly would have been the simple solution to her problem, she would have stayed and married Hartley Rotherham.

Louisa's father was a good man, despite the absent mindedness which sometimes made him appear a little too easy, but her mama was all sternness and lecturing, and she knew that if she had told her parents the real reason for her declining Hart's offer of marriage almost as soon as she had said yes, neither of them would understand it.

The truth was, Louisa did not want to marry at all. She did not want to have children, and knew that however good and kind a man Hartley Rotherham was, marriage, and all the expectations that a husband naturally had of his wife, would prevent her from seeking to fulfil a dream she had kept secret these ten years. If she was to pursue this dream, she could not marry. At first, when Hart had asked her, she had thought it an excellent scheme, for marrying Hart Rotherham would have removed her from Waverly and the tyrannical rule of her mama. But upon consideration of several facts of great import, Louisa had waivered. Hart was a good man; in fact, she could call him a friend, but if she married him, the respect she had built for him as her friend would be quickly torn down by his demanding an heir — and if she was to pursue her own dreams, there would be no place for children in her plans.

Beside her, "Camilla" stirred and yawned behind a delicate hand. 'Forgive me, I think I must have dropped off. Are we stopping? I am so famished I feel I could quite do justice to an entire plumb-cake!'

Louisa laughed. 'Then we shall stop, and very soon. The sun is quite low in the sky — it must be nearing dinner time. There is a small town ahead, for I saw it coming over that last hill and see how the road winds down? I suspect we shall soon be tucking into as much tea and plumb-cake as you desire!'

True to her word, the carriage made its steady way down the winding little road, and the town came into view. Now they were moving into less populated Derbyshire countryside, and each hour had seen the females viewing pastoral scenes far different to those of home. As soon as her companion had fallen asleep, Louisa had withdrawn some papers and pencils from a portfolio book wrapped in cloth and had begun to sketch and draw with great attention the scenes which enthralled her. Louisa had not travelled very much and each new bend in the road revealed a new image of transcendent delight to transfer to paper, a memory from which she would later work to create a permanent oil painting. In truth, painting and drawing were her *raison d'etre,* and her works were always pronounced delightful, on the occasion that she permitted the eye of another person to glance over them. These occasions were rare, however, since while at home her talent was praised, it was still regarded by both her parents as a girlish pastime only, a skill which might help her acquire a husband, perhaps, if he wished to have a wife who was as adept with a paintbrush as she might be in producing children.

But Louisa had been careless with her papers, and when Alice happened to glance over the scattered drawings which had been ill concealed by a hat box, she reached for them. 'How pretty!' she exclaimed before Louisa could prevent her from taking them up and going through them all. 'Why, you have captured the rooftops of this town and the trees and fields so very well! But what a dear little dog! Is he yours?' Alice had pulled from the bundle a drawing of a little King Charles Spaniel, his doey eyes looking pretty and soft.

'Oh, yes, that is Button,' Louisa explained sadly. 'I had to leave him behind, I am afraid. I miss him dreadfully. Do you have a dog, Camilla?' she asked.

'Oh, no,' replied Alice blandly. 'I shouldn't be allowed one as a governess and all that. I should like one very much though, if I wouldn't have to brush him all the time, that is!' She silently congratulated herself on being clever enough to remember, for she knew that Miss Spinner would never have been allowed a dog at Lewisham. 'But this sketch of flowers along the road is better than anything I have seen! I myself am so deficient with a pencil,' she laughed, placing the papers back on the seat, 'that I have given up trying to fashion anything recognisable as itself long ago. Mama has said I must concentrate on my needlepoint and dancing. But I confess I despise needlework as much as I do sketching! But your sketches are very good. You must take my likeness for me,' she added eagerly. 'I have never had one before! I wager you will capture my likeness just as well as you have captured this flower!'

'Certainly I can take your likeness, if you wish it, dear Camilla,' replied Louisa, rather astonished, 'but do you truly despise sketching and needlework? What is left for you to teach your charges, then? You must be the sort of governess who teaches only French and botany! And for what reason must a governess need to learn dancing? I thought it would be a skill barely put to use, from what I have heard of the unfortunate lives of governesses!' Noting the girl's pink cheeks, she hurried to add, 'But of course, you have come from a household who encourages their children to dance! Then of course you must know the steps to teach them!'

'Oh, yes,' stammered Alice, her cheeks flushing in vexation at her mistake, 'the girls I taught were very proficient dancers indeed, and they were expected to practise all their steps before they attended any balls. I was their partner, you see, for they could not practise with Stephen — I mean their older brother — for he was always at school and never home for long. Oh, look there — we are not far from town now! Shall we take a room together, do you think? It would be so cosy to be together!'

Louisa accepted this abrupt change of topic without comment, although she eyed Alice for a long, knowing moment. The two women soon found their horses well stabled, and themselves in plain, but tolerably comfortable lodging, which was able to provide them a small but cosy room with a fireplace, and a pretty view of the hills. The inn was rougher than to what Alice was used, but she did not care, she mused, for nothing mattered now but to gain her aunt's house, and ensure she was not made to return to her father's house! And as for Charles Deed, she refused to shed any more tears over the cowardly man-child with whom she had once thought herself in love! She defiantly struck tears from her cheeks as this thought came to her and sniffed angrily. She would show him!

They dined lightly upon thin beef broth, fresh crusty bread and a hard yellow cheese, and although Alice was temporarily disappointed to hear there was no plumb-cake to be had presently, the innkeepers wife promised them some to take with them tomorrow, and supplied them with such excellent strawberry tarts to supplement their supper that Alice, who had a decided proclivity for sweets, was not disappointed.

After they had dined the evening was still early, and Alice took herself to her room to fetch a book, while Louisa sketched before the fireplace, in the public parlour. Coming out from her room again, Alice collided suddenly with a young man on the stair who happened just at that moment to be passing her doorway. The young man had let out an 'oomph' and then, coming to his senses, had bowed and offered profuse apologies to Alice who was staring in disbelief at him.

'Mr Percy!' exclaimed she, in consternation.

'Miss Featherstone!' he echoed in astonishment, then collecting himself, bethought to ask, 'How do you do? I had not expected to see you here, in such a rough establishment as this. How come you to this place, so far from Lewisham? Are your friends here? Your father and mother?'

Indeed, so ill-prepared as she was to actually meet with someone who knew her, Alice could barely gather her wits enough to stammer, 'I — I am travelling with a friend, a very dear friend, of my mother's and who offered to give me a little change of scenery. But what might you be doing in these parts Mr Percy? I thought you to be at Foal's Keep?'

'I was at the Keep with my father,' replied Percy gravely, 'but I have been at Wickston looking over a horse there, and now I am on my way to Town again.'

Foal's Keep was the seat of Mr Gregory Percy, Thadeus Percy's father, in Shropshire, not so distant from Lewisham Hall. Alice had been introduced to both men on the occasion of her come-out, a good deal more than a year ago, and although on first meeting had thought him handsome, she had quickly taken a dislike to the young man.

This, had Alice been able to admit it herself, had had less to do with the young man's general manners and appearance than it had had to do with his seeming indifference towards Alice herself.

Mr Thadeus Percy had been quite unobliging on the occasion of his asking her to dance the fourth and fifth dances with him, for despite her being in the best of looks that particular evening, he had forgone all civility and failed to gaze at her when she had pretended to be gazing elsewhere, had declined an opportunity she had provided to return a calculated touch upon the arm as they had passed each other in a figure eight, and even worse, he had failed to offer any of the usual compliments to her appearance. She had found herself perplexed and not a little out of sorts at his indifference. This omission was made all the more vexing since Alice was used to easily catching the attention of gentlemen when in society, even before she had officially come into society.

And after the dance, when he had escorted her back to her seat, she had cast him a calculated little glance from behind her fan, but he had merely drawled, 'Pray don't trouble to make eyes at me from behind that fan, Miss Featherstone, for I have had enough young ladies going out of their way to fix my attention. Perhaps you might try such tricks on those gentlemen who find that sort of thing fascinating!'

These insults had been quite a trial to Alice, who, not yet having decided to fall in love with Charles Deed, had been quite ready on her first official ball, to receive all the compliments to her looks, all the besotted glances from young men, to which she had aspired.

Now, all the while she was giving the young fellow stammering, faltering replies as to her business in such a northern county, she was also recalling her particular dislike of him and very soon a certain chilliness intervened between them, and she was obliged to be polite only on account of not wishing to raise any suspicion toward her being so far from home.

The young man, however, seemed not to remember his rudeness to her the previous year, and proceeded to cheerfully enquire as to whom she happened to be travelling with in case he might know the lady's family.

Alice thought quickly. 'Oh, I think that would be unlikely, Mr Percy, for she does not originate in Derbyshire or the south of England. I believe the lady's home is in Suffolk.'

'Oh, but I think you might at least give me the chance to decide that, Miss Featherstone, unless there is a reason you don't wish me to know such details,' said the young man cannily.

Alice at once primed her lips and quelled her rising vexation. The arrogance! She gave a little laugh. 'Why, how silly of you, Mr Percy! Why would I wish that? I will tell you at once if you really desire to know. The name of the family is — it is — Algernon,' she improvised wildly. 'My friend's name is Miss Mary Algernon, from the far north, very, *very* far way, in Scotland,' she added firmly. 'Do you know the Algernon family of Scotland, Mr Percy?' she added, innocently.

Thadeus Percy was not at all nonplussed. 'Not at all, Miss Featherstone,' he replied cheerfully. 'But I should be very glad to make Miss Algernon's acquaintance nonetheless, if you will permit me to accompany you downstairs.' The young man bowed politely and offered his arm, which was not accepted. He eyed her with a half-smile. 'It is not unseemly, you know, for we *are* old acquaintances, after all!'

'Old acquaintances! I have met you but for one evening, more than a year ago, and you hardly spoke two words to me, Sir,' Alice reminded him more acerbically than she had wanted to be. 'I mean to say, we did not have much opportunity for talking, did we?'

'No indeed,' he replied, 'but I hope I may remedy that now? I seem to recall that you were a little out of sorts on that evening. Perhaps you were tired?'

'I hardly remember, I am sure,' replied Alice coolly, remembering quite well how he had treated her with as much diffidence as he would his own sister. 'At any rate, it is nothing to the point now, for that must have been a year and a half ago, and I barely remember that night.'

Percy raised an eyebrow. 'Do not you?' he said enigmatically. 'Then I shall remind you. You wore a white spotted muslin, with deep blue ribbons the same colour of your eyes, and a pearl decoration in your hair. We danced a cotillion and an Irish jig, and you were partnered after that by Mr Collins and Mr Rowbottom. I remember it all very clearly.' He smiled fully then, and his eyes twinkled.

'You *did* notice me then!' Here she coloured in confusion. 'What I mean to say is, you were so cool in your manner that I thought you must disapprove of me very much.' She was now quite disconcerted and felt her cheeks flushing. 'But one can never tell what a young man is thinking,' she added off-handedly, 'for men, I collect, are a different breed to women and never give away their feelings if they can help it.'

'While I can hardly deny such an accusation, I think it is not just men who can be accused of such a crime, Miss Featherstone,' replied he, laughingly watching her blush. 'Now, do introduce me to your friend, and then I must attend to some business in the town. Come, do let me take you down.'

He held his arm out so charmingly that Alice, as anxious as she was to avoid the trial that would be sure to follow downstairs — the confusion of "Algernons" and "Spinners" and "Featherstones" that would be revealed to the two other parties — could not think how to refuse and allowed Mr Percy to lead her downstairs. Her mind raced over the possible scene of introduction, and how on earth she was to somehow let her friend know not to be surprised if Mr Percy was to chance to refer to herself as 'Miss Featherstone', and call

Louisa 'Miss Algernon'. The thought gave her even more anxiety, and she could hardly think of anything else. But they were already advancing to the parlour, and it was with a rush of relief that she found that while her drawing papers were still on the table, Miss Fortesque was not in her chair after all, and was nowhere to be seen.

'Oh dear!' she breathed with a sigh of relief, 'I think my friend has gone to fetch a wrap and is not here.' Alice was anxious that Louisa should not come back at any minute. 'Why, I really ought to go after her and see if she is well; she suffers most dreadfully from bad headaches you know,' she added inventively. 'Well, it was most excessively kind of you to bring me downstairs, Mr Percy, but I would not for the world delay your business. Good evening!' She gave him a most brilliant smile.

Percy, finding himself summarily dismissed in this most hasty manner, bowed gravely and wished her a good night. As he retreated, Alice sighed her relief. That had been a close call! All this business of changing names and so on was all very well, but it made one quite confused and was not conducive to sanguine spirits! She hoped that Mr Percy would not think to mention seeing her if he went back to town, for the drawing rooms of Mayfair were rife with chatter and gossip and news would soon reach Lewisham if he did. But she and Miss Fortesque would be gone first thing tomorrow and it was unlikely that she would see him again. All Alice had to do was remember to act more like a governess, answer to "Camilla" and get to the sanctuary of her aunt Aggie's house as soon as she was able!

Ten

But "the best laid schemes o' mice and men gang aft a-gley" as Robbie Burns once wisely noted. Alice was just congratulating herself on a fortunate escape from Mr. Percy, when she was forced to admit the truth that providence can sometimes appear the most contrary beast in the world. She and Louisa were just stepping into their carriage after an early breakfast the following morning, and the postillions just loading the last of their trunks onto the backboard, when no other than Mr Thadeus Percy emerged from the inn door and caught sight of them both. Alice, catching him with his eye already fixed upon her, gave up the vain attempt to hide but when he made as if to step over and wish them both a good morning, she looked away as if she had not seen him, and said urgently to Louisa, 'Do quickly rap upon the ceiling, Louisa, and let us proceed smartly!'

This was uttered with such urgency that Louisa at once perceived both Alice's distress and the young man who was about to accost them, and she did as bid and rapped smartly upon the ceiling. The coachman at once whipped up his horses, and the carriage rolled off at a pace which the young man could not match. When Alice turned to look behind them, Mr Percy was watching after them in some astonishment. Or was it amusement? She could not tell, but it did not signify since she would not see him again.

She turned forward again and bit her lip. What an unfortunate coincidence to have met the odious fellow just now! If only he did not mention seeing her when he went to Town! Still, she thought it was unlikely anything would come of it, since she was barely more than a passing acquaintance to Mr Percy, and she shrugged off her anxiety.

Louisa, however, was watching her with raised brows. Alice gave her a cheerful smile. 'I was so eager to be off that I could not wait longer! What a lovely day, and how blue the sky is today! I am wild to be on the road again! There is nothing like a carriage ride on a lovely day, do not you agree, Louisa?'

Louisa gave her a grave smile in return but if she thought there was anything amiss with Alice's haste to be gone, she said nothing of it. Instead, they talked of the scenery before them, the temperate day, and the various books they had read. Alice tried to remember to speak of her fictional life as governess and retold amusing stories from her own time with Miss Spinner. Miss Fortesque seemed diverted enough by these – in truth, she seemed to Alice a sweet creature indeed, and Alice did not like to be untruthful to her, but needs must, and if she was to execute her scheme to go to Aunt Agatha, she still needed Miss Fortesque to believe she was a governess on the run from her wayward and wicked employer.

After an hour to two had passed, Alice, checking the roads behind her periodically felt that all danger had passed, in case Mr Percy had decided to follow them. He had not seemed quite convinced of her story, and she would not like to have to meet with him again. But he was for Town, and she for Yorkshire, and it was not likely he would pursue her; it was not as if he even liked her!

They entered Yorkshire country around one o'clock, its fertile green fields, jutting rock formations and stony walls which lined the road charming sights to both women. Louisa brought out her sketch book and happily employed herself making little drawings of the scenes they passed, while Alice contented herself with looking from the window and imagining the surprise her aunt would get on her arrival in only three more days. She would have to ask her aunt to give Louisa something for the kindness of carrying her into Yorkshire, but her aunt being quite rich, and Alice a great favourite, she did not think this would be a difficulty.

They stopped to bait the horses around half past two o'clock and to take an early dinner. The Sow's Ear was a tolerably cosy establishment, although it could not provide them with a ladies' parlour, but only a public parlour, which was busy with a multitude of ladies and gentlemen of assorted qualities. Here the two women took their meal and coffee, finding a table to themselves, while their driver did the same in the kitchen.

'It is just as well we are not overnighting here,' remarked Alice, 'for I hold we would be hard pressed to find two rooms fit for ladies; the place seems full to brimming with travellers! Look, two carriages have arrived just since we have been at table!'

It was true, for a number of carriages had departed, and more arrived since. Alice, who had been leaning to look from the window under the guise of enjoying the scene, was glad to see that no one the least like Mr Percy had arrived.

Their appetites sufficiently satisfied, the two women went out to summon their driver. They were just about to enter the carriage again when Alice, keeping a careful watch should an unwelcome horse and rider enter the courtyard, caught sight of a man, just dismounted from his beast, entering the back door of the inn and she caught her breath with a little gasp. It was none other than Mr Percy! Thank goodness their carriage had been standing in a corner so as to be hidden by the others!

'Louisa! Miss Fortesque, do hurry! I am — I am so eager to be on the road, let us be off at once!' She did not wait for the postillion to hand her in, but lifted her skirts and almost leapt up into the carriage.

Louisa, at once comprehending her friend's distress, followed hastily, and at once rapped upon the roof even before the boy had shut the door. 'Go! Make haste!' Louisa cried, and the carriage rolled smartly around the other carriages onto the road.

No one had appeared at the inn door to see them away and Alice turned back to the road ahead, angry that she should be followed. It was not as if she were a child or being abducted by some rake! Quite vexed at Mr Percy's conceit in following her, Alice bit her lip. Odious fellow! What must he be about, following her, when he had told her that he was for London? Why, he must be following her on purpose, for London was exactly in the opposite direction! Now she would be obliged to concoct a plan to throw him off her scent if she was to gain her aunt's house in three or four days' time! With some clever manoeuvring, she was almost sure his scheme of following her might be circumvented. But what he was thinking of, pursuing her after one chance meeting, she could not fathom at! He was as little interested in her as she was in him, and it puzzled her as to what he might mean by such a course!

But Louisa was giving her such a look now, that Alice knew she must find an explanation quickly. She was prepared to improvise shamelessly to ensure her arrival at Innesfalls.

Louisa had already begun to urge Alice to speak. She said gently, 'You may rely upon my discretion, my dear Camilla — of course you may — but won't you do me the honour of sharing your anxiety and thus relieving you of just a little of it, perhaps?'

Her looks were so obliging, so ready to help, that Alice thought she might be able to do something to forward her own interests. She spoke tremblingly, ensuring her voice wavered just a little more than it would have had it been merely a Mr Percy, distant acquaintance, who was in pursuit. 'Oh Louisa, I can barely speak for terror, but that man you saw looking at me this morning is the man from whom I have been fleeing — none other than my former employer, Mr — Mr Brown! And he is come after me! I saw him at the posting inn just now, although he did not, I am certain, see me. But it is clear that he has discovered me and pursues me to apprehend me and return me to his house! Oh, I cannot go back there, Louisa, I cannot! Please will you promise not to hand me over to him?' Alice turned beseeching eyes upon her new friend.

'Why, no, dear,' replied Louisa calmly, 'I should not like you to go back to an employer who is wicked as you have implied. You shall certainly be quite safe with me. I shall simply inform this Mr Brown that you are with me, under my protection and that he must not accost you under any circumstances or I shall most certainly engage the law to intercede. Perhaps we ought to seek assistance even now?'

'Oh no, pray do not! I couldn't bear it — to be humiliated in such a way. I am but a humble governess, and if the law were involved, I might be seen as some kind of — of coquette, a light-skirts! Let us carry on and get us to my aunt's house just as soon as we can, Louisa!'

Louisa, older and wiser, wondered what the girl was really doing on the road, although she did not doubt that someone, whoever he may be, was following her friend. But she conceded to Alice's wishes without a murmur of doubt, and the two women were soon fallen asleep in the carriage as it made its jolting and bumpy way.

'Bring me my draughts, and call Plowright to come directly!'

For all her illness, Lady Rotherham had not lost a certain vigour to her voice as she called to her servant. The young girl was quick to obey, since her mistress had seemed to faint away immediately after stepping from her bed. Recovering quickly, Lady Rotherham had returned to her bed, aided by her servant, and when she was tucked in place, and given a sleeping draught, the doctor was called once again to make the short journey from the village which had now become familiar to him.

Within the hour, Dr Plowright had seen Lady Rotherham more comfortable and, besides prescribing more draughts, had sat gravely by Lady Rotherham's side. 'You have been overdoing things,' he scolded her. 'You cannot expect to gallivant around the gardens without incurring something of a punishment, you know!'

Lady Rotherham eyed him from the pillow. 'Gallivant? I hardly think I could describe myself as gallivanting anywhere these days, Doctor, but nevertheless I shall endeavour to keep more to my bed, if you think it will ease these dreadful fainting spells!'

'I have left you some draughts, Lady Rotherham, which ought to do the trick for now.'

Lady Rotherham closed her eyes for a moment then opened them again. Her steely blue eyes fixed the doctor. 'Tell me the truth, Doctor Plowright. Is it my time to meet my maker?' Her gaze did not waver.

Doctor Plowright gave her a slight smile and squeezed her hand. 'I daresay you have some life left in you yet, Lady Rotherham. I wouldn't say it is your time just yet. But,' he added sagely, 'it is always prudent to put our affairs in order sooner rather than later, when we near the end of our lives on this earth. Sometimes the good Lord takes us more quickly than we expect. I have seen many a creature on this earth taken by surprise when passing from this world to the next. Now, I don't say that is your fate, Madam, but it would not hurt to get that son of yours back here to be near you and get those little matters of business which concern us all safely done with, if you take my meaning.'

Lady Rotherham sighed and lay back on her pillows. Hart had been gone only three days and already she felt her strength draining. If only he would bring her a daughter-in-law, she could leave this world as satisfied as she had been in life.

The doctor was sent away, and she spent an hour dozing under the effects of the strong laudanum she had been given to help with pain. When she woke again it was to the sound of the front doorbell, and moments later, Liza knocked on her chamber door and peeped around.

'Oh, you are awake then, Madam. There's Mr Thomas Middlemount come to visit, if you will have him, Ma'am. Or I can tell him you are too unwell to receive, if you prefer,' she added doubtfully.

'Middlemount?' exclaimed Lady Rotherham weakly. 'How unusual! I wonder at his coming... I suppose he is probably come to see Hart and doesn't know that my son is gone away to Yorkshire.'

Middlemount, she knew, was in the habit of playing at cards and gambling with her son, and while Hart always seemed to have the greater luck, Middlemount often came off the losing hand. Yet he seemed a good natured enough young man and friendly with Hart; she supposed when a young man was beholden to another, it was politic to remain in good standing with one's creditors! She wondered if it was for this reason that he had come to Hartley Park. 'Come and help me sit up, Liza, and make me tidy, for I perceive I must look like a partridge that has fallen out of the pear tree, as I am!'

A quarter hour later, a rather Corinthian-looking young man in a dark coat, high hat and high cream cravat tied in a bounteous waterfall, was shown into Lady Rotherham's private chamber. 'Good morning, your ladyship.' He bowed elegantly and with a languid grace. 'I hope I have not intruded — it is very good of you to see me so early in the day. But I see you are indisposed? Perhaps I should call later?' he added politely.

'Not at all, Mr Middlemount. You find me a little indisposed, but not so much as to prevent my seeing one of my son's acquaintances. Do sit, will you? Just so — there now, are you comfortable? Excellent! So you have come to see Hart, I presume? He is not here, however.'

'No, indeed he is not,' agreed Middlemount personably. 'I have just left him in Bottomvale, almost on the border of Yorkshire, Madam.' There was a gleam of pity in his eye, which Lady Rotherham did not like the look of. She wondered at Middlemount's object in coming to tell her he had seen Hart in Yorkshire. She hoped that news of the engagement had not gotten out. If this was the case, Hartley would not be at all happy!

However, Lady Rotherham, who took great pride in never allowing her calm demeanour to slip, met Middlemount's gaze with equal composure. 'Indeed, then if you have seen him, you surely must bring news of him, for I cannot imagine you to have ridden such a distance in so short a time if you do not have something very particular to say on the matter?'

'You have guessed correctly, Lady Rotherham. I certainly do have news of your son — and I do so hope it will pleasant news! — but the rub of it is that you might not be aware of a certain circumstance which seems to have occurred — and I know not whether you ought to be informed of it, Madam.'

'Good heavens!' exclaimed Lady Rotherham, 'I hope Hart has not met with some misfortune or had some carriage accident or other! I always tell him not to drive so fast but he will never attend me!'

'Oh no, Madam,' Middlemount said placidly, 'quite the contrary! Rotherham seemed very well when I last saw him. It is only that the circumstance of which I speak is somewhat of a delicate matter, given what I know, and because it may not be known to you, I feel some... hesitation... in speaking.'

'Then you must tell me at once, Mr Middlemount, or I shall have paroxysms from being kept waiting!'

He bent confidentially toward her. 'There is some talk, Ma'am, that Rotherham has become engaged to Lady Louisa Waverly, which news I was apprised of three days ago. I shall not say how I learned of it, for it seems that the engagement was to be kept private.'

'That,' exclaimed Lady Rotherham sternly, 'was meant to be kept quiet for now. I am aware of the engagement, and I cannot imagine what would have brought you here to discuss such a delicate matter with me, given the circumstances.'

'Lady Rotherham, if this was the only intelligence I had been privy to, please be assured I would never presume to mention it, but I happened to be in the vicinity of Bottomvale when your son was present, although he never saw me, as I was in some haste to leave. I was expected back in town and therefore I had not the leisure to make my civilities to him. But I thought to come as soon as I could hasten here, to inform you that Rotherham has most certainly married, and seems to be travelling into Yorkshire with his bride!'

'I beg your pardon? Married? Travelling in Yorkshire?' Lady Rotherham, despite her usual composure, was somewhat taken aback. She was aware that her son had gone into Yorkshire to seek Lady Louisa, but surely Hart could not have had time to locate Louisa Waverly and marry her, all in the space of four days! 'I believe you are mistaken, Mr Middlemount. My son is certainly in the vicinity, on private business, but as for his marrying Lady Louisa already, that can hardly be so, for they are due to marry here, just before Michaelmas. Clearly you have mistaken someone else for my son.'

'But that is just the thing, Lady Rotherham. It was for a certainty Rotherham, for I saw him unmistakably, and I would lay a thousand pounds down that it was he. Furthermore, Madam, he was with a young lady, whom I can assure you is certainly his wife, for I heard the servant refer to the Lady as "Mrs Rotherham." I thought, in light of the intelligence I had received of the engagement, that you ought to be acquainted with the news. I hope you will give me leave to wish you joy, Ma'am!'

The young man yawned and stretched his toes, as if there was nothing in the world which had given him more satisfaction, and

Lady Rotherham decided at once that she liked the young man even less than when he had entered her rooms. He was clearly after compensation for the information. 'And you are certain he was travelling into Yorkshire, not out of it?'

'He made off in that direction, Ma'am, therefore it was not difficult to guess his object was to proceed north, not south. Now, if you wish me to take him some message...' The Corinthian gave her a slight smile.

'He must be going to Lady Louisa's relations — I believe she has connections in that country — Penniston is the name of the place I recall,' she mused. If Hart's object was to travel to his wife's relations, then she thought he would in all probability remain some time. But she *must* have him home, and she could not understand his hesitation in bringing Louisa straight back to Hartley Park if he had found and wed the very lady his mother had chosen. Surely he would wish to bring his bride home to her? She could not account for his going north at such a time! But never mind, he would be brought home in record time, and Louisa too, and she knew how to accomplish just such a task. She knew Middlemount was angling for a reward, and also that he was presently in debt to her son for a rather copious sum.

'Mr Middlemount, I have a commission for you, and I shall sweeten your pocket nicely if you will carry it out for me. Oh, pray do not bother to appear so surprised. It was, after all, the purpose of your visit to me.'

The young Corinthian's eyes lit upon hers in avaricious speculation. 'I am at your service, Madam,' replied he smoothly. 'If I can help in any way at all...' he trailed off with a deferential bow of the head.

'I desire my son to bring his wife home immediately. I commission you to get to Penniston, Yorkshire, just as soon as you can, and ask for the house where Lady Louisa is residing. Mr Rotherham will be there, I am quite certain of it. Tell him I am dying, if you must! He must bring Mrs Rotherham home to Hartley Park so that I can lay my eyes upon her before I pass from this world! I shall give you a generous sum for your troubles plus travel expenses, Mr Middlemount, if you can get him here within the fortnight! Here is one half to go on with.'

When a young man with a debt to pay is given a chance to repay it with so little effort to himself, it cannot be passed up. Accepting the coins she drew from her reticule, he drawled, 'I am at your service, Lady Rotherham. You may count upon me to bring Rotherham and his bride to Hartley Park before next week is out.' Placing his tall hat upon his head, he drew on his gloves and bowed. 'I shall not disappoint you, Ma'am.' He tipped his hat elegantly and was gone from the room.

Camilla had packed her trunk with the meagre assortment of old gowns and hats and gloves that she owned and was now waiting patiently for Rotherham to return to the inn from his business in the town. She had breakfasted alone, wondering what business had taken Rotherham out so early. All the trunks were now loaded into the carriage, and she herself was waiting in the courtyard, dressed as usual in her dull brown bonnet and much-faded brown gingham travelling cloak. There was no sight of him, and she sighed. It really was too bad of Mr Rotherham to be so late, for every minute was precious in her pursuit of Alice!

But she had not long to wait, for only a minute later she spied the very gentleman striding towards her with a young lad in tow. The boy carried several boxes, which looked to her female eye, suspiciously like gown and hat boxes. A moment later and a few words exchanged, and she was proven correct.

'I have presumed on your good will, Miss Spinner,' began Rotherham congenially, 'to take the opportunity of procuring a few items of clothing which I perceive will advance our scheme; here are three or four gowns, which I think will fit quite tolerably, some gloves, a travelling cape, and two bonnets which must take the place of your governess's bonnets. Oh, and here are some new nankin-boots and a pair or two of pretty shoes. Your size, I think,' he added shrewdly, 'for I have an eye for these things. Here, do feel how soft they are, and do stop giving me those governessy looks. You know how they unnerve me!' His eyes were laughing at her.

Camilla was open-mouthed. 'You — you cannot — you *must* not! You merely mock me, Mr Rotherham! You mock my brown cap and boots, and my humble garb suitable for a life of service! It is very wrong of you, you know!'

'Now, now, Miss Spinner, you have it quite wrong, you quite mistake me! I only think of preserving our little secret.'

'I can hardly accept these items, Mr Rotherham, which you must know! To accept such gifts would be tantamount to a confession of being your... your mistress!'

To her utter vexation, Rotherham laughed. 'Come now, Miss Spinner! I'll brook no refusal, you know! When you remarked that your gowns will hardly convince others of your right to share a carriage with me, you had not mistaken the matter, and I took it upon myself to correct the fault immediately; here are some fairly decent gowns, nothing grand, I assure you, but they will ensure that there is no doubt that we are equals, and certainly nothing to incite any suspicion that you are not my wife. In truth, my actions were to protect your reputation, not to injure it!'

He said this with such a look of innocence and boyish charm, that for a moment Camilla forgot herself. 'But you hardly know me! You are already doing me such a service that I cannot accept these greater gifts, and certainly not without promising to repay you every cent once I am established back at Lewisham!'

In truth, Camilla doubted if her meagre salary would be equal to the repayment of such a price as would procure four good gowns, two bonnets, as well as gloves and boots, but she would never admit this to Rotherham! If it took her a year's salary, and she must go without her little comforts, she would still repay him, for she hated beyond anything to be in debt to another person! It was a kind of millstone around one's neck to be in debt to others, and she had always paid her way.

'Certainly,' he replied offhandedly, 'if you wish it, but money is no object with me you know. I hardly notice where my money is spent for I have so much of it, and if it is not to be put to such use as to clothe a worthy female, and further a very good cause indeed — what is the value of riches when they cannot be used for good?' His eyes challenged her.

She was powerless against his reasoning, unless she was to make herself look vastly unchristian indeed, and so she tried another tack. 'But how came you to find such items, all ready-made and in my size?'

She was still in some disbelief, and almost wished to accuse him of some strange trick against her.

'Oh, that was pure luck, I must confess. I did not have the convenience of time to have them made up new, but the seamstress to whom I applied was quite congenial and showed me these, which she had made ready for a young lady who did not expect them until next week. With a modest degree of effort and the application of some compliments to the lady's needle,' (here, his eye twinkled mischievously) 'she readily gave them into my care for a very rational sum, and, well, here they are! Now do not, pray, give me such severe glances for I shall feel very bad indeed if you do not like them!'

She wondered what he was about, and what his ulterior motive must be, for no one had ever gone to such trouble on her account before. 'Why do you exert yourself to such a degree, Mr Rotherham, all on account of a mere governess who has mislaid her charge?' she asked suspiciously. 'I am not even worth your notice; in normal circumstances, even were I to be tutoring your children, I would receive only a quarter of the attentions you have paid me.'

'I suppose I cannot bear to see another human being in trouble, if it is in my power to help. I have always been the same; Mama berates me for the weakness, and weakness it is, I suppose, although I cannot but help myself. I am all harsh exterior, Miss Spinner, all iron and marble on the outside,' he added, smiling, 'but nothing but an unset blancmange, I assure you, on the inside.'

Camilla's life had taught her not only pride and dignity, but humility and she saw that Rotherham had meant well. 'Unset blancmange? Now there is a picture indeed!' she laughed, 'Very well. I suppose I must thank you. I am indebted to you sir. I shall repay every cent in due course. But I shall not give up my brown bonnet,' she added with a spark in her eye, 'however much you dislike it, for I must not forget that I am in service, as much as we might pretend that this is not the case.' She put her hand to her bonnet protectively and looked him steadily in the eye.

Rotherham smiled impishly. 'I would not dream of making you give up such a prize, but do me the favour of putting on one of these others for now, and the pretty pelisse I have procured for you also, since to continue in the way we have come will surely rouse suspicion soon enough! Here you are—' he contrived to open one of the hat boxes, and setting aside the lid asked, 'is this not a pretty bonnet?'

The boy who had laboured beneath the multitude of boxes, was watching this exchange with impatience, and now tugged on Rotherham's sleeve. 'Sir?'

'Oh, of course — here you are boy — now be off with you, there's a good chap!' Rotherham had handed the lad a silver sixpence, and his eyes gleaming with joy from this unexpected bounty, the lad ran off.

Camilla had meanwhile lifted the bonnet up from its nest of straw and gasped. 'It is much too handsome a bonnet for myself, I assure you! I cannot wear it — indeed, I cannot!'

'But you must, Camilla, or our schemes will fail, and you might lose Alice. Do put it on, dear girl, and pray stop being so modest. Your face, you know, is very pretty when you are not casting me injurious glances — the colour suits your eyes and hair, and will, I think, lift your plain gown admirably.'

The bird's-egg blue satin poke-bonnet, with its creamy ribbons, was just what she might have ordered for herself, had her governess's wages allowed such an extravagance. Sighing, Camilla untied the ribbons which held her own old bonnet in place and replaced it with the new one. Her curls fell prettily from the sides of the bonnet, although she did not notice Rotherham staring. She had not become used to compliments, and her cheeks were still blushed with rose from Rotherham's calling her "pretty", and "dear girl", as it were nothing out of the ordinary. His flattery, while she could hardly think it sincere, made her belly do little leaps and starts, and she could not meet his eye.

Rotherham now signalled the postillions to hand in the extra boxes, and after he singled out another of them, pulling it aside, he signalled to Camilla. 'Now, shall we get on at last? We must find a trail of your charge and her beau very soon I wager — these are good horses and will go at pace, never fear!'

Camilla allowed herself to be handed into the carriage and took up her usual place on the bench opposite Rotherham. Once they were away, trotting down the main street and headed north again, Rotherham handed her the other box, which contained a matching pelisse in the same blue silk, trimmed inside with the warmest wool, finely decorated with a little fur, and embroidered with green vine leaves on the lapels.

'It is finer than anything to which I have ever been used,' remarked Camilla, fingering the silk. 'I feel very strange, as if I am being very dishonest indeed to make people think I am a finer lady than I truly am.'

'What is the difference between a fine lady, and a governess, I may ask?' Rotherham asked her amusedly. 'I perceive the only outward difference is in clothing, certainly not in education, for I have been in company with as many 'fine' ladies as I have wished, and not all of them can boast the same education, nor indeed manners, as you may rightfully do, Miss Spinner. I collect that only clothing may suit the purpose of being called such a thing. It is my considered opinion that Miss Spinner is as fine a lady as I have met with, even in her dull brown cloak, and perhaps finer than most I have had the misfortune to enjoy any tolerable degree of acquaintance with.'

Camilla, having cast off her old travelling cloak and put on the pretty pelisse, now gave him a shy smile which, if she had known its effect on her companion's heart, she would have held back for fear of making him a good way to being fascinated by her. But she knew nothing of his thoughts, and said very earnestly, 'You have been kind, Mr Rotherham, although I am not certain I deserve such praise. But I am persuaded. I shall wear the pelisse, and I shall pay you for it the very moment I can return to my post at Lewisham.'

Rotherham seemed momentarily transfixed upon her face, and did not reply to this, and a little embarrassed by his intent regard, she turned to the window to study the scenes which were passing before her eyes. It was too kind of him to supply her with clothing to advance their scheme and protect her reputation, and she rather doubted her ability to repay the sum she would now owe him. She should now be obliged to go without books and gloves and stockings for a full year, she thought with dismay! Nevertheless, she could not accept the items as gifts, for her pride and her reputation would never allow such a transaction. She would forgo all little comforts rather than be indebted to Rotherham. But indebted she was, for now, she mused. She fell into a light doze, allowing the rocking of the carriage to lull her into slumber, but about an hour later she was jolted into wakefulness when she realized they had stopped. Rotherham stood on the road talking to the coachman.

'What has happened?' she asked, peering from the window.

'One of the horses is lame,' replied Rotherham cheerfully. 'I am afraid we must stop at the next village. It is not far, but the poor beast must walk, or he will never recover. It has a stone in the hoof, but I have taken a look at the poor creature and cannot get at it.'

'Oh!' This *was* ill luck, for it would put them even further behind Alice, but Camilla knew that there was nothing for it but to make their way to the nearest village.

It was a slow journey, and even though the little village was not so far, it took them a good hour before they found themselves in the stone-walled road which led through a quaint old village. Finding their way to the cottage which was recommended them by a passing lad, the two beasts were tended to, and the stone removed.

'The poor creature will want a bit o' rest, Squire,' mumbled the farmer to whom they had applied for assistance. 'You want to rest 'im up a bit, or that bruise wil'nt heal. Rest 'im overnight and 'e'll be just like new on the morrow. Ye better see me lady up at the 'ouse for some lodgings and a meal. You ain't goin' anywhere to-day, I'll be bound!'

So they did as urged, and found themselves with a hearty, simple dinner to sustain them, and clean lodgings for the night. Their coachman was accommodated similarly in the haybarn. The farmer had taken them to be husband and wife, as Rotherham had intended, and so the accommodation they were shown to consisted of a narrow bed barely fit for one. Camilla waited until the farmer's wife had gone before expressing her disapproval, but Rotherham had already anticipated her request.

'I shall preserve your reputation, Miss Spinner, by seeing myself downstairs shortly. If the coachman can be comfortable in the haybarn, then so may I. Besides, that bed looks as if it can hardly accommodate a child, let alone two people!'

'You are very good,' she replied primly. 'I only hope I do not need to call for assistance in the night, for there is no lock on the door at all!'

Rotherham chuckled. 'Just pull that solid dresser up to your door, Miss Spinner; I am sure that will be all that is needed to deter the old fellow from snatching your maidenly virtue from you with his wife asleep in the next room!'

She formed a retort, but caught sight of his laughing eyes, and primed her lips. Impossible man!

The night passed uneventfully, however, and when Rotherham met her quite jovially at breakfast the next morning, and the farmer's wife had gone away, Camilla said crossly, 'You express so little anxiety about my being murdered upstairs in my sleep, that I can hardly think you had any concern at all in leaving me alone here!'

'Oh, but I had none at all, for all you needed to have done was given any intruder one of those prodigiously cross looks of yours and that would have deterred him more than I could have done had I been next door,' replied Rotherham pleasantly, helping himself to toast and preserves. 'Besides, I am sure that if you had been murdered, you would never tell me whether you were or not!'

Camilla, despite herself, smiled into her tea. 'I suspect you are quite right, Mr Rotherham. I would never countenance giving you the satisfaction!'

They finished their meal and found their carriage made ready and waiting. Minutes later they trotted up and out of the village and headed north once again.

* * *

They made good time, entering Yorkshire country by noon, and getting behind them a good few hours before they thought of stopping. By and by they turned into a watering place of tolerable quality, the Sow's Ear, and pulled up the tired beasts which had drawn them thus far. Being a rough establishment, it did not boast many servants to unload what was now a multitude of boxes and trunks, but for two tired travellers, it was enough for them to set foot upon the ground, stretch long cooped-up limbs, and order up a dinner and rooms. About them, several carriages and horses were being brought in and out, and several other travellers strolled and went in and out the door. Camilla looked about eagerly for any sign of Alice, then sighed to see no sign of her.

When the innkeeper came out, Rotherham gave the orders himself. 'A decent room for my... my wife, man, and one for me — and have our trunks taken up as soon as possible, if you will, for we wish to order a meal, having been on the road all day.'

'Certainly, Sir, my wife will get you up a bit of a meal, if you don't mind it being a bit haphazard, since we have been busy all day — but

I collect there is still half a pigeon pie left and some cheese — and there's a baked apple from our own trees for a desert — but as for the room, Sir, I can only offer one, since my house is full tonight.'

'Oh, no!' exclaimed Camilla in dismay. 'I mean to say, is there not something that can be done?'

'No indeed, Ma'am, for I have but one room left and that will soon be gone if you do not take it now.'

'Devilish bad luck!' Rotherham glanced at an anxious Camilla. 'Well, man, can you not find me a closet? I'll sleep in the barn, even!'

The innkeeper looked askance at the husband and wife and said with a wide grin, 'I'd be obliged to believe the lady snores, Sir, if you don't have care, for you be so adamant not to sleep in the very same room! Haha, it ain't nothing I aint seen 'afore, Sir, though I can see I have offended your wife with my foolish jest. Ne'er you mind, Mrs, I was only funning, as you can see!'

Rotherham laughed, not at all put out by the man's jest. 'Now that is all very well, man, but perhaps it is *I* who snores? I'll be grateful if you don't offend my wife, if you please — Mrs Rotherham *never* snores, I assure you!' He gave Camilla the most familiar wink.

Camilla did not know if she was blushing at the familiarity suggested by such a comment or by his coming to her aid like a doting husband, but while she turned variously three shades of pink all at once, her chance to preserve what shreds of her maidenly virtue were still intact was being dashed into pieces quite completely.

'I am sorry for it, Sir,' continued the innkeeper, 'for I can see you and the lady are well-to-do folk, and I be terrible sorry to not be more at your service and give you two rooms as you ask, but it's a full house I have, and even the closet and barn is full up. I only have one room left, Ma'am, if you and your husband here don't mind it being a little on the cosy side!'

Share a room! It certainly would not do! She had made concession enough by putting on the clothes he had got for her, but to share a room! Camilla was about to suggest that there was nothing for it but she and Rotherham to carry on to the next village, but Rotherham had already accepted the innkeeper's offer. He cast her a glance, giving a stern warning with his eyes which she dare not object to.

'That will do just as well, will it not, Camilla, dear? I am sure you can endure my snoring for one night, *darling!*

While Camilla was trying hard not to blush even more at the familiarity which had once again caused little leaps within her insides, Rotherham had turned back to the innkeeper. He agreed on a price with the man and soon their trunks were being brought to a room of exceedingly modest proportions, and which boasted a rather small bedstead with a curtain, a washstand and pitcher, and a smallish cupboard. It was more a room for one than two! One bare, very hard-looking chair adorned the fireplace which had been lit and was crackling feebly in the grate.

The doors shut behind them. Taking in the scene before her, Camilla was heartily dismayed. The room was cosy indeed, so cosy that there was not a whit of room on the floor betwixt the narrow bed, the washstand and the walls, let alone a chair that would support a man's weight for hours of tossing and turning! Her eyes met Rotherham's in dismay. 'Where on earth will you sleep?' she cried.

'I think that must be quite obvious, Miss Spinner!' he replied, with one of his impish looks.

He thought to share her bed? But she supposed that to expect him to sleep in that hard little chair was uncharitable of her, since it was his money which was paying the bill. She reluctantly supposed that there was no alternative. Her mind was in tumult. Once again, her stomach did little somersaults at the thought of being obliged to lie down on the same bed with him.

'I — I suppose there is no other solution...' Had she taken leave of her senses? Did she find the idea of his sharing her chamber — her bed — attractive? Desirable? But she had certainly taken leave of all reason, all decorum! But the idea of his sharing a chamber with her, however innocent, gave her the most... the most... unthinkable sensations!

Rotherham was eyeing her as if every thought in her mind had already been clear to him. He saw her face and laughed. 'My dear Miss Spinner, I assure you, I shall be quite comfortable sleeping in that chair.'

'Oh! I thought you meant to — to—'

'Share your bed? Not at all, but I must say its excessively considerate of you! Very accommodating! I am gratified indeed!'

'You know *very* well I didn't – I mean I never–' she fumbled, her face now as pink as a rosebud. 'You are very unkind to tease me so!'

His eyes danced. 'Never mind, Miss Spinner! Believe me when I assure you that I shall preserve your female modesty as surely as if I was your brother.'

Still suffering under his tease, Camilla eyed him primly. 'I assure you, Mr Rotherham, that I shall scream loudly if you so much as leave your chair, Sir!'

'Certainly, Madam, and I shall scream with you, if you think it will assist matters!' replied Rotherham helpfully, having opened his trunk and begun searching for a fresh cravat.

Camilla could not but help herself. 'Why, you are the most – the most – vexatious, obnoxious creature of my acquaintance!'

Rotherham was unmoved. He bowed low. 'If it helps, I can leave you here and you may make enquiries of your own as to Miss Featherstone, if you can get a carriage, that is. Does that please you more?' His eye twinkled.

'You think yourself astonishingly amusing, I collect.'

'Certainly, I strive for nothing more than to divert and amuse my friends, Miss Spinner. I am glad you find me so entertaining! Pray, don't trouble to remove that fomenting look from your face on my account – it makes your eyes dance very prettily and I have no aversion to looking at them in that case!' Here he chuckled as she banged down the lid of her trunk more vigorously than she had needed.

'I shall do no such thing! I mean to say – you really are the most irritating, aggravating–'

'Yes, yes,' Rotherham laughed delightedly, 'do encourage yourself to stay in a rage with me. I tell you, you really are in perfect looks when you are angry – Camilla *darling*!'

About to throw her hairbrush at his still laughing, dodging figure, she stopped just in time to see the maid step in the door. She was as happy to see them both as Camilla was not.

'Good afternoon, Mrs Rotherham,' greeted the girl cheerfully. 'I was only come up to see if you needed any assistance dressing for dinner, Ma'am? Mrs Rodney sent me, seeing as you have no one to do for you.'

Camilla's bright red cheeks at being referred to as "Mrs Rotherham" almost gave her away, but silently berating Rotherham himself for the smile straining at his lips to see her predicament, she calmly replied in the negative and sent the girl off.

Rotherham was chuckling to himself and she bristled. Abominable gentleman! He appeared to be relishing her discomfort as much as *she* was finding it a taxing strain on her nerves! Besides which, to be standing in a bed chamber with him, and have them both sharing those little intimacies which would generally be carried out when two married people were to share a room — she could not tell if she was shamed or fascinated! Being quite perplexed at the feelings which were assailing her, she strove for an appearance of calm at least and said sensibly, 'I see you mean to mock me and take your amusement at my expense. If you must, then I suppose I cannot prevent you. But do me the favour of waiting until we are alone before embarrassing me, if you please!'

He had the grace to look contrite, although she doubted the sincerity of it. 'Touché, once again, Miss Spinner! It was very bad mannered of me indeed to take advantage of you like that! I am quite sorry! Only I am so singularly fond of amusement that my friends say I choose quantity over quality, and therefore have very poor taste in it, I own. But I shall endeavour to take pity on your poor nerves and behave myself better. Now, don't be cross anymore and come let us to a meal. I could eat at *least* three of those pigeon pies the innkeeper mentioned!'

Camilla, slightly mollified by Rotherham's apology, sat down to table as composedly as she could under the circumstances. She had dressed for dinner, reluctantly putting on another of the fine gowns Rotherham had purchased for her, a pretty pale apricot muslin with green ribbons. She had taken some pains with her hair, reasoning with herself that all the ladies she had seen here were so well dressed that she was certain to stand out if she did not take some care with her appearance. She finally went down to dinner a little in awe of the picture she had made in the glass before she had left her room. She wondered if Rotherham would make a comment on her appearance, but then had laughed at herself for conceit. If playing the part of Rotherham's wife was to have the effect of increasing her vanity, she would surely be better to put on her dull brown gowns again! But although he had given her an admiring glance, he had said nothing when she had come down to the dining room, and she did not know if she was relieved or put out that he seemed not to notice the pains she had taken to be in looks.

Now as they were brought in several dishes, she marvelled at what magic it was that all innkeepers wives seemed to have, always insisting that they had 'very little but what humble offerings as was left over from yesterday', and then could put up such a feast as was before them. The pair, both ravenous from hours on the road, managed to consume a great deal of the pie, a baked sturgeon, buttered greens, and several boiled potatoes, before they were able to pass a few pleasantries.

Once the afore mentioned apples were almost gone as well, and the custard which accompanied them, Rotherham begged her pardon and stood. 'If you will forgive me, I shall see to some enquiries as to your Miss Alice and her beau. It is possible they have stopped in here to overnight, for it is the best posting inn for some miles. I may even hear something of Lady Louisa, if I am fortunate. I suspect neither of our parties would suffer the misfortune of a carriage accident if they could take a better road. I shall make some enquiries and return directly.'

Camilla, her belly full and her toes warm, was grateful to sit quietly while Rotherham undertook the enquires of Alice and Charles Deed. She sat before the fire, contemplating the evening she was to spend in the same room with him, and sighed. She would remain in full dress, and be ready to bolt at the slightest hint of his taking advantage. Although Rotherham appeared in general so much the gentleman that quite apart from his taking it upon himself to purchase her some clothes, she could not fault him in anything else, so far as they had come. Still, never had she been put in so many untoward circumstances, so many trying situations. But if nothing else, she had always relied on fortitude to carry her through when faced with trials, and now was no exception. She would suffer it quietly and hope that no one would ever suspect them of not being husband and wife!

Rotherham was back very soon. 'I have just made some enquiries with the innkeeper, and it has yielded a very interesting intelligence. I suspect you will be quite relieved by it.'

Camilla leaned forward in great eagerness. Perhaps the delay with the horses had not disadvantaged them so much as she thought. 'Have you found Alice? Is young Mr Deed with her? Are they here?'

'I cannot give you that assurance exactly, but here is the most fascinating fact of the matter. A young lady meeting your description of Miss Featherstone was indeed here yesterday, and departed this morning. However, this young lady does not travel with her beau. She travels with another female, an older woman.'

Camilla was disappointed. 'Oh, then it cannot be Alice at all! She would be with Charles, I collect, unless something has happened!'

'Ah, but I have not apprised you of an interesting circumstance which was mentioned by the innkeeper. The young woman who meets the description of Miss Featherstone was heard to be called by her female companion, "Miss Spinner."

'But that is *my* name!'

'Indeed,' Rotherham supplied helpfully, 'and I rather think this must be a confirmation that the young lady mentioned is indeed your Miss Featherstone.'

'But,' replied Camilla in some consternation, 'why would she use my name, and whatever has become of Charles Deed, then? For knowing Alice as I do, it is my considered opinion that nothing would have prevented her running away with Charles but the most unavoidable circumstances!'

'Perhaps the lad could not get away, or was prevented in some way?'

'Perhaps,' replied Camilla, sensibly unmoved for her charge on account of her deeming the whole scheme being such an ill-planned evil, 'although I cannot vouch for it that he has not gone and backed out of such a hair-brained scheme; he must know his father would disinherit him. Besides which, I never saw any particular strength of regard in him for her. I dare say he has seen sense or been discovered, and left her stranded! Then she will not be going to Gretna, I think. I collect she must be going on to Yorkshire, to Innesfalls, where she has relations — an aunt of whom she is rather fond.'

'Yes, and under the guise of being you — Miss Camilla Spinner!'

Camilla had begun to grow rather vexed. 'Yes, she is certainly bold as to that! What a mischief! I cannot say she has not been rather brave to continue her journey alone, but under the disguise of my name! Only think what she may do to ruin my reputation in the meantime!'

It took Rotherham a few moments' coaxing to persuade Camilla from her outrage.

'Now then, Miss Spinner! She can hardly ruin your reputation if she is travelling quietly with this lady who is obviously Quality, herself. I think you might be made quite comfortable in this intelligence, for now you know we are on the right road, after all, to pursue your charge. It appears she is quite the resourceful young lady. She clearly thought herself safer to travel under a pseudonym, than her own name. Very clever of her! But I do wonder why she would prefer the deception, for she obviously bethought herself quite safe from pursuit by *you*!'

'Well,' mused Camilla, now somewhat gotten over the shock, 'she ought to have known that I would immediately see right through her little ruses; she was not at all as sly as she thought herself! "Miss Spinner" indeed! But she cannot know that I am in pursuit! I suppose I can only be grateful that I shall have a good chance to find her and bring her home to Lewisham! But whom do you suppose this other female to be? Can she be a woman of good sense to carry a young girl travelling alone, into Yorkshire?'

'I cannot say who her companion is, nor anything comforting regarding her character, I'm afraid,' replied Rotherham, 'except the innkeeper's wife said she was well-dressed and obviously a woman of breeding.'

'Nothing else?'

'Oh, she thought she might have heard Alice refer to her as "Miss Fortesque." The name does not ring any bells with me, and I cannot think of any young ladies who might be attached to the families I know of hereabouts. Your Miss Featherstone must have imposed herself upon this female to carry her into Yorkshire. But at least you have the comfort of knowing that if you simply make towards the aunt's house, you may very well find the young lady.'

Camilla heard the singular, 'you' and inferred his meaning to be that he meant to discard her so that he was free to make his own way after his Lady Louisa. Stung, she said with a suddenly wounded pride, 'Oh, certainly, I shall do just that. I have detained you from your own object too long, I think. Tomorrow I shall certainly order up a new carriage and a woman to accompany me, for I am sure this inn appears to have as many free carriages as the last did not!'

Rotherham, however, eyed her with amusement and said, 'And here I was, rather enjoying being a married man! Now don't, pray, give me one of those looks again! I was merely sporting with you. If it is to Innesfalls you are bound, I can engage to carry you there with no great inconvenience to myself.'

Camilla conceded that pride might have had its way and insisted she decline the offer of his further company, but she was too anxious at the prospect of going on alone, and grateful not to be obliged to order up a carriage of her own. Besides which, she had little enough coin left for such an outlay. She thanked him, but could not help but add, with a degree of acerbic tartness, 'Your reward, Sir, for my having plagued you this far, and giving you the most painful exertion and trouble, must now to be finally free of me if you can! I am astonished that you have not dropped me and my trunks on the road forthwith!'

'What an ungentlemanly notion you have of me!' he exclaimed with feigned astonishment. 'And yet I am bound to deliver you where would go, Madam, since I am nothing *but* a gentleman, despite your wild imaginings three days ago that I might murder you in your sleep, or worse!'

Her mouth dropped open. 'How did you—'!

'Oh, the look upon your face quite made your thoughts clear. You are not as clever as you think, Miss Spinner; indeed, you wear every thought upon that stern countenance of yours! But go on, do concede at once that so far I have behaved very well indeed, for someone whom you thought might murder you in your sleep, or take advantage of you!'

'There is still tonight, Mr Rotherham,' she retorted primly, then regretted her impetuous comment, for he had given her the most lecherous grin.

'Indeed, there is!' replied he, amused at her blush.

'I know you sport with me, and I do not like you any better for it,' she responded, unwilling to approbate his jesting manner toward a topic which was of so serious a nature. 'It is my reputation of which we speak, which it appears you look upon so lightly as makes me think you not at all anxious for it, although you profess otherwise!'

'Believe me, Miss Spinner, I am as anxious for your reputation as I am for your happiness. I have certainly been giving your reputation a great *deal* of thought! After all, I am to share a room with you!'

Camilla, whose stomach had just begun to tingle in a very unusual manner at the thought of Rotherham's sharing a room with her, added to her own confusion by flustering, 'Is that the clock? It chimes eleven, I think. I — I believe I should go up to bed — I am very tired indeed — I shall rely on your not disturbing me when you come up, if you please—'

Rotherham's eye twinkled suspiciously. 'Never fear, Miss Spinner, I professed just now a great anxiety for your reputation. You will be relieved to discover I am, after all, quite determined to preserve your modesty by taking this very good chair by the fire here. Only do be a dear and leave me some hot water in the morning after you have finished making your ablutions!'

Now, she did not know if she was relieved or disappointed. 'Really Mr Rotherham! You intended to sleep before the fire this whole time, did not you? But you are beyond vexing, for you let me believe you intended to share my — my bed!'

'You know I like to see you cross, Miss Spinner! It makes your eyes sparkle fetchingly indeed! Now, do put down that cup, for I believe you might throw it at my head and then I won't sleep for the bruise!'

* * *

Later on, tossing for some hours in the little bed, Camilla was grateful to have been after all, granted the room to herself. She had now been obliged to own some feelings she had not wished to examine in Rotherham's presence. Being inherently a sensible creature, who had no inclination to be like other disingenuous young ladies, for whom self-delusion was as natural as deluding others, it took her less than ten minutes to ponder the unusual feelings which Rotherham had caused to rise up in her, and shortly thereafter, she came to a rather sober conclusion. She had never been in love before, and did not suppose herself so now, but as for the feeling Rotherham aroused in her, she had not been so few years in the world that she did not recognise attraction to a gentleman when it kept her awake at night! She supposed that at the age of five-and-twenty, she by now ought to have felt a very natural inclination to wish herself married and perhaps have a family of her own, but she had never thought that as a governess, she would ever be in the way of meeting anyone of her own lowly rank in life.

It was natural, too, she told herself, that by being thrown into his company every day, in accepting his kindness toward her, and allowing herself to be in his power and his protection, that very natural inclinations might arise from such a circumstance. But as for love, she neither needed nor desired to feel such a complicated emotion, and especially for someone of Rotherham's rank. It would be a foolhardy thing indeed to allow herself to fall prey to a passing inclination for a man who sat well above her in rank and in circumstance. And even besides that, she had no reason to believe that he would flout convention by failing to preserve those separations of rank which were so necessary in society. She must not allow the gift of a few clothes,

clothes which gave her the appearance of gentility, to alter her own determination to conduct herself in such a way as would not bring shame and humiliation upon herself by imagining a preference in him which did not exist. If there was a preference of her own, for him, she must surely stamp it out!

But one thing she was now obliged to acknowledge; that Rotherham, by his kindness, and his consideration of her reputation, by his impeccable manners towards her, had now proven that he was indeed a gentleman. She would no longer suspect him of anything else but an impartial and unbiased regard for a woman in difficult circumstances.

Still these thoughts did not have the effect of making her more comfortable. Rather, they increased her sleeplessness, until, thinking she might read and then discovering that she had left her book in the little room in which Rotherham slept now, she could not too closely scrutinize her next action, that of leaping from her bed and going directly downstairs with her candle to the very room!

Wrapped in a shawl, she padded barefoot to the door of the parlour, which was slightly ajar. Peering in, she was astonished to see Rotherham, not asleep, but sitting upright, very still, with his hands toward the fire, seemingly deep in thought! She was so astonished that she must have made a small noise for Rotherham at this moment turned, and all astonishment at spying her at the door, immediately got up and came to her.

'What is it, Miss Spinner? Are you well? Or are you a vision,' he added dryly, 'a dream come to me in my sleep to tease me?'

'No, not at all — I am as real as you, or I think I am!' He seemed out of sorts, and she stopped, embarrassed to have caught him so. 'I could not sleep and only came for my book... it is there, you see it, on the chair.'

He fetched it for her, but he held it in his hand and when she reached for it, he would not let it go. 'Are you sure you are not a dream? But you must be, for I was just now thinking of you, and I have conjured you up with my thoughts, I collect. You do not shiver from cold, and yet the night is cold. Therefore, you must be a dream!'

'Why should you be thinking of *me*, Sir? But I assure you, I am as real as this book. And I do not shiver, simply because I am not cold. Well, I am beginning to be a *little* cold,' she added, not sure if Rotherham was foxed or ill or worse.

But Rotherham immediately led her to the fire. 'Warm yourself then, a little, Miss Spinner, and pay no attention to me, I was in a daze from being mesmerized by the fire, that is all.'

Conscious that she was in her night-things and they were only covered by a thin shawl, Camilla spread her fingers out to the fire, which was still bright, and after a minute of companionable silence which, despite all her previous determination only half an hour before, she found herself loath to end, she was about to say something when she realized that he had fixed his eye upon her for some time. When she turned her head, he turned sharply away, and she was perplexed. What was his meaning, fixing her with his gaze like that? And why was he thinking of her before she had come into the room?

'You find me in an ill mood tonight, I fear,' he said with a half-smile.

Camilla, seeing Rotherham troubled, found her own feelings disturbed in his behalf. 'Then perhaps you ought to relieve yourself of them, Mr Rotherham. Nothing prevents sleep so much as contained, disturbed feelings!' She ought to know, she thought, herself having been disturbed by her newly-recognised attraction for Rotherham.

'I have been cogitating on the disagreeableness of having one's future set out according to duty — although you may disagree, Miss Spinner, but you are a governess and therefore free to choose your path in life — or at least which family you shall work for or not — I must never falter from the path chosen for me, for I have a duty to the name "Rotherham."'

'I think — your mother's wishes are very important, are they not? But she may claim fairly that you have a duty to her, bound by real filial affection and loyalty, as much as by your name. Surely you must honour your mother in a way that supersedes even the strictures of duty?'

He raised a brow. 'Of course, and that is why I am determined upon a course which, while it may not lead to my happiness, will give my mother some comfort in her final months.'

'I cannot value these things lightly, Mr Rotherham, for not having had my own mother or father's affections to rely upon for some time, I suppose I have come to value them more highly in retrospect, than if I had not learned to do without them.'

'Yes, I forgot that you have been alone for many years. It cannot have been easy, I think, to leave your former life and go out as a governess. But you do not have to please anyone else, other than yourself, whereas I must find a replacement for Louisa, and marry before Mama dies. I shall not be content until I have found a woman to take home as my wife. I must do my duty, and you are right — my affection for Mama means I must do my duty, for I am not such a man as to value duty highly for itself alone.'

'Yes,' she cried warmly, 'you must consider your mother's wishes; it is above everything the highest duty one can do as a Christian, and as a gentleman.'

'But finding someone to whom I can imagine tying myself for three decades or more — someone that she will approve, a woman of breeding and rank — that is the part of duty which I dislike Miss Spinner. My own choices, my own inclinations cannot be consulted on the matter. I must do everything to please Mama, whose right it is to request such obedience.'

Camilla contemplated the weight of his words, the manner in which they were uttered, and suspected him, unreasonably perhaps, of having some idea of her attraction for him. She coloured, stung, and knowing at the same time that he was right to remind her of his duty to his mother. He could not, he had said, consult his own inclination, but must please his mother. It was all she needed to bring her out of the trance she had been in since she went to bed. This was not a fairy tale, where some Cinderella married her prince charming. She must think of him no more!

'I find myself suddenly tired—' she faltered, vexed at herself and at this ridiculous inclination for blushing wildly wherever near him. 'I think I will not read, after all — I shall leave you to sleep.'

'Yes,' he said musingly, 'we ought both to sleep. Goodnight, Miss Spinner.'

She left him more confused as to her feelings than she had gone, and when she discovered that he had retained her book and that she still had nothing to amuse her, she sighed and blew out the candle. It was some time before she fell asleep pondering the irony of being attracted to a man who, due to rank, circumstance and family expectation, was the last person whom she could entrust with her future happiness.

It is very well that Louisa had fallen asleep in the carriage beside Alice, or she would have had reason to question her new friend more thoroughly. Alice, having had some three hours in the carriage before they had signalled the driver to find a posting inn in which to overnight, had spent that time feigning sleep. She always thought best with her eyes closed, and besides this, she did not wish to fend off well-intentioned attempts at conversation when she was trying hard to think!

Only once Alice had assured herself that her companion was deeply asleep, by dint of whispering loudly, 'Miss Fortesque? Louisa?' had she sat up and peered back the way they had come for some time, anxious to see if they were being followed. By and by, she muttered an unladylike exclamation and fixed her pretty rosebud mouth in a line so severe as might have convinced anyone watching that Alice was in quite a February mood. Her eyes were as stormy as could be, and she sat in deep contemplation for some time, periodically checking behind them each time they topped a hill or covered a long stretch of road.

There was, however, just cause for Alice's being so very out of sorts. She had discovered that they were indeed being followed, by a rider so far into the distance as to be a tiny dark blemish on the dusty roads behind them. The rider was, certainly, a good hour in their wake, but it would not take much for a gentleman with a good horse and an even better idea of the roads hereabouts, to guess their direction and make the same posting inn by night fall.

What rotten ill luck, Alice thought vexedly, to be followed by that odious brown-nose, Mr Percy! There was nothing for it now but she would have to throw him off, or change her plans! Seeing that she had little chance to throw him off in her present circumstance, it did not take Alice long to decide upon a new course of action. She must remove herself from the carriage of Louisa Fortesque and find other transport! But first they must detour a little.

When Louisa woke, she was inclined to pull into the first posting inn on their route, but Alice begged her to tell the driver to take them a very little out of their way, for fear of their being followed by the very Mr Brown whom she was so in dread of. Louisa, comprehending Alice's distress, agreed immediately. The poor, tired coachman was directed to go past the next posting inn and veer off towards another village slightly to the west. It was not far off their way, but Alice knew that in taking the longer route, she would have a better chance to throw off Mr Percy who followed so close behind them.

By the time they drew into the pretty village of Oakdean around four and a half o'clock, Alice had concocted a further scheme and she now set about putting it into action. She knew that she did not have much time.

As soon as they had bespoken rooms in the inn, she shut herself in, took out her little writing case and penned a hurried note. Folding it almost before the ink was even dry, she addressed it and placed it on the bedside stand. Now she went downstairs in search of one of the house maids, a silver coin in her palm. A few minutes later and a satisfied Alice nipped back upstairs hastily, a small bundle under her arm.

Now she set the bundle down and opened it out. 'Yes, that will do very well,' she said decisively to herself as she folded up the items and put them away again. She washed her face hastily, changed out of her pelisse, put on a light shawl, and went downstairs again to meet Miss Fortesque for dinner.

To Louisa's amusement, Alice made a hearty meal of the ham and potatoes, lamb pie and new peas, and the strawberries and cream. 'You always seem so excessively hungry, my dear, when I can manage only half of what you eat! And yet your figure is so slight! I declare I don't know where you put it all!'

'Oh,' cried Alice in very good humour, 'Miss Spinner says the very same thing, only she says I must have hollow limbs for I never gain an ounce in my figure!' Then she blushed very hard indeed for she had realized her mistake. 'I meant to say, Miss — Miss Spoder, my friend. Bless me, I always say such silly things when I am not myself! How excessively tired I am!' She feigned a yawn. 'Will you mind very much, Louisa, dearest, if I retire early? I can hardly sit up!'

Louisa, who had detected the error immediately, only smiled, for Alice just had confirmed what she had all along suspected; "Miss Camilla Spinner" was not at all a governess and likely not a "Miss Spinner" either! But since she was certain her friend was most definitely escaping the man who was following them, she felt that she might do worse in offering what service she could to the desperate young woman. She nodded kindly. 'Of course, dear. Do go up and rest, and we shall meet at breakfast tomorrow. We shall leave promptly at ten, mind, so don't be late!'

Alice promised, with her fingers crossed behind her back, and she hoped the good Lord would not be *too* cross with her when she met Him, for telling so many untruths in such a short time! But there was nothing else to be done if she was to escape the odious Mr Percy!

She spent a restless night, and as soon as it was barely light she was up and packing her things. It was only six o'clock and outside it was just daylight. Clouds were gathering at pace on the horizon, blocking out the morning sun, and Alice did not want to be standing in the rain trying to beg for a ride! She quickly threw off her night gown and put on her petticoats. Then she unravelled the bundle she had solicited from the maid earlier. Within its folds were a plain cambric work dress, a stained apron, and a rough mob cap. These items she hastily put on over her fine undergarments, drew the laces of the dress tight herself, and surveyed herself in the glass. A little maid with suspiciously glossy curls looked back at her and she stuffed the pretty dark tendrils more severely under the cap until she looked quite the picture of servitude. That would do!

Throwing her gown and bonnet haphazardly into her open trunk, she looked out the window. The main road was on the opposite side of the building, although there was another narrower road hard by, but it seemed deserted and there was no one lurking by the hedge which ran along the laneway and separated the inn from the road. She bit her lip thoughtfully as she surveyed the distance between the window ledge and the garden below. It was but a tolerably shortish drop to the ground, she thought bravely.

Heaving both her trunks over to the window and hoisting them up onto the ledge took some effort, but after a little groaning and unladylike cursing, she had them both balanced atop the wide ledge. There was a convenient patch of thick bush below the window and it was into these that she now dropped her trunks, one by one, her two hat boxes following, with not so much as more than a dull thud. Next, she gathered her serviceable cambric skirts, and by grabbing hold of the drapes she contrived to get herself onto the ledge also. Not wishing to take an injurious fall onto the hard wooden trunks, she chose a spot next to the bushes, and easing herself over the edge, skirts hitched past her bloomers, she lowered herself as far as she could before dropping to the ground.

The ground below met her with rather an unfriendly address, and a little huff of air escaped her lungs. Keeping her eyes closed, she waited until the sudden dizziness had passed and she was about to sit up when a low chuckle caused her to open her eyes in shock.

'I cannot say I have ever seen a young lady quite as agile as yourself — the way you cast those trunks over the edge of the window was something I shan't forget. But I suppose I ought to enquire if you are injured? It was rather a drop!'

Before Alice stood a young man, well-dressed, with a wonderful waterfall of a cravat and a smart blue tail-coat and tall hat. His drawling tone and his open amusement caused her to colour up. 'You — you did not see me jump from the window, did you? But how ungentlemanly of you to watch!' The memory of her skirts hitched to her chin caused her to take a sharper tone with him than she had intended.

'I could hardly miss it, for my carriage happened to drive past just as the spectacle was unfolding, and I could not pass without stopping to ensure you had not broken all your bones!' His voice was languorous, as if he had had all the time in the world and had stopped merely for his own entertainment.

'You needn't have bothered,' she quipped acidly, quite annoyed with this laughing youth, 'for I am quite alright, as you see!' She realized that his carriage, with his liveried coachman and pair in front, now stood in the little laneway she had thought unfrequented.

But he did not bite back, so amused as he still appeared. Laughing a little he offered his hand and helped her up. 'Now you have bits of grass and leaves attached to your dress, just there, you see? That's better. So do tell me, is being in service here so abominable that you must take to jumping from the windows to escape? Cannot you just give the master your notice and get a character and go to the next town? That would have saved you the difficulty of breaking a limb if you had fallen the wrong way!'

'Oh!' replied Alice quickly, 'I don't need a character, for I am leaving service and going to my aunt's house, two days carriage ride from here. I don't suppose you are going north, are you?' she added hopefully. 'I wouldn't be any trouble at all, only I have no way to get to my aunt's!'

The young fellow surveyed her thoughtfully. 'Damnit! I had much better go on, you know, for I am making a good time to Yorkshire, and cannot afford to be behind! You had much better find yourself another ride, if that is what you are after.'

Alice turned beseeching eyes upon him. 'Oh Sir, please won't you take pity on a poor servant girl? I must get to my aunt's, for she is ever so ill, and I have no other way but to take my chance on the road with whomsoever might take pity on me, and even then I must chance the fates that I will make it alive to my destination!'

The fellow lifted a manicured brow and sighed. 'Oh, very well, I expect the company will relieve the tedium of travel somewhat. I don't mind admitting that barrelling up here in such a haste, only stopping to change horses, has been a bit of a bore. I don't like sleeping in carriages, gives one a dreadful sore neck! Very well, you can come along, so long as you don't mind only stopping to change pairs. And you must pay for yourself, mind, for I am not in pockets presently!'

'Of course,' said Alice eagerly, and pleased that her scheme had been so quickly accomplished. 'My name is Alice. Alice... er, Smith. I am much obliged to you, Mr — er?'

'Middlemount. Now where exactly are you going, that you must jump out of windows to get there?'

'Well, I do hope you are going in my direction. Where are *you* bound for? I must get as far towards Innesfalls as I can.'

'I am for Penniston,' drawled the young fellow, 'some devilishly remote village north of here, so I shall have to drop you off before I arrive if you don't mind it. I believe Innesfalls is two or three hours west out of my way.'

'Penniston!' Alice was taken aback. How strange that the very place Miss Fortesque was bound for was the same destination of this gentleman. However, it did not matter, so long as she could get as far as Innesfalls. 'Why, if you can put me down as near my aunt's as you can, I shall be greatly obliged to you, Sir. You are not going to take dreadful liberties with me, are you?' she added suspiciously, her blue eyes narrowing under the jaunty mob cap.

'I should hope not!' replied he haughtily, eyeing her dowdy, serviceable dress and mob cap. 'I am a gentleman and have nothing to do with maid servants at the best of times! I hope I have a little more taste than to be interested in chits of girls who run away from their employers! As much as a fine set of pink bloomers might tempt another man,' he added languidly, 'I am as indifferent to a serving girl as I would be to my own sister.'

'Oh, good!' exclaimed Alice, much relieved to hear this sincere refutation of her charms. 'Although it is not very kind of you to remind me that you saw my skirts up. I should think a gentleman wouldn't go about saying such things to females of *any* rank, even servants!'

'Just go get your trunks, there's a good girl, for I must get on and it looks to pour down soon. I am on a commission for a very important Lady, and there is a good sum of money at stake. Here, let me get my man to take that — I suppose he had best carry the trunks, but you may carry the hat boxes. What the *devil* can a maid want with hat boxes?'

But to Alice's relief he did not pause to hear the answer to that question. He hailed his driver over, and between them they carried Alice's things to the carriage, which was still waiting, horses stomping impatiently, in the laneway. Alice, looking careful about her, was satisfied that it was still so early that no one was about and they had managed to complete the task unseen. Even if someone had spotted her, she would only look like a little maid doing her master's bidding. Clambering aboard the carriage, she sighed in satisfaction. Let Mr Percy try to follow her now!

'*Dear Miss Fortesque,*

It gives me no pleasure to relate to you that, certain of my Unfortunate Fate should I find myself at the mercy of Mr Brown, who followed us these last two days, I have decided that I have no choice but to Throw Him Off, which means I must leave you and travel onwards by other means. Do not be anxious for me. I assure you that I am quite able to fetch for myself.

I collect you shall have no problem engaging a woman to accompany you to Penniston from here, for it is but a short distance, only a day and a half.

But do me the favour, if you happen to be accosted by Mr Brown before you arrive, to tell him not to pursue me as I am going on to my aunt's house, only don't pray tell him which town exactly I am bound for, since I believe him desirous of Kidnapping me!

Dear, kind Louisa! I will forever be obliged to you if you will protect me just a little longer.

Until we chance to meet again, I remain your True Friend,

Camilla Spinner.'

Louisa sighed and put down the paper. She could not guess what her friend was really about, and in what trouble she had gotten herself embroiled, but she did believe that it was something to do with the gentleman who had followed them from the posting inn, the day before, and if he really was as bad as Camilla had implied, she had no choice but to protect her friend as well as she was able. Well, she would face that obstacle when she arrived at it, but for now, she would take her young friend's advice and procure a woman to go with her the last few miles to Penniston.

She hoped, and indeed had reason to hope, for a kind welcome from her mother's brother who, for all his idiosyncrasies and foibles, had been everything kind and generous to her since she had been a girl, and she had no reason to think him averse to the sight of her now. True, Edmund Stacey would have aged a little more, since it was two years since she had laid eyes upon him, but having spent several summers in his company, she thought of Penniston with calm and equanimity. And when she thought of revealing her secret to her uncle, revealing her desires and wishes, she thought that he might not be averse to giving her shelter until she could secure her future. And so she folded the letter, tucked it in her pocket, and went to see about breakfast and the possibility of engaging a woman for her comfort between Oakdean and Penniston.

She had just sat down to breakfast, and was sipping her tea, when a young man entered the breakfast room and seemed to scan the room as if looking for someone. Louisa dipped her eyes, for she had seen at once that it was none other than Mr Brown, the man whom her friend Miss Spinner was trying to escape! He must have discovered that they had given him the slip and come further on to Oakdean! Well, he was too behindhand, for Camilla had already made her escape!

She kept her head low, then, realizing that the gentleman had never laid eyes on her, and that her young friend's sudden departure meant that the young fellow had no way to know that she herself was connected with Miss Spinner, she lifted her eyes and continued to sip her tea placidly, although she was cogitating most vigorously on what she ought to do next!

The young fellow, not finding the face he was looking for, sat down at a nearby table and took up a newspaper. Louisa watched him covertly from half-closed lashes. Now, she had lived long enough, she thought, to perceive a fudge when she saw it and she had known that her friend Camilla was very likely not a governess, nor was her name in all probability Miss Camilla Spinner. Louisa had ascertained enough to deduce that Miss Camilla Spinner was probably the young lady's governess, and that the young lady who called herself Camilla was a gentlewoman. But why she would be running from this man she could not guess.

If Camilla was not a governess, then she could have no employer called Mr Brown. Therefore, Louisa thought shrewdly, the young man from whom she was running was likely not a Mr Brown but a young man of some other name. He was, clearly, a gentleman, as his manner of dress was impeccable, besides which his bearing and manners seemed every part the gentlemen. She could not imagine this man making lewd advances to a young woman, let alone a governess who would be quite below him!

Louisa decided to test the strength of these assumptions. Feeling herself to be quite safe since there was no way this fellow could identify her with the lady he sought, she got up from her chair and walked past the young man, and, seeming to trip on her step a little, dropped her reticule. 'Oh, I do beg your pardon, Sir!' She anxiously peered below his chair where she had thrust the item.

The young fellow was all polite attention. 'Forgive me, I am such an oaf! I must have brushed your arm as you passed. It is entirely my own fault. Here, allow me—' and he reached to the floor to retrieve the dropped reticule.

Louisa blushed prettily and reclaimed her property. 'You are very kind, Sir. I — I did not hurt your arm as I went past? I did rather stumble into you.'

'No, not at all, but you — are you hurt in any way, Miss? May I call for something for your comfort, a glass of something perhaps? You look unwell,' he added as Louisa put a hand to her forehead.

She bestowed upon him one of most gentle smiles. 'Perhaps I will sit down just for a moment. I believe I got up too hastily just now and became dizzy. Oh, thank you, you are too kind!' She took the chair he had pulled out for her at his own table and allowed him to call for a glass of sherry.

'May I call someone for you, perhaps?' asked the young man with concern. 'A companion? With whom do you travel?'

Louisa composed her face. 'I travel alone, I thank you, but I have my woman with me. She is just now, er, packing my trunks. I shall be better directly, and we are to leave this hour. I am going north, you see, to the town of Penniston. My uncle, Mr Stacey, resides there and expects me.'

'I do hope you will have a safe journey Miss — er?'

'Miss Fortesque.'

'How do you do, Miss Fortesque? Thadeus Percy, at your service. If there is anything I might do for your comfort before you leave, please do not hesitate to ask.'

'Thank you, Mr Percy. In which direction do you travel, Sir?'

'I travel northward, as you do, or at least, I was, but I am not sure where I am headed just now.'

Louisa gave him a most inviting smile and hoped he would continue.

Mr Percy hesitated. 'I — I was in some anxiety about a young lady, you see — a young lady who was known to me, and whom I met with in Derbyshire, far from her home and all her friends. I suspected some sort of foul play, or that she was in trouble of some kind, and so I have been following her, and it is here I thought to find her. But I find that I was mistaken, for she is nowhere in this place, for I have been all over, unless she is hiding in one of the bedrooms. Or she is not here at all!'

'And what is the name of this young lady? Perhaps I have met with her while I have been travelling?' Louisa wanted very much to believe that this young man was indeed a friend of Miss Spinner's, but she wished to verify his innocence first.

'Why, her name is Miss Alice Featherstone, of Lewisham Hall in Shropshire. Do you know the lady? She is reported to have been travelling with her governess, Miss Spinner. The strangest thing is, however, that she told me herself that she was travelling with a friend, a Miss Mary Algernon, from Scotland.'

Now Louisa was hard pressed to remain silent. Should she tell this Mr Percy what she knew? But in doing so, however innocent and well intentioned he seemed, she would be violating a trust that she had with Miss Spin — Miss Featherstone — she corrected herself. His story seemed to fit what she had seen, and she felt that he was telling the truth, but still, she owed Miss Spinner — Miss Featherstone — some loyalty born of their blossoming friendship. 'I do not think I have met a Miss

Featherstone since I have been on the road,' she said quite honestly. 'Did this lady say why she was travelling north? Perhaps she is only going to visit relatives? Perhaps your fears for her are unfounded?'

Mr Percy sighed. 'I have heard reports only yesterday, from her friends in Shropshire, that indeed the young lady I speak of is missing from her home, and no one seems to know where she has gone. The newspapers have reported her disappearance, and the report says her governess has disappeared with her. I rather thought she was travelling with the governess when I last encountered her in Derbyshire, and have been following what I believe is their carriage ever since, but although the carriage has brought me here, to this posting inn, I see no sign of either the governess or of Miss Featherstone. I am at a loss as to what to do next. I believe the young lady is in danger, or may be, and I can only think she must be running away to friends in the north.'

Mr Percy looked so much in a state of apprehension for Miss Featherstone's comfort that Louisa now suspected his heart must be involved. He must be sincerely attached to her friend to follow Alice in his anxiety for her safety! She looked him over. He was obviously a young man of some consequence, and seemed of good birth and fine manners. He would be a good match for any young lady, she thought, and might suit her friend very well. She wondered what it was that Camilla — Alice — did not like about Mr Percy, for she was obviously taking great pains to avoid him! Louisa made a decision.

'I believe I can help you, Mr Percy, but you must not tell Miss Featherstone that I had any part in her discovery. I believe you mean well for my friend.'

'Your friend!' exclaimed Percy. 'So you do know her! So you are her friend, Miss Mary Algernon?'

She smiled. 'I suppose I am, Mr Percy. Indeed, Alice has travelled most of the way with me from Derbyshire to here at Oakdean — yes, Mr Percy, it is my own carriage which you have been following these past four days — and she only took her leave, rather abruptly I'm afraid, this very morning.' Louisa smiled as she recalled the rather dramatic little note she had found addressed to herself. 'I believe your Miss Featherstone intends to go on to Innesfalls, Mr Percy, to her aunt there. But if you think Miss Featherstone in any danger,' she added with quiet amusement, 'I rather think you don't know the lady as well as you might. For she is the most resourceful young woman I have had the fortune to know, and I think she has fetched very well for herself this far.'

Louisa did not tell Mr Percy of Alice's wild deceptions and escapades, nor of the manner of Alice's sudden departure, most probably jumping from a two-story window, that very morning. He would, she thought with smile, discover these things for himself if things progressed that far.

'I see,' said Percy in some astonishment still, to find he had been outwitted. 'I am obliged to admit that on that score, I am not surprised. She always seemed prodigiously full of pluck to me, even last year when I met her at a ball. So, she is going to Innesfalls, is she? That is indeed an adventure. But I wonder what has happened to the governess, then? Miss Spinner I think her name was.'

'As to the governess, I cannot tell you, for Alice never mentioned her to me, except to take her name, and I have known your Miss Featherstone only as Miss Spinner since she has travelled with me.'

'Resourceful indeed! I must thank you for the intelligence, Miss Fortesque. Do you happen to know what became of Miss Featherstone after she left you so suddenly this morning?'

'Why, I hardly know, Mr Percy. She left me a note — here it is — you may read it yourself — as you see she says very little. I believe she may have tried to find some other person to carry her as far as Innesfalls.'

Percy looked over the note and handed it back with a smile. 'Kidnapping! The lady has a wild imagination, if nothing else! I suppose she had you thinking I was as licentious a rake as ever there was and that she needed protection from me, did she? Resourceful indeed!' There was a tinge of admiration in his tone. 'But if her plan is to be carried to Innesfalls, it won't do. I have it on the best authority that it is about to rain rather heavily. The roads will not permit a carriage to pass through to Innesfalls in that case. It will be overrun by the rivers which suffer very little bad weather before the fords are covered over. I am a little acquainted with the road in these parts, so I shall advise you to be careful when you travel onwards. But you are for Penniston, and so will have a good road. No, I suspect Miss Featherstone will find that, if she tries for Innesfalls in bad weather, any carriage will be turned back.'

'In that case, Mr Percy, I suspect if you travel onwards to Penniston you may find what you are looking for, for if Alice cannot go to Innesfalls, she will certainly try for Penniston, knowing that I am due to arrive there myself. Her object will likely be to petition me to carry her to Innesfalls after the rain stops.'

'I believe you may be right. I shall, with your permission, call at Penniston as soon as I arrive tomorrow.'

'Certainly, Mr Percy. My uncle and I will receive you with gladness. But now I must engage a woman to travel with, and so I must beg your pardon while I go and arrange my affairs!'

'By all means. I shall hope to see you again at your uncle's house. Mr Stacey, I believe you said his name was? I shall enquire when I arrive. And I can only hope to find Miss Featherstone safe and sound there as well. I cannot imagine what dreadful occurrence has driven a young lady from home and her friends there, and I will only be satisfied once I have discovered her and ascertained that she in no danger.'

'You are indeed a true friend to Miss Featherstone, then, Mr Percy. But I must confess, I am not Miss Fortesque — I am Lady Louisa Waverly, although I will thank you not to mention the fact to anyone hereabouts, for I, too, have my secrets, Mr Percy.'

Her blue eyes sparkled at him and he smiled back. 'Very well, my Lady, your secrets shall remain your own. All I desire is to find Miss Featherstone and see that she is safe. I have already guessed that a return to Lewisham at this time will not do, so I can only hope to try to help the lady in any way I can to reconcile with her friends in Shropshire.'

'Call upon my uncle and me at The Grange, tomorrow afternoon around two o'clock, Mr Percy, and if I know anything of Miss Featherstone, you shall hear it then!'

* * *

Once the rather liver-complexioned woman who was to do for Louisa's last night on the road had been ensconced in the carriage, they rolled off, and took the high road out of Oakdean, heading north once again. True to Mr Percy's prediction, the sky had already clouded over quite darkly, and large dark droplets had begun to patter into the dusty road ahead, making mud and dirt where before had been fine, brown dust. Very quickly the rain turned into heavy downpour. Without Alice's buoying and scintillating company, Louisa was much less entertained than she had been these last three days, and apart from a few attempts at conversation with Susan, she became silent herself. The day had become cold too, and she allowed Susan to draw a warm cover over her knees as she watched the rain spatter the leaves and trees as they passed along.

So, Camilla Spinner was really Miss Alice Featherstone. It was not as if she had not known the girl was hiding secrets in those blue-violet dancing eyes of hers. But Louisa was comforted to know, despite all Alice's untruths and fudges, that the dreaded Mr Brown had turned out to be Alice's saviour, if she was in need of one at all.

Louisa pondered the intricacies of love and marriage, and hoped that perhaps her friend might come to see Mr Percy as someone she might consider a friend. Again, she wondered at Alice's aversion for the man, and decided that a young lady, so full of pluck and backbone, might need a strong hand to keep her in check, and that Mr Percy might very well be the person to take on such a task!

Louisa's thoughts turned to her own situation and she wondered, too, what Rotherham's reaction had been to finding himself jilted so quickly. She hoped very much that he had not been too stung by her sudden change of heart. When he had asked her to marry him, she had been so astonished at the prospect, and so keen to leave the confines of Waverly, that she had said yes almost without thinking. But knowing that Hart was expected to produce an heir, and her own thoughts being almost as far from child-rearing as they could be, she had quickly regretted her impetuosity and recanted her promise.

Perhaps, she told herself, Hart would have understood her situation if she had explained, but there was no denying that she could not have entered the halls of Hartley Park and faced Lady Rotherham, when she had no intention of bearing anyone's child. Her own hopes and wishes were quite different, on that score. And that, partially, was why she had come to Penniston, for from there, she hoped very soon to be accepted into a household which was not far from the village her uncle lived in, and it was in this household, Louisa felt, which lay the only chance of true happiness she might have.

She now pulled from her reticule a letter which had been folded out many times, so worn were its creases. She ran her eye over it again now, drawing comfort from the strong handwriting of its author.

'Dear Louisa,

In your previous letter you asked me to call you 'Miss Waverly' and say you do not wish to use your title, but that you wish your works to be considered on their merits alone. Then, I hope you will forgive the impertinence of my calling you by your first name, but we have had so frequent a correspondence now that I feel we must be either forever sisters, or if not, then we must be forever unknown to each other! In your friendship I confess I find a comradeship which even my poor husband does not understand. To meet another woman with a passion for art which is equal to her talent, is a rare treasure. Let us be 'Mariah' and 'Louisa' to each other then, forever more!

As for your coming into Scotland, let me first ask you to be very sure of your decision. The path of true happiness is rarely paved with gold. I applaud you in choosing this path, but you must know that it will not be an easy one. However, whenever you are ready, our doors will be open to you, and I shall nurture your talent as if it were my own child. For indeed, all my works are my children and what better way to nurture our children that to give them the opportunity to experience full and unlicensed creative expression. We are women, Louisa, and so we must fight for what comes naturally to men, but that is not to say that we cannot win that fight. God willing, Richard and I shall welcome you to Clevedon whenever you can honour us with your company.

Until then, believe me to be your friend
Mariah Cosway.'

Louisa folded away the letter and placed it carefully in her reticule again.

She would ask for asylum at Penniston, and write directly to Mrs Cosway to give notice of her arrival. Then, God willing, she would begin a new life, where she would be free to paint, to take lessons from one of the most admirable female artists of the time. Then she would send for Button, dear little Button, and make a new life for herself, where she could be free to express herself through art. Perhaps one day female artists would even be able to exhibit at the Academy or anywhere men might exhibit, without having to change their names to a man's or attribute the work to a husband. But even if that were not possible in her lifetime, Louisa had no intention of ever changing her name to Rotherham or anything else! It was Louisa Waverly she would stay, and it was with 'Louisa Waverly' that she would sign her paintings. She would not rely upon her title. Whether her peers were male or female, she was determined to be judged equally among them, on her talent alone.

She was late. Dressing had taken so long, and she had taken so many pains with her hair, that she chided herself for foolish pride. Camilla took one last glance at herself in the tiny looking glass before going down to breakfast. She had put on one of the gowns which Rotherham had procured for her, and she marvelled at the creature in the mirror who stared back at her. The morning dress was pale blue with an elegant white stripe. From below the capped sleeves, gauzy white fabric flowed gently and along the hem bluebirds fluttered around her feet. She had never seen anything like it and marvelled once again that he had found something to fit her size so exactly. Her chestnut brown hair and eyes were warmly accentuated by the cool tones of the gown, and the little kid boots which sat neatly below the hem were as comfortable as her sturdy governess boots had not been.

Playing the part of Rotherham's wife, she had come to admit to herself, was both exciting and dangerous. She was obliged to admit that her feelings for him had only grown, and she must take the first opportunity to find Alice and be done with fantasies, to return to the life she had carved out for herself as governess. But they had two days before them yet, before she would be deposited on the doorstep of Alice's Aunt Agatha, two days more of sitting in the intimacy of a closed carriage, experiencing the intense pleasure of conversing with Rotherham, of having him to herself. She smiled at her reflection, almost laughing at the swooning schoolgirl who smiled back.

Downstairs, Rotherham was already at breakfast but when she entered the little breakfast room, which was now almost deserted due to the lateness of the hour, he looked at her appreciatively.

'You look very well in that gown. I flatter myself I have as nice a taste in gowns as I do in hessian boots and top coats,' he remarked as she sat down. 'But I have made you blush, Miss Spinner.'

She glanced at him, her cheeks a little pink despite her determination not to be discombobulated at his flattery. 'I am merely overheated,' she replied, busying herself with toast. After their rather intimate exchange the evening before, she wondered how he could be as composed as she was not. She kept her head down, recalling how he had seen her in her night gown. 'Did you manage to sleep at all, Mr Rotherham?' she asked, trying for an indifferent tone.

'Not at all,' he replied jovially. He poured tea for her and she tried not to notice the length of brown skin which was exposed as he reached out his arm. His fingers were long and brown too, and just speckled with dark hair. She shivered.

'Are you cold? I shall close this window. It is excessively cool this morning, I fancy.' He did so and waited until she was comfortable, then began again. 'I did not sleep, Miss Spinner, as I told you last night, because I was thinking of my future. I have come to a decision, and I wish to ask you something.'

She sipped her tea as composedly as she could. He would now talk of duty, his mother, and what he must do to secure her happiness before she passed from this world. She knew that he was obliged to marry to produce an heir, that this is what his mother had decreed, and she knew that she herself could have no part in those plans. 'You know that I sanction only whatever will give your mother the happiness and peace that she deserves before she passes from this world, Mr Rotherham. You must do your duty, even if it is uncomfortable for you.'

He gave her an odd, amused look. 'I am glad you feel this way, Miss Spinner, for I have decided that I must marry you.'

Her eyes grew wide. 'Marry *me*? But you do not — that is, I am not — we are not—!' She could hardly speak for astonishment. Was this some unkind tease? Or worse still, did he perceive her feelings and think to taunt her?

There was a gleam in his eye. 'You wish to say we are not

attached, Miss Spinner? Not in love? Perhaps not. But we *have* been married for five days already, and I find I can tolerate you surprisingly well. Despite that sharp tongue of yours!'

'Tolerate me? That is praise indeed!' She laughed, but it was rather of confusion than mirth. 'But I confess, I am all astonishment, Mr Rotherham. Why me? What of Lady Louisa — you do not think she will receive your second advance favourably? Surely you must try her again before you think of matrimony to another?'

'Louisa has made it quite clear she will not have me, and I am loath to force the matter. I suspect she has made up her mind. Besides, a man never likes to think of a lady being persuaded into matrimony against her will. Either she does, or she does not, want him.'

'And a lady never likes to think of being a man's second choice,' replied Camilla tartly. 'Either he does, or does not, want her.' She felt strangely hurt, because she knew that he did not love her but was soliciting her hand merely for convenience. Still, the idea of being Rotherham's wife was intriguing.

Noting the expression on her countenance, he laughed. 'Are you feeling put out, Miss Spinner? Did you expect declarations of undying devotion and passionate regard?'

'Not at all,' she replied with forced casualness, her heart fluttering a little to think of what form his declarations of "passionate regard" would take. 'I suppose I have been taken off guard a little. A woman supposes that, when she is asked to marry, there will be *something* of tenderness and affection between the two parties. I would quite misunderstand the matter however,' she added calmly, 'if I had expected these things from you, for if we unite, I am quite aware that it will be no love match.' She tried to hide the little stab which these words gave her, and determined to be ever more on her guard against falling any deeper into this silly infatuation with Rotherham than she had already progressed!

Rotherham seemed about to speak, then hesitated, and finally said in an odd tone, 'Indeed, this is not a love match, but a sensible arrangement between two mature adults. It will benefit us both. I need a wife, and you need a more certain future than to teach brats until you must suffer to retire and live off some stipend which is as near to poverty as might well be considered such. You could do worse than accept me, you know!'

'Do you *really* wish to marry me? There are no other ladies to whom you can propose?'

'Despite that sharp tongue of yours, Miss Spinner, I feel oddly comfortable with you. I have not felt as if I could tie myself to any other woman in matrimony, except for Louisa. You, Miss Spinner, are my only hope of bringing some semblance of peace to my mother. And as my wife, you will want for nothing.'

She might want for love, she thought silently, hardly believing that he had just proposed to her. 'And what of your mother? I am not from a family of quality, nor do I have any dowry. My father left me poor, Mr Rotherham. Surely you cannot want to saddle yourself with such a one, and your mother will know that I cannot fulfil her requirements for you so far as rank and circumstance goes. When she discovers I am merely a governess—!'

'As to that, you must agree not to tell her.'

'Not to tell! — but how could I avoid doing just that, when she asks me about my background, my family! I should not like to tell untruths, Mr Rotherham. To marry you, knowing that we do not have your mother's approbation — well, it should not sit well with me.'

'Have not you been implying untruths for the past five days, Miss Spinner?'

She stared at him. 'But — very well, I am obliged to admit it, but fooling your mother, tricking her, that is altogether another thing. A great unkindness!'

'If Mama was to think I have married just such a woman as she wished me to, and I give her some comfort in the last months of her life, would you deny her that? Is that what you call "unkindness"?'

Camilla played with her upper lip, tugging at it in thought. 'You really are quite serious! You truly contemplate marriage to a mere governess, to bring comfort to a dying woman?'

Rotherham saw that he had almost won her over. 'It is a great opportunity for you, and you would be doing me a great service, if you were to agree. Now don't, pray, make me get on one knee and beg you!' he added, smiling.

'I thought you declared only last week that it was *you* who were to be in *my* service, since you ruined my bonnet,' replied Camilla tartly, although her eyes softened the sharpness of her retort. She could hardly believe that only a half hour previously she had been considering this very possibility, of being married to Rotherham, and now the opportunity was being offered to her as if she was a Lady of Quality with nothing more to concern her but to make a good marriage. It *was* an opportunity, she thought, but would she be satisfied to be married without love? Would *he*?

'Quite so, Miss Spinner, but as I have more than repaid you in gowns, bonnets and good dinners, I feel things have become somewhat over balanced. You must equal your side now, by this small service to me!' He smiled winningly.

'Small!' exclaimed she. Trifling indeed! If she married Rotherham, it would change her life. She hesitated then said, 'I am not a romantic, Mr Rotherham, as you know. Thus far in my life I have desired nothing more than an adequate wage with which to sustain myself and a place to put my head at night. But I always thought that if I did marry, it might be for love. If I was to marry you, it would be a marriage without love. Would you be satisfied with that? Would you not, in time, become dissatisfied with our arrangement?' *Would he take a lover?* she thought, and immediately wished she had not!

He met her gaze. 'Camilla, I cannot say that I have ever been in love. Therefore, I have no compass to guide me in that regard. What is love but two persons devoted each to the other, to the happiness of the other? I cannot promise you love, or that which others promote as love, but I can promise you devotion, and the happiness of friendship; are these not the basis of what we call love?'

Camilla thought for a moment, then held out her hand to him and sighed. 'Then I accept your proposal, Mr Rotherham, if you will not think me conniving or climbing for accepting you. I did not expect it, but perhaps we may make each other happy in time, in our own ways.'

'Thankyou.' He smirked. 'I shall do my best to give voice to my most tender, transporting sensations and satisfy your taste for—'

'—vulgar, false sentiments?' She laughed. 'I think you are quite safe, Mr Rotherham, from feeling obliged to satisfy such tastes for I have none of those, I hope! Give me water over wine, mutton over partridge, and the joy of a simple sonnet over a thirty-stanza'd "Ode to a Grecian Urn".'

'No odes, Miss Spinner? Then I certainly shan't purchase Lord Byron's latest book for your wedding present!'

'Oh!' She was nonplussed. 'I had not thought of it — a wedding present? I have not been married before, Mr Rotherham. You are not the only one with no compass!' How strange, she thought, to suddenly find herself engaged to be married. She had never had to think of such things before and she said so.

'I would not worry, Miss Spinner, neither have I. I suspect we will muddle through in our own way!'

But now it occurred to her that she would still have to find Alice and return her to Lewisham. She must go on to Innesfalls! Rotherham however, had already thought of this. 'I shall take you on to Penniston with me, for I still intend to discover Louisa and ascertain if she is safe. I have the duty of friendship, although years of intimacy make duty no hardship. After I have seen that she is safely with her uncle, I shall take you on to Innesfalls, and if necessary, we shall conduct Alice in my carriage back to Lewisham, before I take you on to Hartley Park.'

'I think that will do very well,' mused Camilla. 'You are very kind to think of it.' She blushed a little. He had already considered her feelings and wishes regarding Alice and had prepared a scheme to accommodate them!

'And what shall we tell them, when we arrive at Penniston? Lady Louisa will think very ill of you, to be sure, to find that no sooner had she rejected your suit than you have found someone else?'

'Lady Louisa,' remarked Rotherham with amusement, 'will be very pleased that she will not have to refuse me to my face a second time! I rather think she will be happy for me, after all! Now, you must be obliged to suffer a small detour into Scotland, if you don't mind. If your Miss Featherstone had no need for a clergyman at Gretna Green after all, we most certainly do! I intend to make an honest woman of you, Camilla Spinner, this very day!'

The mud on the roads and the darkness in the sky had both increased since Alice had settled herself in the corner of Mr Middlemount's carriage, and now they were to pull into a small town signposted 'Meadleton' where Mr Middlemount wished to stop for an hour or two. The rain had increased from drizzle to steady pour.

Middlemount had languidly told the driver to pull up at the Lion.

'I daresay you'll be alright sitting in the carriage. I shall just have one pint of ale, to keep me going, you know. I say, shall I bring you out something to eat? Perhaps I can get some apples and a bit of pie. Have you any coins about you, Miss Smith?'

He eyed her innocently, but she was not taken in. 'I suppose you intend to be inside the ale house sometime, Mr Middlemount, for I know young men well enough. Well, I am not going to give you any money — oh, but if you can get me something to eat I would be much obliged, for I own I am starving! But don't be too long, Mr Middlemount, will you, or I shall have to come and find you and that would be embarrassing, would it not?'

'Aye, I suppose it would. Aren't you a canny one then!' He laughed. 'I don't know what you are up to, Miss Smith, but I shan't give away your secrets. Not unless you don't help me. Well, give me a coin or two then and I shall just get myself one pint and a piece of pie for yourself. I promise I shall not be long. After all, you owe me for carrying you this far!'

Alice felt that he had just gained the upper hand and she did not like to be in such a position. Still, she had little choice. She fished around in her little cloth coin purse and pulled two coins from its depths. 'Very well, Sir, but do be quick! I shan't mind driving the horses on my own, you know, if you are too long!' Satisfied, she smiled back at him, and almost laughed when he gave her a spiteful glance.

'Very well. Just wait here and I shall be back in a trice!' He took the coins from her and disappeared into the depths of the ale house. His driver had long since disappeared into the house, quick to take this opportunity of slaking his thirst. God knows how many hours it would be before he would get refreshment again, and Alice supposed she could blame neither man for stopping. She sighed and hoped that they would be quick.

Fifteen minutes later, neither Middlemount nor the coachman had come back, and Alice began to fulminate. Young men were altogether quite unreliable! First that scoundrel of a Charles Deed, now Middlemount! But she sat another thirty minutes before she ventured out of the carriage, leaving the horses stomping in the rain, morosely chewing on their hay. At least *they* had been given a bundle of hay by the coachman! Alice hadn't even had *that* much consideration!

She ran through the rain, not caring if her cap and dull brown gown got wet and dirty, for it would only serve to disguise her further, she thought. She had never been inside an ale house before, but she bravely pulled open the door and peered into the darkness. There were twelve or so men sitting in the dim light at three long tables, and the smell of ale pieced her nose. She scrunched it up and looked for Mr Middlemount. When she spied him sitting at a card game, she lost no time in stalking over to him, and sitting beside him. 'Well,' she said loudly, in rough accents 'and where's me grub what you promised me? Ah look, what a nice Queen in your 'and! Now is that high or low? I can't niver remember!'

It was enough. Middlemount pounced upon her, grabbed her by the arm and propelled her towards the bar. 'Alright you pestilence of a female. Don't you try to fool me, I know you are no serving girl, despite your grubby gown and clever act. Here is your pie, see, and here's some cider, and then we will go, but I've just won two crowns and was about to win another game, if it wasn't for your plaguing interference! If you want to ride any further with me, you had better mind your manners from here! Or I'll put you out in this rain and leave you and your trunks in the mud, Miss Fiddlesticks!'

Alice, eyeing him, saw that he was serious. She sighed and turned to her meal. She ate her pie then drank deeply of the cider, which she was rather inclined to like on principle since she was not allowed cider at home. Soon she began to feel rather sleepy, and seeing that Middlemount was still at cards, she concluded that he must be winning enough to keep him in the ale-house for a longer time. Well, she thought, he would soon lose and then he would come back to the carriage. There was nothing for it but to wait in the carriage for him. She went back to the vehicle, curled up on the seat and was soon soundly asleep.

Several hours later she woke, cold and in darkness. Wondering why she could not see a thing she peeked from the door, only to find the carriage had been put in the carriage house for the night, and the horses unshackled from their traces. These two were now tethered in two narrow stalls nearby and snorted sleepily when they spied her. She went immediately to see that her trunks were still in the rear, and finding them safely stowed, and her hat boxes still inside the carriage, she was about to turn away when she noticed that Middlemount's own trunk was slightly open, having been incorrectly closed. Peeking into the trunk thoughtfully, Alice reached in, and drew out a silk stocking with several guineas tucked into the toe. It was, she was sure, Middlemount's winnings from his card game, and he had almost surely put it in his trunk for safety, so that it would not be taken from him while he slept inside. Which meant that he almost surely had seen her asleep in the carriage and had not thought to get her a room. The impertinence of that Corinthian youth!

Laughing a little to herself, and feeling not at all guilty, she emptied the stocking of its four coins, pocketed the pretty sum, and then went to the stable door. Opening it, she perceived it was almost daylight, and realised that they had been stopped since yesterday afternoon! Presuming Middlemount to be lying in a comfortable bed somewhere inside the ale house, she fulminated a little, but decided there was nothing to do but wait for him to show his face. She settled upon a pile of straw, and waited.

An hour later, Middlemount showed up, his coachman in tow. He did not look in the least worse for wear, and seemed to Alice's eye to have slept rather well. His cravat was tied in its usual bounteous fall, and his impeccable blue coat as well-looking as ever. 'Ah, I forgot about you!' he drawled when he spied her sitting beside the carriage. 'I trust you had a comfortable night, Miss Smith? I am sure it would have been quite pleasant, considering a house maid is usually obliged to sleep on a narrow cot; I vouchsafe that all this lovely hay and straw was likely more comfortable than your servant's quarters at that posting inn!'

Alice met his lazy, impertinent smile with one of her own. 'It was very comfortable, Mr Middlemount. Much nicer than my narrow cot in the milking house.' Her tone was arch. 'How did you do at cards yesterday? I hope you won?' she added innocently.

'Oh, well, as to that,' he said languidly, 'I shouldn't mind saying that I did win a small sum, in fact. Quite enough to buy me a cosy room for the night, although I am confoundedly behind time, now, when I had hoped to reach this devilish village in time to intercept Roth — but never you mind, young lady, just help the coachman get the horses into their traces, will you? I am sure you must know what to do, being a servant girl and all that.'

Alice, who had never in all her life been obliged to get a horse into anything at all, almost refused, but seeing the amusement upon her benefactor's countenance, she decided to make some show of helping, and then suffered to see him laugh knowingly at her as she made token gestures of assistance to the young fellow.

The horses, keen to be up and moving, however, were cooperative, and the coachman soon had them in their traces and the carriage ready to depart. It was still raining outside, and the mud deep, so by the time Alice had clambered aboard the carriage, the hem of her dull maid's gown was thoroughly dirtied and wet. Her pretty boots, which she had not thought to replace with sturdy maid's boots, were similarly ruined, and she looked at them ruefully as they drew out onto the road. Alice might be playing the part of a maid, but the gentlewoman inside her balked at the sight of the ruined boots! It was just as well she had changed her pretty gown for the servant's clothes, she thought. Never mind, at Aunt Agatha's she would order a new pair of boots directly, just as soon as she had taken a long, hot bath and found a clean gown!

They had somewhat gotten behind in making time to Penniston, and for a few hours Alice did not bother to look out for a cross roads which indicated the road to Innesfalls. But after a few hours in which her travelling companion made the occasional lethargic remark regarding the weather and Alice's leaving mud on the carriage floor, she began to worry.

'I really must be dropped off on the road which leads to Innesfalls, Mr Middlemount. I am quite anxious that we have passed the turning — do you think we might have gone by it?'

But the Corinth, having no interest in anyone's affairs but his own, had little helpful to add to these ponderings, and Alice was obliged to watch through the rain for her signposting. Another hour passed and the rain became heavier, making their progress slow. Alice spared a thought for the poor coachman who was sitting out in the weather, in a great coat, but no other protection, and once again pondered the ills of being poor. She did not know which was worse, being a governess like Miss Spinner, and having no home of one's own, and having to teach naughty and ungrateful children (here, she felt a stab of guilt, for she knew that she herself could well have been called ungrateful in the past) or being a coachman and having to drive one's master through all weathers.

After another hour had passed, and the signposting told them that they were most definitely on the road to Penniston, Alice allowed that she had missed the turning. 'It is too bad! I shall have to go all the way to Penniston,' she mused aloud, 'for there I know I shall find Miss Fortesque, and perhaps she can help me to get to my aunt's!'

'Miss Fortesque? Who on earth is Miss Fortesque?' remarked her companion in bored tones. 'What does a maid have to do with a "Miss Fortesque"?'

'Oh, do be quiet! You know very well I am not really a servant, Mr Middlemount. You told me so yourself! I am a lady,' she added haughtily. 'I merely took the disguise of a maid as I was being followed by a rather unsavoury and persistent young man, and was obliged to throw him off my scent. I am going to my aunt in Innesfalls to live with her there.'

'Yes, well, I rather think had you been put down at the right turning, you would not have been able to pass the road to Innesfalls due to this confounded rain. I believe the road is impassable in such weather. You had best remain with me and go to Penniston, as you say. Only don't expect me to take you anywhere else; you have already ruined my card game once!'

'Oh, I shan't need your help, thank you all the same Mr Middlemount, for my friend Louisa will take me, I am certain. I only need to be put down in the village, and will surely find her uncle's house for I know his name.'

They jolted along rather slowly, since the roads were so wet, but by and by, as the afternoon wore on, a small village loomed ahead of them, and very soon they were rolling down the rough cobbled streets of Penniston. Middlemount stopped the carriage at the square. 'I shall put you down here, Miss Smith, if you don't mind, for I must discover the whereabouts of old Stacey and see if my quarry is in presence there.'

'Mr Stacey!' exclaimed Alice in some consternation. 'Why, that is the very residence I am bound for! How odd! What a strange appearance it will make with us both turning up at the very same time, but it is rather convenient, for I may travel directly to the house with you! Do go on and make your coachman enquire for us as to the place!'

Middlemount, thinking what a cursed coincidence it was to have to take the young woman exactly where he was bound himself, sighed. Cursed women! When would he ever learn to say 'No' to a pair of beseeching violet eyes!

He ordered the driver to enquire as to the residence of old Mr Stacey and soon they were pulling into a wide paved driveway which led to a rather stately, old fashioned home of Elizabethan build, styled 'The Grange' according to the plaque upon the gates. They had only turned in when Alice noted that another carriage, not far behind them, had also turned in. The carriage pulled up outside the house, and Alice noted that the other carriage had followed them to the door.

The rain having stopped, Alice did not wait for the servant to come to the carriage door but opened it herself and sprung lightly from the vehicle. Middlemount followed her, and they both looked to see who had followed them up the driveway. A pretty black and gold carriage now came to a halt behind their own, the horses snorting in the cool air, relieved to be stopped at last. As Middlemount and Alice watched, the carriage door gave way to a gentleman, who in turn handed out a rather self-conscious lady in a pretty gown and bonnet.

Alice stared at the couple. 'Miss Spinner!' she cried in astonishment.

'Alice!' cried Miss Spinner in relief.

'Rotherham!' cried Middlemount.

'Middlemount!' exclaimed Rotherham. 'What the devil—'

'Rotherham!' cried a fifth person from the front door. 'Miss Spinner — I mean, Miss Featherstone!'

'Lady Louisa!' cried Rotherham.

'Miss Fortesque!' cried Alice, ever more astonished.

'Miss Spinner!'

'Yes?' replied both Alice and Camilla together.

Louisa descended the steps and came to the fray. All persons were speaking at once.

'Whatever are you doing here?'

'You are dreadfully dirty! Why are you dressed as maid?'

'I came directly to fetch you home, Rotherham, on account of—'

'How come you to be with Mr Rotherham, Miss Spinner? And what happened to your clothes?'

'But, I thought you in Shropshire! Did you not—'

'What a fine chase you have given me, you naughty girl!'

'But why does Mr Rotherham call you Lady Louisa?'

'What do you want with me, Middlemount, to follow me thus? I hope Mama has not—'

'I thought you at Innesfalls by now?'

'And why are you with Mr Rotherham? What has — no, no, Miss Fortesque, I missed the turning to Innesfalls and came here instead — the bad weather, you know!'

As the little party tried hopelessly to make themselves understood, a horse and rider now trotted smartly up the drive. He was hardly noticed among the party gathered however, so lively was the mayhem which had overtaken them. He stood for a moment, nonplussed and observing the little crowd of astonished faces, hearing their exclamations, and then was suddenly observed himself.

'Mr Percy!' cried Alice, blushing. 'I mean, *Mr Brown!*'

'Mr Brown,' cried Louisa. 'I mean, *Mr Percy!*'

'Miss Algernon!'

'Whatever in the world are you—'

'Who on earth is Mr Percy, and who is Mr Brown?'

'Miss Smith! How—'

'Miss Smith? Who is Miss Smith!'

'Will someone please, *please* tell me, *who* is Lady Louisa?'

With this commanding tone, the little crowd was suddenly silent. Alice stood looking at them all, suddenly exhausted. There was only so much adventure a lady could enjoy in one week. She sighed and asked again. 'Who is Lady Louisa?'

Louisa smiled. 'I am Lady Louisa Waverly. And I collect you are Miss Featherstone.'

Alice sighed again. 'I suppose the cat is rather out of the bag then, is it not?'

'I am afraid it is,' replied Louisa placidly. 'But now that you are all here, why do you not come in and take some tea. I suspect there might be a little explaining to do so you might as well all make yourselves comfortable for the moment!'

Rotherham was sitting with Louisa in a corner of the drawing room. The others were variously spread throughout the room, apart from Middlemount who had gone away already, having imparted to Rotherham his mother's urgent summons to Hartley Park and made certain of his immediate return. 'Don't be long, there's a good chap, for I promised your good mother you would hurry home directly!'

'Oh, you did, did you? I suppose she gave you a princely sum for fetching me, too!'

While Middlemount had reddened and muttered, Rotherham had taken stock of the situation. 'Well, never mind that, but you owe me three guineas if you have not forgotten our wager from two weeks ago, and I am sure that you might afford it now that Mama has sweetened your palm. *There's a good chap!*' he echoed with a barely repressed laugh at the look upon Middlemount's face.

The other man eyed him warily. 'Well! I daresay I could have paid you yesterday, old chap, had you reminded me, but you know, your mother never gave me anything but a guinea to get here, since payment was upon delivery, you see! Then I had a devilish time getting a suitable pair, and had to give those thieving postillion boys at the King's Arms double what's usual just to get 'em changed over so I could get on! I'm quite out of pocket already or I'd pay you directly!'

Alice, overhearing Middlemount's pink-cheeked bluster, intervened. 'Oh, but Mr Middlemount,' she exclaimed, 'you must have forgotten the guineas you got yesterday when you stopped at the Lion at Meadleton! Remember, when you won at cards?' she added innocently.

Middlemount cast her a pointed glare and said casually, 'Oh, *that!* Yes, quite so! I won a guinea or two, it is true... but I was obliged to spend that on our accommodations there, and after our dinner and breakfast there is nothing at all left of *that,* you silly girl!'

'Our dinner and breakfast?' cried Alice in great surprise, 'I don't remember getting any meals at all! But then, being left in the carriage in the stables for the night, I suppose you forgot me! But that is nothing to the point, for I have your four guineas from your cards right here, in my pocket, where I put them for safety! Here you are — are you not excessively glad I looked after them for you?' She smiled up at Middlemount's rising vexation as Rotherham gave her the most admiring glance.

'I rather think people must underestimate you, Miss Featherstone, which they would do well to curb.' He laughed. 'Now, Middlemount, do pay up, for I collect you won't need four guineas going home. One will suffice I am sure!'

Middlemount, glaring at a laughing Alice, was obliged to hand over three of the four guineas, and had soon retreated from Mr Stacey's residence with the tiny measure of dignity as had been left him.

* * *

Now Rotherham turned back to Louisa, with whom he had been conversing. 'And so you see I felt it my duty to see if I could find you, and give myself the comfort of knowing you safe, at least. I did not come to propose again, for I was persuaded nothing would budge you if you had not decided in my favour.'

'And so you married Miss Featherstone's governess, Miss Spinner, in my stead! What a little minx the child is to have deceived me into thinking *she* was Miss Spinner! And a governess, too! However, only think what pluck she has! I confess I admire it, but don't tell her so or I rather think she will try to benefit by it!'

'And you are not distressed by the news? I was rather anxious that you would not be hurt by my hasty change of allegiance.'

Louisa was tranquil. 'I own I am a little surprised by the speed at which you found a new prospect, but I am not injured by your decision. I am glad for you, Hart, really I am. I wish you both very happy.'

Disturbed by murmured voices from the other side of the room, Rotherham was amused to see that young Miss Featherstone was now deep in conversation with her former governess, while Mr Percy kept half an eye on those proceedings from his seat next to old Mr Stacey. Periodically, Alice appeared to glare at Mr Percy, at which ferocity he merely smiled politely, which seemed to incense the girl even more. Both Alice and Miss Spinner seemed engaged in rather a spirited conversation in which the governess glanced at Percy every now and then and seemed to be arguing with Alice over something.

Rotherham surveyed them absently, then turned back to Louisa and bestowed upon her a slight smile. 'You are excessively forbearing, then, Lou.'

She said placidly, 'Hart, dear, I never really wanted to marry you, and I am dreadfully sorry that I mislead you, only I answered you in haste. I saw in your proposal a way to escape the confines of life at Waverly. But I meant what I said in my letter to you. You know me well enough by now, I think, to know that if I have made up my mind, I cannot be easily persuaded out of it. I have already told you that I do not see matrimony in my future. I want only to paint. Forgive me, but I could not bear to argue with Mama over it, and especially over the money which she and Papa so need for Waverly. It was easier just to go away than to stay at Waverly and have them to try to change my mind. And I knew you would come to Waverly to do the same.' She looked contrite. 'I am only sorry that I did not tell you sooner and save you some pain.'

'Since being at Waverly has not promoted your happiness, it is true that I thought that you might have been happier at Hartley Park. We have been friends for many years, after all. But you must forgive me, Lou, for being so thick-skulled as not to have guessed at your feelings, and the impossibility of our marrying. I see now that it would have been a disaster, for both of us, for you are right, I must produce an heir, and you — you must not marry to please your friends — you must follow your heart... wherever it leads.' He smiled kindly.

Louisa smiled back at him. 'You and I have always been the best of friends.'

'So we have. And you know we always will be so. Have you written to Waverly yet?'

'I have written to Mama and Papa. They will be disappointed, for they were counting upon the benefits to Waverly. Do — do you think me selfish, Hart?' she added anxiously.

Rotherham caught her hand. 'Even I, as a man, can own that women get little chance to follow their dreams. If you have the means to do so, why should you not? Waverly may be floundering a little, but surely your parents can retrench — or lease Waverly and go to Bath or some such place as many old families are obliged to do when in reduced circumstances.'

Louisa laughed. 'A retrenchment, I am persuaded, would do it. If Mama's spending is brought in line, I am sure they will manage without such a drastic change! Oh, I have asked them to send Button on, for I cannot go into Scotland without my darling boy! If I had known you were going to follow me into Yorkshire, I would have had you carry him to me!'

'And when do you expect to travel into Scotland?'

'I have written to Mr and Mrs Cosway only this day. I shall expect to leave here within the month, perhaps to stay many months with them. I shall learn all manner of new techniques,' she added, her eyes glowing, 'and Mariah says I shall exhibit my best works with hers at the salons in Europe next summer. It is a very great opportunity for me you know. One which would be impossible,' she added soberly, 'if I were a mother and a wife.'

'Then I wish you all imaginable happiness, Louisa. You are a fine painter. Perhaps you are paving the way for future women artists. You are bearing a great torch, lighting the way for the future generations of female artists. I cannot ask you to give that up.'

'You have been nothing but kind to me all these years, Hart. I do hope your mother will not be too disappointed. She is such a proud woman. But your Mrs Rotherham gives all the appearance of refinement and conviviality, despite her low beginnings. Nevertheless, a governess is not such a lowly position that she should be embarrassed by it, and I am sure that, given the chance to get to know her, your dear mother surely will not balk at your sudden change of allegiance, nor her low rank. Why, she looks quite a gentlewoman sitting there next to Miss Featherstone, as pretty as a picture!'

Hart glanced at his new wife and could not but agree with Louisa. In the dress of a gentlewoman, Camilla Spinner had never looked so well, nor less like a governess!

They had been married two days ago at Gretna Green, without undue ceremony, and with only two by-standers for witnesses. Then, with a degree of sudden, unaccustomed awkwardness they had entered the carriage together, not as pretend man and wife, but legally bound together for life. Rotherham had, like his wife, said very little as the carriage brought them closer to Penniston, for both had been thrown into a kind of pensiveness from which the other was necessarily excluded, and lost in their respective thoughts they had only emerged from reverie once the carriage had pulled into the last posting inn to bait the horses and overnight themselves.

The following morning, he and Camilla had entered the carriage once again, a comfortable amity having revealed itself between them. She had had nothing sharp to remark, and he no taunts to tax her with. If she had been slightly pink of cheek at breakfast, he had liked to think it the pleasant aftermath of their first night of marriage, and he had been at pains not to notice, so that she should not be embarrassed even more. They had passed the morning each well enough pleased with their lot so as to make an intolerably long journey as pleasant as possible. In truth, Rotherham had been just as acutely conscious of their new situation as had Camilla, and, being at least tolerably acquainted with the principles which must guide her behaviour toward him, he had determined not to be expecting her to be immediately at ease with her new situation.

Besides this, the long hours in which they had sat silently together in the carriage had allowed him his thoughts, and he had used the time to consider just how he was going to inform his wife that it was not just his mother's happiness he had consulted when making Camilla his wife, but his own! He had long come to acknowledge that her company was not a trial to him, nor was she hard to look upon, but it was only when she had come to him the previous night, her long hair loose and her white gown as pure and refreshing to him as her mind and soul, that he had been obliged to admit that he was falling in love with her!

Such an admission had shocked him, for he had never envisioned himself falling for a governess, but as much as his mother was a proud woman, he himself had never had much regard for the divisions of classes. Still, to fancy himself falling for a woman was a strange sensation indeed, and he was not sure he liked it. He had never felt himself in love with any other woman, however much he might admire Louisa. He recalled his words to Wilkes, about preferring a warm temper over a bland one, and laughed, for he had surely found the warmest-tempered woman he had ever met, all verbal spars and strong opinions!

How he might broach the topic with Camilla, and reveal his growing feelings, he was not at all certain, for he did not wish to frighten her into repenting her decision to become Mrs Rotherham. But having spent the better part of the morning in the carriage with her again, he held some hope that quite soon he might declare his feelings, when he was sure of their being well received.

Louisa was watching him now as he himself had been observing his wife, and she broke into his reverie with a smile, 'I have never seen that look upon your face before, Hart. I own it is strange to see you in love, but it is rather amusing to see you so.'

He laughed a little self-consciously. 'Is it so obvious? I am glad it gives you such diversion, but there is still Mama to be convinced. Middlemount followed me here, you know, with a commission to discover me and bring me home without delay.'

'But what can be so urgent that you cannot stay, now that you are here? Mrs Rotherham may rest a day or two surely, before making such a long journey back to Hartley?'

'Middlemount brought news that Mama has taken a dangerous turn. Knowing my mother, it is likely not as bad as all that, but nevertheless, I cannot think of delaying our return if it is true. I suspect it is more that she has somehow heard of my being married, and believes I have made you my wife. I collect she will not be so pleased to discover it is a different Mrs Rotherham I shall be bringing to her. '

'She will soften, I am sure, as soon as she gets to know your bride. And she shall be sure of an heir, which was her object in urging you to marry. She must accept your choice!'

'I hope for Camilla's sake that you are right!'

Rotherham now took his leave of Louisa and went to his wife. She and Alice had been deep in discussion, but now that they were interrupted, Alice turned to appeal to Rotherham in a great agitation.

'Mr Rotherham! I am prodigious glad you have come over to speak to us, for Miss Spinner — I mean, Mrs Rotherham — is insisting I must return to Lewisham, and I have assured her I shall do nothing like it! Can you not tell her it is certainly impossible?'

He laughed at the look upon her face. 'Now don't, I pray, use that look upon me, my girl! It is a fine merry chase you have given us all the way to Yorkshire, and I collect that Mrs Rotherham is quite right in her directing you to return to your father and mother. Have you not had enough adventure for one lifetime? You very surely must return, if you have any heart for your friends at home.'

'Pshaw!' commented Alice with spirit. 'Friends at home! Why, perhaps Anne will be wishing for my return, but if I ever see that scoundrel Charles Deed! I shall — I shall tell him that I shall never speak to him again!'

It was Camilla's turn to be amused. 'Would not telling him so rather undermine the intent? No, my dear girl, you shall return to Lewisham, for although I may not return to Lewisham as your governess, I owe Sir George the safe return of his daughter.'

'We had already intended to conduct you home to Lewisham, although I am rather in a quandary now, for my dear,' Rotherham turned to Camilla, 'Middlemount has informed me that Mama has summoned us home on account of having taken a turn and has taken to her bed. I am not certain how serious the matter is, but I rather think—'

'If you will permit me to interrupt, I overheard you speaking.' Mr Percy had come to them, having left his seat by Mr Stacey. 'I wish to offer my services.' He glanced at Alice, then said to Rotherham in low tones, 'I would be glad to conduct Miss Featherstone home to Lewisham, if a woman can be got to accompany her in the carriage. I am a little acquainted with the family and it would be an honour to be of service to Miss Featherstone.'

'I shall do no such thing!' remarked Alice loudly, at the very same time as Rotherham said, 'That is very good of you, Percy! It might answer very well indeed!'

'I assure you,' cried Alice, 'that unless it is as Mrs Charles Deed, I shall never return to Lewisham!' Her blue eyes were bright. 'And since I have been quite mistaken in thinking Charles to harbour even an ounce of duty toward a woman, or inclination to keep a promise, I shall never return at all! I shall go to live with Aunt Aggie! *She* shouldn't make me go home if I don't wish it!'

Camilla gave Alice one of her most stern looks. 'Alice dear, you cannot run away forever. You wrongly suppose Mr Deed to be the author of your troubles, when you have been your own enemy in this entire affair! Your father will be dreadfully anxious as to your safety. And your poor sister will be beside herself! You must begin to think of others and take some responsibility for your choices!'

Alice, finding herself overruled, flung herself from her chair and flounced toward the door. 'You shan't make me go back! You shan't!' and without waiting for the servant, she opened the door and banged it behind her.

Camilla made as if to go after her, but Mr Percy held up his hand. 'No, rather let me go after her. If you will permit it?'

Rotherham, glancing at his wife, laughed. 'By all means, Percy; if you can bring the girl around, I shall get you to whisper my wild horses too!'

Alice's leaving Penniston for Lewisham was, however, settled with astonishing speed. Within the half hour, Percy had appeared once again in the drawing room and given them the particulars of Alice's concession. 'I think she will go without further argument,' he informed them quietly.

'But whatever did you say to her?' asked Camilla, both astonished and amused at Percy's powers to persuade her headstrong charge. 'I must hear what you said to soften her! Especially since she seemed to take every umbrage that you had followed us into Yorkshire! What her dislike of you stems from I cannot say, but if you have persuaded Alice to be escorted home, then you truly are a miracle worker, Mr Percy!'

Percy smiled. 'I could see no point in overcoming her feelings — as strongly as they incline her not to return to her friends — but I merely represented to her all the pleasanter parts of such a return, such as seeing her sister... and I may have mentioned a large ball that is to be held very soon at Foal's Keep.'

Camilla was doubtful, however. 'She agreed to return on the strength of a ball? I own I am astonished at her giving way, if that is the case — it must be a very fine ball, indeed, and she must be far fonder of a ball than I had given her credit for!'

'As to that,' replied Percy with a sly smile, 'I *may* have also promised her that if she were to consent to have herself brought into the vicinity of Shropshire, she should not have to return to Lewisham immediately, but that I should get my mother to invite her to stay for a few weeks. On the condition, of course, that she must write to Sir George informing him that she is safe. Then she may decide to return to Lewisham, or Mama may invite her to stay on for a time. It would be doing Mama an excellent service, really, for company is her great delight.'

Camilla returned his smile, her eyes dancing. 'A great service indeed,' she murmured knowingly. 'How prodigiously kind you are, Mr Percy! I really cannot say what we would have done without your help.'

'Miss Featherstone is a remarkable young lady. I am glad to have the opportunity to be of service.'

Alice had earlier confided to Camilla the truth of her association with Mr Percy, and the source of her dislike for him, and Camilla now understood that Alice's feelings were founded in wounded pride only. To all appearances, Mr Percy seemed a person of education, manners and circumstance, and she suspected it would take only a little encouragement by the gentleman for Alice's feelings to be mollified, and perhaps even won over by a suitor who seemed to have her best interests as his object in following her thus to York. But perhaps another five days in his company on the return to Shropshire would alter her feelings enough to change her allegiance from Charles Deed to Mr Thadeus Percy of Foal's Keep. He was to inherit on his father's death, and was not considered of low means even now. He would, perchance, make a fine husband for Alice, thought Camilla, if the girl would but get past her own stubborn inclinations.

Now, the gratitude that she felt towards this young man, his general benevolence, and his particular attentions towards Alice, prompted her to thank him again, and to speak of Alice's likely gratitude when she realized how very fortunate she was to have made such a kind friend of Mr Percy.

Mr Edmund Stacey was so far from being weary of his unexpected guests that he now pressed them all very earnestly to remain the night at Penniston, and everything relative to their departure the following day was arranged by the old fellow and his niece. Louisa, for her part, was courteous and accommodating, especially of the new-made Mrs Rotherham, and if there had been any self-consciousness of the part of Camilla in meeting Rotherham's recent intended, it was put aside quickly in place of delight and gratitude at being so very kindly received by Lady Louisa.

Once all the details of their departure were settled, Alice, now being almost sanguine in the thought of returning, not to Lewisham but to the home of Mr Percy, was able to meet them all at dinner with composure, and when Camilla observed her charge laughing at something Mr Percy had said, she smiled to herself, for she could guess it would only be a small interval before Alice would think no more of Charles Deed!

Camilla, for her part, had rather a lot to think upon. Only two days previous she had been a spinster governess, expecting nothing more in life than to live out her remaining years with as much comfort as a governess's income might afford, and with no hopes of matrimony in view. Suddenly, she had found herself married and, she admitted to herself, a good way to being in love. She was under no illusion that Hartley Rotherham had married her for any reason other than to please his mother, and to give the lady hope of an heir after she had passed to the next world. The fact that her husband did not love her back gave Camilla a little disturbance, but, she reasoned, many a good marriage had been based on less, and she knew couples who had grown to love each other over time. She was hopeful that in time, Rotherham may come to feel for herself what she had begun to feel for him. But she was careful to show no over-display of emotion or affection with her husband, beyond warm civility in public and little more than this when they were in private together.

The wedding night had, she admitted, been both nerve-wracking and wonderful; she had never imagined that the conjugal duties of a married female might give so much pleasure. She had heard some women complain of their marital duties, but Rotherham had treated her with consideration and kindness, and her nervousness had quickly been replaced with wonder and pleasure. She wondered if he had felt the same, but she had enough experience of the world to know that men were driven by their animal natures; to procreate was as much a duty as it was hers to comply with that duty.

She had come down to breakfast the next morning only a little self-conscious, but Rotherham, paying her special attention and regard, had soon dissipated her embarrassment, as if what had taken place the previous night had been the most natural thing in the world.

Therefore, Camilla was, for the most part, satisfied with her new circumstance, and felt herself to have been justified in agreeing to Rotherham's proposal. The only matter to give her pause was a guilt, no matter how Rotherham had persuaded her, that they had married without the knowledge and approbation of Lady Rotherham. She was not by nature a dishonest person and it weighed upon her heavily that they were to continue to deceive her mother-in-law. But she had not a creature whose advice she could reply upon, and for now she must trust her husband, and hope that they were not committing what might be a great wrong against the lady!

It was then, with no small amount of trepidation the next morning, that she contemplated the journey ahead, which was to take her to Hartley Park. They had seen Alice, and the woman who had been engaged to do for her on the journey home, drive off ahead of them. Percy had mounted his horse and trotted off after them, since he would attend the carriage all the way back to Shropshire.

Camilla had watched them off and then gone back inside to take another cup of tea before she and Rotherham set out on their own five day journey back to the West Midlands and Hartley Park. She laughed a little bitterly to think of the irony at their having played at husband and wife all the way to Yorkshire. What strange turn of providence had given her up to the fates, she knew not!

Their carriage set out, a waving Louisa at their backs, on a fine Yorkshire morning, and apart from a little nervousness at meeting her new mother-in-law, and no small degree of hesitation at knowing she must commit a deception in not revealing her true rank, she was *almost* perfectly at ease.

Rotherham was quite sanguine, however, as they jolted along the road south. 'Mama has her heart set upon my marrying someone of rank, and I own I cannot approve of telling her the truth when I know she has so little time left in this world. If it were some deception we were committing in order to gain by it ourselves, then I might feel as you do, Camilla, but as it is, there is no one to gain by it but a poor woman in ill-health, who deserves a little happiness before she passes. Surely you would not deny an old woman near her time that small comfort?'

Unable to argue with such a Christian way of thinking, Camilla soon put aside her doubts and devoted herself to enjoying the journey. They made excellent time, stopping at the various stages to take a meal and bait the horses, or to change their pair and overnight themselves. Each evening Camilla went happily to her husband's bed, there to find the warmth and growing closeness she had secretly come to depend upon. She kissed him back demurely when he kissed her, but she longed to confess her feelings and allow herself to surrender to him completely. But that, she thought after he had fallen asleep with his arm over her shoulder, she must not do, unless she knew that her feelings were reciprocated.

* * *

Five days later, towards midday, their carriage turned into the gates of Hartley Park. The house was a modern-built, spacious residence, which rested upon a sloping lawn and had a pretty aspect due to the extensive pleasure-grounds which sat either side of it. A white road of smooth gravel led to the frontage, and an abundance of verdure and trees surrounded the house.

Camilla was unable to prevent a flutter of excitement to be entering the gates of what was to be her home, but this was tempered with natural nervousness at meeting Lady Rotherham. Rotherham had sent a note ahead before they had left to inform his mother of their impending arrival, and now, having been expected all morning, a number of servants rushed out as soon as the carriage came into view around the trees, and were awaiting them both as Rotherham stepped first from the carriage then handed his lady out.

Of course, Wilkes, always at his master's service, was the first to welcome them. Eyeing Camilla somewhat warily she thought, with his glistening bright blue eyes, he nodded at Rotherham. 'Welcome home, Sir. May I be so bold as to wish you both joy.' He gave Camilla a little nod as if in approval of what he saw before him.

Camilla smiled at him, but the butler had opened the front door wide, and she and Rotherham were obliged to keep moving up the steps. Wilkes stayed deferentially behind his master but followed them closely.

As they passed into the house, the butler welcomed them. 'Good morning, Sir. Mrs Rotherham. Lady Rotherham awaits you in the drawing room.'

'Thank you,' replied Rotherham. 'Wilkes, where are you? Ah, take my coat, will you? Now tell me, how does Mama go on?' Rotherham handed the old valet his coat. 'I had Middlemount bounding all over the countryside after me, last week, after Mama gave him orders to send for me. She must have rather sweetened his pocket, to get him so quickly up to Yorkshire! He told me she'd had a turn and demanded my immediate return to Hartley. Is it so?'

'Lady Rotherham had a tolerably serious turn, I believe, Sir, but is in better health presently. Her woman has been in attendance constantly. Doctor Plowright was here yesterday,' added Wilkes, 'and told her to take as much rest as possible, but she has been sitting up in the drawing room waiting for you since ten this morning.'

'Thank you, Wilkes.' Rotherham was already removing his gloves. He handed these over also. 'Have Mrs Rotherham's things taken up to the blue rooms, will you? And have my things moved there also, after you have sent up some spruce beer. You know how I regard tea!'

He was already leading Camilla up the steps and into the grand hallway. Her boots made little echoes on the marble floors as she took a few steps into the large entry hall. Wall hangings, paintings, vases of flowers, and pedestals sporting cherubic marble busts all stood variously about, increasing her notions of the grandness of the place. Of all this she was to be mistress! She hardly knew if she ought to be impressed or terrified!

'Oh, Hart, I am so anxious your mother should like me!' she said in low tones as she clung to his arm. 'What if I displease her?' She smoothed her silk gown, still unused to such finery. 'What if she asks about my parentage? My history?'

'That,' replied Rotherham with a short laugh, 'is not unlikely, given my mother's fondness for rank and money, but you shall simply tell her the truth; you are a gentleman's daughter, who met with hard times. There is no need to inform her that you were forced into work. Had your father lived, you would have remained a lady, and would not have been forced into teaching brats their times tables!'

'Yes,' replied Camilla doubtfully, 'I suppose you are right... but is she so *very* intimidating?'

'I am sure, with that tart tongue of yours, that you will hold your own!'

'Tart? I collect that 'tart' is as tart does, Mr Rotherham,' she said severely. 'If you think my tongue 'tart', then perhaps the application of sweetness would do much to alleviate your thinking it so!' But the smile in her eyes softened the reprimand, and she thought of the 'sweetness' with which he treated her at night. All in all, she was, she thought, a great deal more fortunate than she deserved.

He looked down at her, smiling, and her stomach did little flip flops. Their eyes caught and just for one moment, she thought he was going to kiss her. In the same way he had kissed her the previous five evenings, in the privacy of their chamber. Her heart began to pound.

But to her disappointment he hesitated and pulled away a little and the moment had passed. 'Come, we must get the inevitable over with, and present you to Mama. Now Camilla, pray don't look like you are going to an execution! She may bark, but even old Wilkes has more bite in him than does Mama, I assure you!'

With this dubious reassurance he led her upstairs and soon they were entering a large room in which a multitude of flowers in vases and flowery chintz sofas were placed. On one of these, a woman in a soft chemise and bed jacket reclined, half sitting, and when they entered the room, she held out her arms.

'Hartley! At last!'

'Mama.' Rotherham went forward, taking his mother's hands in his own, and kissed her gently on the forehead. 'You look pale! What is this I hear about a turn last week? And do tell me, how much did you promise Middlemount to get him to come bounding about the countryside to fetch me home? I suspect all his outstanding bets shall be paid off by the end of this week!'

His mother laughed weakly. 'Never you mind about that. Now — let Louisa come to me! Oh, my goodness!' She eyed Camilla in astonishment. 'Who is this? And where is Lady Louisa?'

Rotherham intervened firmly. 'Mama, this is my wife, Camilla. Camilla, Lady Rotherham.'

Camilla stepped forward a little more, so conscious of the disappointment that her appearance must bring to the older lady, that she was quite guilty to meet the woman's eyes. 'How do you do, Lady Rotherham? I am very pleased to make your acquaintance.' She curtsied and allowed the woman to run her eye over her new daughter-in-law.

'I see.' The older woman assessed her shrewdly. 'Well, I must say you are prettier than Louisa, although your figure is not nearly as fine, but still, you carry yourself with a great deal of assurance. Yes, you will do, I think. You are nonetheless welcome at Hartley Park.' She gestured grandly for Camilla to sit. 'I apologise for my astonishment at seeing you, but I had expected Lady Louisa to return with Hart. You did,' she turned now to her son, 'see Louisa? You found her?'

'I did, Mama, but it was too late even so, for I had already met Camilla and been charmed into making her an offer of my hand.' He smiled, glancing at his wife. 'I did promise you I would bring home a wife, and you recollect I never promised it would be Louisa Waverly.'

'Yes, I do recall it. But Hartley, I am not displeased. Your wife is a gentlewoman, I perceive, and looks to be a good enough girl! So long as she can bear children and is of a good enough breeding not to disgrace the shades of Hartley, then I shall be satisfied!'

At this, Camilla felt a stab of guilt, but Rotherham had already assured his mama that Camilla was as much a gentlewoman as Louisa and as for degrees of handsomeness, did not the agreeableness of one's appearance depend upon whomsoever was doing the observing? She caught his eye and he smiled at her, and she felt her heart race. *Did he think her pretty?*

His mother, ringing the bell for tea, set about asking some rather excavating questions of Camilla, who strove to remain composed under the scrutiny.

'And your family? Where does your father have his seat, Mrs Rotherham?'

Camilla beseeched Rotherham with a pleading look.

Rotherham said quite smoothly, 'Camilla's family comes from Derbyshire, Mama, but as her father died only recently, leaving her alone in the world but for a few friends, it is a sensitive topic which we might do better to canvass some other time, perhaps.'

'Oh,' cried Lady Rotherham, much affected by this dreadful picture. 'Poor dear! But you do not wear mourning? How long ago was it that he passed? No, but I must not force a confidence on a topic so fresh. You are quite right not to wear mourning for more than six months, for I collect it is so unfashionable now to affect a black-veiled face longer than that; a young woman is sure never to marry again if she does! You are quite right to dispense with such old-fashioned ideas! Now that I look at you, I see that you have a certain charm — why your eyes are vastly lively, and your figure handsome enough, now that I see it in the light. Little wonder you have caught Hart's eye!'

To these kind profusions of sympathy and compliment mixed, Camilla only smiled, and Lady Rotherham, after a conversation with her son, declared herself to be made almost quite well again just by the comfort of knowing her son finally married.

Spruce beer appeared, and little white cucumber sandwiches, and while Rotherham partook most appreciatively, Lady Rotherham leaned in to Camilla.

'I am obliged to tell you my dear,' she remarked confidingly, 'that it has been my fondest wish to see Hart married, for without the promise of an heir, I was quite beside myself with worry that Hartley Park would pass to our despicable nephew, Lionel Abercrombie! The Scottish are such outlandish creatures, do not you think? No? Well, I could not let that old toad take over Hartley Park; he would rub his hands together in glee if he were to get hold of the place! But you have saved Hartley Park, and given me the greatest comfort, my dear, to know my nephew's devilish schemes to overtake English soil quite thwarted!'

Camilla, not quite knowing how to make a reply to such a remark, was saved the trouble of doing so, for Lady Rotherham had not finished her attack on their neighbouring nation. 'Is it not Samuel Johnson, in his great wisdom, who said the very thing? "The noblest prospect which a Scotchman ever sees is the high road that leads to England" Ah, yes old Abercrombie won't have the pleasure of laying hold of English soil, now that you are to provide us an heir!'

'Mama!' scolded Rotherham, half laughing. 'You will make Camilla blush, and think I have only married her to produce children for Hartley! Camilla, don't, pray, attend Mama, for she loves to say outrageous things!'

Camilla, who was very well aware that while he had not married her for love, her husband had most certainly married her to produce an heir, only blushed anyway and said, 'Must you not rest, Lady Rotherham? Should you like me to read to you, or—'

'Goodness no, child! I should very much like to have you both sit with me a while. Tea is just coming, although my son, as you see, never takes tea after breakfast. I declare you must be both exhausted travelling such a vast distance in such a short time. What was it, five, six days on good roads, more if it rains? Well, I suppose it will do, however, for a bridal tour — my son, you know,' she added to Camilla, 'never thinks of these things, for he is not at all a romantic, so you must not expect too much, but I dare say a five-day tour of Yorkshire and Derbyshire is no small thought — it must do, for now.'

'Mama!' Rotherham was laughing. 'Pray don't tax my wife with too many of my faults, or she will run away just as I have caught her!'

The tea things came and they spent another hour with Lady Rotherham before her husband took Camilla to their rooms. These turned out to be spacious, airy with three large windows, and she had her own dressing room, and an elegant wardrobe in which to put her new gowns. She turned to her husband. 'It is lovely, Hart, it truly is. I — I feel myself to be the most fortunate female that lived.' Her eyes shone.

'Oh, I am not finished with you yet, Mrs Rotherham' he drawled. 'You are mistress of Hartley Park now. You must have a new wardrobe. If you so much as dare unpack that awful brown bonnet of yours, I shall feed it directly to Fitz! Not that he would eat it, for even *he* has better taste in bonnets!'

Despite her laughing protests, she conceded to having a new wardrobe ordered, still in a daze at the sudden change in her fortunes. But it did not take much to extract from her the promise that she would order three new evening gowns, some new shoes, and a selection of morning dresses, for as Rotherham argued, she must look the part of his wife, not only for propriety but so that his mother would not guess her lowly origins.

Camilla was still in somewhat of a daze of being swept from the humble world she had inhabited so long, to the rather illustrious position of Mistress of Hartley Park, and she was glad her father had been so particular about her education and sent her to such a good girl's school. In that regard, at least, she would not be a disappointment to her mother-in-law!

Twenty

Lady Rotherham began to talk, in the first week of Camilla's being at Hartley Park, of a ball given in her honour, and although Camilla at first, somewhat embarrassed, said that she needed no such thing and that she preferred no fanfare to announce her presence, Rotherham was firm.

'It will give Mama something to look forward to, and besides she already has her heart set upon it. She might be sharp witted, Cam, but she is still feeble and weak, and I think we ought to humour her wishes for the pleasure it will give her. Besides, it is expected that you will be officially introduced as my wife.'

Camilla, feeling that he must be right, allowed herself to be persuaded, and entered into the planning with her mother-in-law, submitting her preferences when asked, and helping as much as she could with the details. Not that she had ever been to a ball before, she thought nervously, but she was on a daily basis being swept up into the dreamy fantasy of it all, as part of her new life with Rotherham.

Lady Rotherham seemed a little stronger as the week went by and Camilla was as attentive to her as she could be, her affection for her husband's mother growing each day. Hart's mother made no attempt to question Camilla on her family and connections out of a sensitivity for Camilla's feelings for which Camilla was grateful, for she did not like to be dishonest with the woman who was her mother-in-law.

Rotherham, too, was just as attentive, and when he came to her at night, Camilla felt that she was the happiest woman in the world. He was a little too polite, too reserved, during the day, but this she thought would begin to change over time, as he began, she hoped, to fall in love with her; indeed, there were times she almost confessed her feelings, but his reserve with her during the day made her wary and she was happy to wait until she knew his affections had been fully secured.

The day of the ball had been set for the Saturday, and Rotherham had made certain that the new gowns had well and truly been delivered. Camilla had been in a state of quiet wonder as she tried on the dresses. She had been to few private assemblies in her lifetime, and now she could hardly prevent herself from imagining what it would be like to dance with her husband.

Invitations were sent, and the rooms prepared, and Saturday arrived bringing with it a letter from Alice. Camilla took up the envelope at breakfast and opened it eagerly.

'Alice is still with Mrs Percy, she writes,' Camilla informed Rotherham, 'It seems as if she is very happy there... and it is just as I suspected! Percy has made her an offer and she has accepted! Well,' she added dryly, dropping the paper, 'It is a very fortunate outcome for her, I think, although I rather think he has his work cut out for him!'

Rotherham laughed. 'He does indeed. But I rather think some of my friends will say the same of myself! Now, I see you wish to throw that toast rack at me, which only proves my point... what is the expression? "Beware a horse behind and a woman in front?" There is that governess look again! Shall I sit in the corner?'

'You could,' she smiled, abandoning any attempt to look stern, 'but you know you promised to bring the hothouse flowers up to the ballroom for your mother, so I don't recommend it.'

'I did, didn't I? And I'll take any other errand you give me. I am attempting to be the most amiable husband in the world to make up for my deficiencies in overblown husbandly sentiments,' he teased. 'Do you like my efforts?'

'I am much impressed... although I never wished for sentiment! In fact, I lo — I like you better when you don't talk!'

'Then I shall be at pains to please you with my very long silences,' he laughed, reaching for the butter.

Camilla did not reply for she was making herself very busy with the tea-pot to cover her awkwardness. She had almost said the word which hung between them, and it was fortunate that she had prevented what might have been an even more awkward moment. She fussed with the tea-cups.

'I received a letter of congratulations from Lewisham Hall yesterday, which I had almost forgotten to mention. Sir George was most gracious about my abandoning the family, and tells me they have engaged a young governess to see Anne to her eighteenth birthday. I think they will be very happy to have Alice off their hands... although relations between Lewisham Hall and Sir Alan have sunk to the point of Sir George's telling Deed point blank that if he ever sees young Charles again, he will pepper him with buckshot! Only think of them inhabiting the same village!'

But, Camilla thought to herself, she was glad Charles had proved cowardly for she knew that if they had ever married, Alice would have quickly found the young man insipid and boring. In escaping Lewisham, and accepting Mr Thadeus Percy, Alice had found a man of ten times the calibre of young Deed!

* * *

They had a light dinner at four, and by seven Camilla was dressed, and her hair had been put up by the chamber maid. Looking at herself in the mirror, she marvelled quietly at the transformation she had undergone. No more did she look like a governess of humble origins, but a true gentlewoman. Her gown, a pale pink and deeper rose-sprigged India muslin, was diaphanous, and made her skin glow in the candlelight. It swept in delicate folds over her bosom and fell gently over her strong figure, softening her lines and giving her unaccustomed curves. She pulled on the cream kid shoes which her husband had bought for her when they had still been playing at husband and wife, and she marvelled at the way life had turned out.

'You look beautiful, Ma'am,' said Belinda, who had been putting the finishing touches to her hair. 'A real picture. Listen, the music is starting! Are you not just *wild* to dance, Ma'am?'

At this moment, Rotherham stepped into the room. She met his eyes, and found her heart was pounding in her breast. She resisted the urge to run and kiss him. Instead, she said calmly, 'Well, what do you think? Will I pass muster as your wife?'

'You look very — beautiful,' he said with a smile. 'Come, your first guests have arrived and we must receive them.' He held out his hand, and glowing, she took it.

'You look very well yourself, Hart. I have never seen you in such finery,' she added quietly.

They went downstairs, her hand on his arm, and began to meet their guests. Various families of, she was certain, great gentility and breeding, paraded in front of her and one by one she accepted their kind wishes for her future happiness. Two ladies now made their way towards them both, the older woman very obviously the mother of the younger, dark-haired female. Rotherham squeezed her arm, and murmured, 'Unfortunately, Cam, I cannot spare you the misfortune of having to be introduced to—'

'Lady Forster, and Miss Forster,' was the announcement by the footman, as the two females made low curtsies to their hosts, but when the younger woman raised her head and met Camilla's own eyes, Camilla discerned a chilly unfriendliness in them. 'How do you do,' she said politely, as Rotherham took Lady Forster's offered hand. Then she looked again, and her smile froze as Rotherham bowed to the ladies. It could not be! But how unfortunate! Miss Forster, Miss Jane Forster if she recalled correctly, was slightly known to her! She had been present at Lewisham Hall only a year ago, as one of a party of guests who had been invited to the Hall by Sir George to amuse his daughters. Camilla, as Alice's governess, had had little to do with the fine ladies of the party, of course, and had not been included in any of the outings the females had enjoyed, but she had sat quietly in the drawing room on several occasions as the young ladies played at cards, while Miss Spinner had kept a quiet eye on the proceedings from her corner. Even then, Miss Jane Forster had not addressed but two words to the governess in the corner, but Camilla, recognizing the young woman at once, was immediately on her guard that she might indeed be recognized, and her background as a humble governess exposed to Lady Rotherham.

Still she might not be recognized, she hoped, since her situation in life was now far different... it would be a great misfortune if humble Miss Spinner of the brown bonnets and governess's aprons was recognised now, in her fine gowns and greater consequence as mistress of Hartley Park! She suspected that Miss Jane Forster would have paid as little attention to a governess as she would to any servant of the Hall, and so allowed herself to relax just a little into her husband's arm.

'So, this is your new bride, Rotherham!' remarked Lady Forster, eyeing Camilla up and down in rather an impertinent way. 'Very pleased to meet you, I am sure! My daughter Jane and I had such an amusing wager on the way here, Mrs Rotherham, that you would be in the latest fashions from town, but you have exceeded even our expectations! What a perfect gown!' Her eyes, however, like her daughter's, had barely glanced at Camilla's gown but were fixed on Camilla's own, waiting for a response. Jane, however, was scrutinizing Camilla. 'But I feel I know you from somewhere, Mrs Rotherham, although I cannot say where... your face — it is familiar, but I cannot recall—'

'I don't recall that we have met,' replied Camilla quickly, with an alarm which she was at pains to disguise. 'I believe you have confused me with another—'

'You will forgive us, Lady Forster,' interrupted Rotherham smoothly, who had sensed Camilla's alarm, 'but we must greet Mr Austin and his daughters who come behind you. Ah, good evening Austin, how do you do?'

Camilla watched the two Forster females enter the ballroom with a mixture of relief and anxiety. If she should be recognized! But that such a supercilious lady as Miss Jane Forster would remember a governess, she doubted, and although she would warn her husband later, she felt so far removed from her old life that she felt it most unlikely she would be recognized as Alice Featherstone's governess. Still, she said to Rotherham very quietly, 'I do not like those two, and you were right to warn me against them! I feel as if they know who I am — the younger one I think I have met before, once.'

'I wondered if that was the case... well, my dear, I shouldn't worry, for they are both as unpleasant a pair as ever my mother invited here. I suspect they are just put out that I did not make an offer for Miss Forster, for Lady Forster had me quite lined up for the job of warming her daughter's marble heart, I collect! No, unless you go back to wearing a brown bonnet, I believe your secrets are safe here at Hartley Park!'

Camilla did her best to laugh at Rotherham's little tease, but when later in the evening, she went down the dance on her husband's arm, she found she was the subject of scrutiny by a pair of chilly eyes, and she wished, not for the first time, that she had not agreed to keep the secret of her background from Lady Rotherham, no matter how unpleasant it would have been to confess!

'How long must you be away?' Camilla had not needed her husband's impending absence to know that she was a deal more than just a little nervous at being left alone with her mother-in-law at the best of times, let alone for an entire week! Although Lady Rotherham had been nothing but kind, the weight of a guilty conscience had wrought its toll on Camilla's mind since she had suffered being almost recognised at the Ball a few days earlier. Therefore, Camilla now heard her husband's scheme of going away with great deal of trepidation.

'I shall be as quick as I can, perhaps only a few days,' assured Rotherham. 'Fitz will be keen to get out for a good ride, and I must see to some business I have put off too long. Besides, although Mama seems to be making good progress and has been up every day, I own I am pleased you will be here, keeping an eye on her.'

'Then don't be too long away, will you please? What if she takes a turn?'

'She won't — why, just knowing what you have given her, the possibility of the heir she has her heart set upon — her health is so much improved upon that alone!'

Still, Camilla was nervous as she waved her husband off the next morning, and found herself missing his presence even more than she had allowed. She had been happier than she had ever known herself as Mrs Rotherham, and had given herself reason to hope that in time, her husband might come to feel for her what she had come to feel for him. Each night, she was entranced to experience the joys that she had only read of in a union which was based on mutual respect and affection. However, she knew that those private thoughts which she was not yet at liberty to reveal to her husband, those sensations when she was around him which enhanced her happiness both at night and during the day, could not be made known to him just yet. She was careful to not allow him to read her feelings too fully, in case she should be reprimanded for girlish foolishness! Both Hart and his mother had warned her that he was not a romantic! But his attentions to her were so kind, so marked, that she had high hopes of his coming to love her in time and, she hoped, before a child was announced, for she would like very much to know that any child of theirs would be conceived in love.

So she waved Rotherham off, and went inside to read to her mother-in-law, counting the days until her husband could be home again and she could know the comfort of his presence.

A week passed, and Camilla began to look forward to her husband's return. Lady Rotherham had been kind enough, seeming to take some comfort from the addition of company which she was lacking when Rotherham was absent, and they together had entertained a veritable string of callers most days, since many of Lady Rotherham's acquaintance knew that she was indisposed for calling herself.

Friday morning brought a little rain. Rotherham was due to return the following day, and Camilla had left Lady Rotherham resting in her room and gone to read in the drawing room. After a short time, however, Miss Jane Forster was announced, much to Camilla's astonishment. Why would any well-bred lady come calling in the rain? She stood to receive the young woman, feeling more anxious than she liked to admit.

'Mrs Rotherham, how do you do?' Miss Forster's eyes scrutinized Camilla once again, and she met the other woman's gaze with a nervousness born of a pressing guilt. She made a curtsey and indicated the other woman to sit. They engaged in civil small talk for a minute or two, Camilla's nerves somewhat on edge as she explained Lady Rotherham was just now indisposed, and was resting. But as the minutes progressed and the civilities wore out, she began to wish herself elsewhere or Lady Rotherham present.

And it was not long before she had full reason to wish the woman had never come to call, for just as soon as tea had been brought in and the servant gone out again, Miss Forster said with a little crowing smirk, 'I believe I have recollected where I know you from, Mrs Rotherham! But it was Miss Spinner then, was it not? It was from my visit to Derbyshire last summer, at Lewisham Hall, was it not? Do you remember? You sat in the drawing room to chaperone all of us young ladies! But how is your charge, Miss Alice Featherstone? Who is governess to her now that she has lost you?' Her cold blue eyes were triumphant as she shrewdly assessed the look on Camilla's countenance at this intelligence. 'I suppose you thought you might hide your origins — that you are really a -a lowish sort of person — and I suppose you have succeeded, until now.'

Camilla met the woman's eyes calmly, although her voice shook a little. 'And what of it? My husband knows full well who — and what — I was then, and he has no great exception to it, or I would not be here.'

'Ah,' said Miss Forster with a sly smile. 'But I wager your mother-in-law does not, for she is too proud a woman to endure having a governess for a daughter-in-law! How dreadful if she were to discover you have been hiding the truth, Mrs Rotherham!'

'What do you mean to do?' Camilla could hardly believe the woman's arrogance in coming to Hartley Park just to crow because she had found out her secret. What was Miss Forster's object in coming to call?'

'I? Why nothing at all, my dear Mrs Rotherham. Although I do believe it will be the death of poor Lady Rotherham when she discovers the truth you have been hiding! Who knows what dreadful affect such a revelation would have on her!'

'Perhaps,' said Camilla coolly, 'you underestimate the love my mother-in-law has for her son. If she knows my husband is happy, she would not, I suspect, force him into giving up the union for the sake of her own peculiar feelings. She is a stern woman, and used to having her way, but she is not without motherly love.'

'Pray, don't preach to me about love, Miss Spinner — I beg your pardon — Mrs Rotherham,' added the lady blandly. She yawned delicately. 'Love is irrelevant in all marriages, and as far as I can see, Rotherham might have married you but he will never love you. He was forced to marry, and it is only because Lady Louisa Waverly turned him down — yes, gossip spreads quickly in a small town — it is only because he must provide an heir that he married you. There was a time I thought he might offer in a different direction... certain affections having been exchanged.' Here she cast her eyes down modestly, but not before she had cast a glance at Camilla to ascertain the effect of her words.

'Some men are so fickle, are they not Mrs Rotherham? But if you think he loves you, a woman far below him in circumstance and breeding, you even you are a bigger fool than I thought!'

Camilla's self-command was challenged sorely but she did not fail. She said composedly, 'Fool or not, Miss Forster, I believe you have said enough. The footman will see you out.'

The servant appeared immediately, and opened the door for their guest. Miss Forster stood and shook out her skirts. 'I feel a vast deal of sympathy for you, believe it or not. You have been duped, and now you seek to dupe others. I have only done you a service by bringing your plight to your attention. I only hope you are not hurt too much when Rotherham seeks his — *comforts* — elsewhere. For a man with the consequence of Rotherham to marry a governess — well, he must have been quite desperate to please his mother.' She laughed. 'You must have realized that the connection between your two families would be impossible! I hope, too, that you have some place to go when you are thrown out of Hartley Park!' With these words, she retreated with dignity, leaving Camilla stunned.

A half hour on the sofa, with her tea growing cold, taught her the foolishness of deception. Guilt ravaged her mind, and she determined that as soon as Rotherham returned, she would urge him to make a full confession to his mother, and beg for her good opinion, if not immediately given, then to be given over time. As for Rotherham's not loving her, and her being a substitute for Lady Louisa Waverly, she was less sure. She had thought herself a sure way towards being secure in Rotherham's affections, although he had not given her a verbal confirmation of it. But the way he kissed her at night, and his small attentive kindnesses to her during the daytime were, for a woman who had never experienced love, all the proof of his growing affection that she had thought necessary. The idea that he was acting a mere part, playing husband to her to please his mother, had not occurred to her and she cursed her ignorance.

But he had been open about their union being one of convenience. She had been foolish to imagine what would never be, for he had been quite clear that he had married her to provide an heir. Having supposed herself tolerably secure of Hart's affections, Camilla now felt herself exceedingly foolish in having agreed to the marriage. But she had been almost sure of his affections being genuine! Her security sank to half of what her assurance had been only a few days previously, and she was in a most painful perplexity to understand his feelings. But then, she thought bitterly, it mattered not what his feelings were, when her own so very strongly urged her to confess — to confess, or to leave, if he would not sanction such a confession!

Such was the seriousness of her thoughts that when Rotherham finally returned around eleven o' clock the following morning, it was to find Camilla sitting in the breakfast room, her toast and tea untouched. She had greeted him with a tender smile and kiss, but soon she appeared listless and wan to his eye. When he made enquiries into the cause of her pallor, she broached the topic with him, and informed him of Miss Forster's knowing her secret. 'It will break your mother's heart to discover my concealment! What if she takes a bad turn? I am every moment regretting our rash decision to enter a union which can bring only pain to those in this house.'

'My dear girl!' Rotherham was astonished, and his tone showed it fully. Camilla had not seen him this moved, his usual amiable demeanour turned severe. Her heart broke a little.

He continued. 'You surely cannot be contemplating telling Mama? She is a proud woman, Cam. She may have accepted that you are not Louisa, but to discover that you are a governess by trade — it cannot be made known to her! You will break her heart and give her a great deal of pain in discovering that any heir you might produce would come from stock of which she would never approve. It cannot — it will not — be done!' Rotherham had never been this stern, this serious with her, and hear heart sunk.

'We — I — have no choice, Hart. I cannot live a lie! I will not! I must confess, or live as if a prisoner of my own wrong doing, until such a time as she discovers the truth by means of Miss Forster. She will throw me out of Hartley, surely!'

'And *this* is how you repay her kindness to you in receiving you so amiably, so warmly, although you were not the Louisa she expected? This is how you repay her for welcoming you into Hartley Park as her own daughter? Do not you suppose yourself excessively wicked indeed for wishing to cause needless pain to an old woman not long for this world?' His face was thunder itself and she flinched at his anger.

'We have entered into an arrangement without the knowledge, much less the approbation of your mother! We have not been prudent, Hartley, and now great suffering must come about because of it! Either we confess the entire truth to your mother and risk her health, or I must go. I cannot remain in this house as an imposter.'

Her resolve was strong and calm, although her heart was cast as low as it could be. There would be no love, no husband, no creature she could rely upon in the world, if he refused her this. She raised her eyes to his cold ones, only to endure the chill in them. He did not answer her and she knew that he would not budge. 'I think it would be better then for us both, if we were to break the matter off entirely.' She said it calmly, for she had endured worse than this, and she did not feel equal to entering into any more discussion. 'I shall remove today. I shall leave it to you to say what you wish to Lady Rotherham. Only, give her my sincerest good wishes and tell her I can only hope to be forgiven in the next world, if she will not forgive me my deception in this one.'

She stood and moved toward the door, Rotherham doing nothing to prevent her leaving. The door shut behind her, and she went in deep sorrow to remove her things from the blue room, and order her maid to pack her trunks.

It was September. The heat of summer, what little of it there was in Yorkshire, had passed off almost entirely, and given way to frosty mornings, cool days, and chilly evenings. Autumnal splendour now girded the great oaks and poplars which dotted the fields and valleys of the fertile and beautiful scenes which lay around the village of Penniston. Camilla had walked in the valley every day since her arrival. She had written to Louisa the day she had removed from Hartley Park and begged to be accepted to be as a guest at the home of Louisa's uncle, on her way to Scotland.

> '*I hope you do not think me impertinent to rely upon such a short acquaintance, but truly, I have no creature in the world but you to depend upon. I rely upon your friendship with my husband to perhaps soften you toward one who might otherwise have no place in the world to go. I have no family, and no friends. But I cannot stay at Hartley Park, and you, of all people, know my secret, and why I cannot remain at Hartley Park.*
>
> '*Write to me at Meadleton, to the posting inn there, and if you give the word I shall only be a day's journey from Penniston. If you are unable to offer me respite, or perhaps if you have already left to go to Mrs Cosway, I shall go on to Scotland myself. There, I shall endeavour to find myself a new governess position. At least nobody there will know of my inglorious past.*'

A six-day journey, one which was now quite familiar to her, had given her the time needed to think about her future, and upon receiving Louisa's very earnest entreaties to come to her at Penniston while she was still at her uncle's house, Camilla had entered the village a day later, grateful to have at least one friend in the world.

Louisa had delayed her own removal into Scotland in order to spend Michaelmas with her uncle. Upon receiving a pale and sombre Camilla into the house, she had been as gentle and unobtrusive as possible, giving her friend all possible attention and solicitude, but preserving the privacy of her friend by making no enquires into the state of affairs at Hartley Park. After a week of this solicitude, however, while they happened to be walking together in the valley, she had ventured to enquire gently into the circumstances which would see Camilla, so recently married, running from her husband.

Camilla had given her a brief explanation of the events of the past two weeks, and the visit of Miss Forster whereby the truth of Camilla's past had been exposed.

Louisa had been perplexed. 'It is a very severe stroke indeed, if what you tell me is true, Mrs Rotherham, and I must say again that I am quite astonished at Hart's being so hard-hearted. But he is very attached to his mother. Lady Rotherham would be most displeased and angry to discover her son had deceived her from the outset.'

'Do you really think it is as Hart maintains, that it would hurt her more to know? She has been so kind to me, but it has weighed upon me heavily to think that I am living a lie at Hartley Park.'

'It would result, I suspect, in the most unhappy rupture of two people. Hart will likely be dismissed from Hartley, and his mother's notice. She is a proud woman,' sighed Louisa, 'and I ought to know it for I have known her these twenty years. And I believe Hart is right in wishing to protect her from another turn; her health is so delicate it may be her undoing. But you are his wife, and his first allegiance must be to you!'

Camilla was sober. Hartley had been adamant about concealing the truth for the sake of his mother, and this she understood; indeed, she herself had urged all care and affection for his mother when he had sought her advice on whether to marry or not. But she felt it to be the greatest evil in the world to place one's mother over one's wife; this was not the 'for better or for worse' of their marriage vows and she felt herself bitterly disappointed, used and abandoned. But soon the truth would be out, she was sure, since Miss Forster seemed quite ready to open up her secrets to the world, and then it would be a worse evil to still be living the lie which it galled her to admit. No, she could not for all the world return to Hartley Park and her husband; he had made his choice clear, and his allegiance was to his heritage and his mother, before her. He had been apprised of her whereabouts, for when she had left she had told him of her intention go back into Yorkshire and on to Scotland. If he wanted her, he would have to come to her.

He had not. Her heart was sunk altogether, and her self-command was greatly taxed to appear as unaffected as she hoped. As the two women pulled their shawls closer and walked toward the village, Camilla tried to conceal her misery.

Louisa however, observing her pale demeanour and watery eyes, took her companion's arm. 'One thing I hope may give you comfort, Camilla, if I may be so bold as to mention the matter — it is with the earnest hope of giving you comfort that I speak of it — but I believe that, despite his behaviour, and his stubborn insistence on sparing his mother the pain of knowing the truth, Hart himself does not think of you as not being worthy of the heir that you would have produced. Indeed, I believe he loves you too much to regard a division of rank as an impediment to your marriage.'

'Love me?' exclaimed Camilla, blushing. She cast her eyes to the ground below her in a confusion of feelings. 'I did not think — perhaps he does love me, in a way — at least, I thought he might love me, although we never married for love, you know — Hart was very clear that it was mutually beneficial arrangement, but I had hoped that over time...'

'I believe he loves you very much,' insisted Louisa. 'Pray remember that I have known Hartley since my childhood and we have spent a great deal of time together. I knew he was in love with you when I saw him watching you when you were here only these three weeks gone. I have never seen so much pride and happiness in his demeanour — on his countenance was certainly love, or something very much approaching it. Perhaps, given time to think on things, and the encouragement of an absence, he will come to reconsider his harshness and realize that he is better off with a wife who loves him, than a mother who controls him.'

But Camilla did not think it very likely, nor did she think that Hartley Rotherham was in love with her in the way that Louisa thought he was. When, after another week had passed and she had heard nothing of her husband, she began to make her object of going into Scotland a reality, and to place an enquiry in the papers for governess' positions in that country. Louisa's own removal was now imminent, and Camilla planned to be leaving Penniston at the same time.

Louisa at that time was gratified to receive a letter from the newly married Alice, who had professed herself exceedingly eager to keep up the friendship forged during her flight to Yorkshire. The letter was full of details of her union to Mr Percy, her gown, the guests who had attended the breakfast, the convenience of Percy's establishment at Foal's Keep, her husband's virtues, his handsome demeanour and the amiable kindness of his mother.

To Camilla, upon Louisa's reading her some of its parts, it was a both a joy to hear from Alice and yet a burden, for dear Alice had had no objections to contend with at home, and had received no small amount of kindness from her mother-in-law to be, whereas Camilla was at pains to remain unembittered at the treatment she had received from Rotherham, and most likely his mother, if and when that illustrious lady should discover the truth. It hurt her that Rotherham had not come to her, even after four weeks of absence, and if he could not even write to her, then she felt that it was upon her own head that she had now reaped the consequences of dishonesty, and had been humbled back into the governess that she had always been.

A suitable position arose, and a very kind and jolly letter written inviting her to come immediately she could remove from Yorkshire. The position was with an amiable family with three little girls and the older two boys away at school. The house was not so distant from the residence of Mrs Mariah Cosway to make a journey there impossible, and so Camilla took comfort at least in the knowledge that she would be near Louisa as she studied art with the illustrious painter, Mrs Cosway.

Now Camilla did not balk at putting off her fine gowns and bonnets; indeed, she was almost eager to cast off the garments that reminded her of her brief former married life and the happiness she had begun to feel, the love that she had begun to develop for her husband.

The morning of her departure she gravely put on her humble brown calicos and muslins and tried to think of herself as fortunate to have had a glimpse of such things, even if they were not to be in her future. 'I have, at least, my memories for company,' she told herself, 'and I have learned to be rational; this must keep me strong against the evils of melancholy recollections!'

She had packed the last of her fine gowns into trunks to be kept for her at the home of Mr Stacey, then followed her one humble governess's trunk downstairs, full of its grey and brown aprons and morning dresses, to await the carriage which was to carry her into Scotland. Louisa had insisted that she take her uncle's coach and have his footman for her comfort, since the Cosways were to send their own for Louisa the following day. Old Mr Stacey having joined his very kind entreaties to his niece's, Camilla had at last been persuaded to accept their kindness, although her eyes were bright with unshed tears at being shown such consideration.

Soon it was the last breakfast she would have with those around her whom she could call friends, and then it was the last cup of tea. She sat with Louisa in the breakfast room, in her dull brown travelling coat, and her one remaining brown bonnet once more in its place upon her chestnut curls. Louisa made a good effort at first to talk of mundane matters, her own pursuits in Scotland, her lessons with Mrs Cosway, and her upcoming exhibition, in which four of her landscapes would be exhibited alongside those of Mariah Cosway. Soon however, it was time to remove, and Camilla began to be sensible of all that she must now leave behind her.

Louisa took her hand. 'You must write to me every week — I shall depend upon hearing from you, very much. How you can bear this dreadful change, I cannot imagine. Don't lose hope that he will write to you — I myself shall write to him and give him your forwarding direction.'

'This truly is my last day of being Mrs Rotherham, Hartley's wife,' replied Camilla resolutely. 'I shall take as much delight as possible in my charges; three little girls, full of life, must go a good way to distracting me, and my former life must soon become a distant memory to me.'

Louisa was sympathetic. 'You look so different, so strange, in the garb of your former trade. It will be no discredit to you, I am sure, to wear your finer gowns. There is no need, surely, for you to resort to the dowdy gowns of your former life? And my dearest Camilla, that bonnet!'

Camilla could not forbear to smile at her friend's accidental reminder of her husband's little teases over her choice of head covering. The smile, however, lasted but a moment or two and became replaced with the sadness which had become her daily companion since leaving Hartley Park.

'I am a governess, my dear Louisa, if I like it or not, and I have worn such clothes for so long a time that it was more peculiar for me to put on the fine gowns which my husband bought for me than it has been for me to return to a humbler form of dress. I may be a mere governess,' she added lifting her chin, 'but I have not lost my pride. I shall return to the trade which supported me after my father passed away, and I have no need to be ashamed of it, nor of wearing the sensible gowns and boots of a governess. Do not say it is strange to see me so!'

'It is stranger to me, dear Camilla, that if all your friends, so disposed to do well by you as they were, were to have their way, you would have wanted for nothing in your future life. And yet, here you are, ready to return to that former style of living which only a few months ago you had no idea that you would be obliged to give up!'

'Indeed,' replied Camilla earnestly, 'it was a very great mistake to think I could ever play at Rotherham's wife and take a rightful place at Hartley. I was foolish — believing that no evil would come of attempting to transcend my rank, to rise above my place in the world! But I shall go forward now, as I am, and I will not be shamed for my future rank as lowly governess. Only I do feel shame for my past behaviour, for what it ought to have been.'

Louisa took her hand. 'And what of Rotherham? If he should come here looking for you? You are still married to him, Camilla. He surely will come after you when he comes to his senses!'

Camilla sighed and shook her head. 'I can hardly say — I cannot tell you what he will do, but if he had any idea of coming after me, any of the regard that you feel he holds for me, surely his absence here is proof of a mistaken notion? It has been four weeks. He will not come. He is too angry with me. I shall go into Scotland as Camilla Rotherham, a governess. If I am asked, I shall never tell my sorry story, but say I am a widow, for it is verily the same thing!'

'Then be strong and I shall see you very soon. I shall remain in Scotland until the spring. I shall come to you whenever I can, my dear Camilla. You *shall* have one creature in the world to call a friend, although I hope I shall not be the only one!'

Now the sounds of the carriage were heard outside. Camilla stood and embraced her friend. 'You and Mr Stacey have been more kind to me than I deserve. Pray write to me often!'

They made their way out to the open door, in readiness to step through it, but footsteps were heard on the gravel outside, then a voice rang through the air which rooted Camilla to the spot.

'Where is Mrs Rotherham? Louisa! Louisa!'

Camilla barely had time to exchange astonished glances with Louisa. In a moment, Rotherham had appeared in the doorway. Camilla had shrunk into the shadows, and Rotherham strode inside, toward Louisa. 'Lou! Thank God! Is she here? Where is my wife? Am I too late?'

'She is here, Hart. You are not too late.'

Camilla stepped out from the shadow of the stairwell. 'Hartley.' Her own heart pounded. Her feelings were a tumult of confusion. Why had he come, after four weeks with no word from him? What was his object?

But before she had a chance to ask him anything, he had taken a few steps toward her and swept her into his arms. His lips came down upon hers and for a blissful moment, she was Mrs Rotherham, in love with her husband, and he with her. But a few moments was all it took for her reason to return with a rush. She pulled away, blushing to be observed by a slightly amused Rotherham, a smiling Louisa, and two astonished footmen. Louisa discretely melted back into the morning room and the footmen returned to their other duties. Camilla and Rotherham were alone.

Camilla calmed her breathing, unable to believe that her husband, the man she loved, was here, and yet with all her heart, she hoped that he had changed his mind about confessing all to his mother. But she would be dignified, she would be mistress of herself. She spoke with calmness, although it was in strained tones.

'Hartley. How do you do? I see you received my note after all.' It was all she could do to remain civil, for while she was hurt that he had not come before this, she wished so much to throw herself into his arms. Yet, she could not give into such unrestraint unless she knew he had forgiven her and was ready to confess to his mother.

'Have I really deserved so much indifferent politeness between us?' He smiled down at her and her stomach fluttered alarmingly. Her resolve to be strong crumbled a little.

'Why are you dressed like that?' He now seemed to notice her garb. 'I thought Fitz had devoured that bonnet long ago!' He smiled but his eyes quizzed her.

'I am just now to remove to Scotland, to a position as governess.' She tilted her chin.

He seemed speechless. Then, 'And you are determined upon going away?'

'I am resolved.'

'I see.'

'How — How does your mother?'

Her coolness had the intended sobering effect on him, and a shadow of pain passed over his countenance. His smile faded. 'That is one of the reasons I have come. My mother has passed away, Camilla. She is gone.'

Camilla turned pale. She half reached a hand to him but restrained herself. 'Oh, Hart, I am too sorry for you. But she had the happiness of knowing her son loved her.'

Rotherham gave a bitter half laugh. 'Oh yes, she had the knowledge that I would do anything for her. Almost. Camilla, I told her. I confessed our secret to her before she died.'

Camilla's eyes widened. 'You did?'

'I did. After you left, I was for a time very angry with you. I felt you had betrayed me by leaving, by refusing to carry on a deception to hide something which I felt would cause Mama great unhappiness. But after a week without you, in which I had time to scrutinize my actions, my feelings, I realized that I had made a grave mistake in asking you to carry out such a deception. A deception which I had instigated, and which had made you very unhappy. You were right. A man's devotion must be to his wife, not to his mother. She has ruled me, Camilla, with an iron fist since I was in frocks, and I realised that I was still being ruled by her.

'It was my intention to tell her three weeks ago about you, and tell her that I was going north to bring you home, to your *rightful* home, and that she would have to accept any child of ours as befitting Hartley Park and the name Rotherham. But just as I had determined upon this course, she took another turn, and was very ill for many days. I sat with her, and had to delay my journey into Yorkshire to fetch you home, for she was not expected to live above a week. One week stretched into two. She drifted in and out of consciousness, but last week, a few hours before she died, Camilla, she became lucid enough to converse with me. It was then that I told her everything. She was very weak, you understand, but she understood me well enough. Then she forgave us, and gave you her blessing. She told me to give you this.'

Here, into Camilla's astonished hands, he placed a gold locket on a gold chain. Her eyes questioned him.

'It was my mother's. She instructed me to give it to you as a sign that she has forgiven you, and that you must take your place as mistress of Hartley. She told me that you must be made to return home. I could not come immediately as I had intended, for I had a funeral to arrange, and I saw my mother into her final resting place this se'en night gone. I came then just as soon as I could. My dear, will you — can you — forgive me my selfishness?'

Camilla had never seen Rotherham in so much doubt of himself, of the outcome. For a man so used to commanding his way, here was a boy, in doubt of his own powers of persuasion. She was speechless. He stood before her, familiar and dear, his dark eyes searching her own. His mother had accepted her! Was it true? She opened the locket, and a miniature portrait of Hart peeked out at her. She closed the little piece again, and tugged absently at her upper lip.

'Was it not only a month ago that you complained of a woman in front being as dangerous as a horse behind?' Her eyes danced.

'Indeed, I most certainly did!' exclaimed Rotherham, holding back a laugh. 'And I cannot be persuaded it is otherwise. But at least I did not say a wife in front was *like* a horse's behind!'

'No, indeed you did not. If you had, you would be in a great deal of pain even now.' She was laughing now, and so was he. 'Hart?'

'Yes, my love?'

'Louisa is of the ridiculous opinion that you are in love with me.'

'Oh, she is, is she?' He took her hands. 'Do you doubt it?'

'No. Oh Hart!' Then she murmured what she had yearned him to know for some time, and they were quiet for a few moments.

Breaking free, she was about to speak again, but a sheepish Louisa had come smiling from the morning room. 'I was almost in the way of giving up hope about you, Hartley Rotherham. And yet here you are, come to admit you were wrong, after all. It gives me joy indeed, to see my two dearest friends reunited. But how could you have justified to yourself your behaviour, I can still hardly comprehend!'

Rotherham, still with his arm around Camilla's waist, shook his head. 'I was a devilish fool, I know. I thought it my duty, independent of my own feelings, to honour the wishes of a dying parent. One who, while not having been a just and fair parent, had been affectionate in her own way just the same. My mother, as you know Louisa, is — *was* — a most complex female. I could not, at first, contemplate the weight of guilt which would have come upon me if Mama had renounced me, or taken a turn for the worse, but after a short time, I came to see clearly her influence over me. My regard for my wife, I have come to confess, is a kingdom beyond my allegiance to Mama, God bless her departed soul. I only hope Camilla can forgive me.' Here he turned fully toward Camilla and took her hands in his once more. 'What say you? Will you remove that dreadful head piece, and come home with me, Mrs Rotherham?'

That his repentance of misconduct should be believed, and even more so, heard with eagerness, should not be doubted, for Camilla was as ready to forgive as he was to repent. At any rate, Camilla could not resist such a tug on her heart, and all was quickly settled for their remaining fixed at the home of Mr Stacey for another day or two, and then to remove back into the West Midlands, this time, Rotherham promised laughingly, by a different route, and with as much time in the world as they chose.

Epilogue

Louisa put down her brush and stood back from the canvas. Cream, rose and white, with touches of blues and greens flowed over the canvas she had been working on. The eyes of a woman, the woman who had been her mentor for these ten months, looked back at her. It was a portrait, and it was good. Louisa's technique had improved so much that Mariah had promised that Louisa would be exhibited at the Royal Academy this year. It was an opportunity to be celebrated.

She had been almost continually in Scotland. She had met some of the most influential painters, writers and poets in these months, and her work had become her life's purpose. To express herself in the medium of canvas and paint was the exquisite bliss that some people found in marriage and child-bearing, but Louisa had always been different, and now she was proud to be bearing a torch, lighting a way for the many other talented female artists denied the right to exhibit on the basis of sex.

She wiped her hands on a rag of muslin and rang the bell for tea. Mariah had given Louisa a studio to work in, although she sometimes worked in the larger studio which Mariah shared with her husband. She removed her aprons, spattered with oil paint, and went to the window to sit and peruse once again the two letters she had received that morning. One was from Camilla Rotherham, who had kindly invited Louisa to spend a month with them at Hartley Park after she had finished her European tour in the spring. She would go gladly, for not only did she wish very much for the society of her friends there, but she had yet to meet the young heir to Hartley, George Hartley Rotherham, but a few weeks old.

The second letter was from her father, and was full of the doings at Waverly.

> *'Your mother and I are a good way to being in pockets again, by the careful adjustment of spending and receiving, so that neither of those pillars of a wise household is too far leaning to the one side. You know your Mama too well to fail to understand how little satisfaction this gives her in the present, especially having been obliged out of desperation to shut down the milliner's account and cease the ordering of fabrics from town, which has put her rather more out of countenance. But I have had the very great foresight to follow up my strictures on spending with more cheering news. I have promised her a long visit to Bath, which is so cheap a place to live and yet provides such a variety of diversion for such a small sum, that I hold she will be diverted enough from the loss of her gowns to be tolerably content. At any rate, your Mama is already somewhat mollified by the thought of Bath, and then after that we shall come to you at The Granges in June. We would come sooner but you know she could not bear the cold winter and spring of Yorkshire country without it affecting her bones. As it is we had but vast indifferent weather for our visit to—'*

Here, Louisa put down the letter, smiling at little to herself, to receive the tea things. Soon she would take up her brushes again, but she welcomed the rest. Breaking off a little plumb-cake, she held it out.

Button, having found his nap disturbed by the delicious smell of fresh-baked cake, got up at once from his place under the table and came to delicately take the offering his mistress had made him. Settling at her feet, his tail thumped gently, and he closed his eyes. He was with his mistress, and while he could sleep at her feet, all was right with the world.

The End

I hope that you've enjoyed this book!

After the About the Author section, you'll find a
preview of

Woodston

About the Author

Kate Westwood is the author's pseudonym. Kate has a background in academic writing and holds a Master's degree in English Literature. Having had a life-long dream to write, she finally turned her pen to regency romance when she turned fifty.

Kate is a huge fan of Austen, and her contemporaries, and strives to recreate an authentic 'regency' experience for the reader.

Kate's hobbies, when she is not writing or reading Regency romance, include playing classical piano, and walking and hiking the beautiful Gold Coast Hinterland. Kate has three adult sons and lives in the beautiful Moreton Bay Islands with her partner and cat.

Connect with Kate

Facebook: https://www.facebook.com/katewestwood.net/
Sign up to Kate's email newsletter at :
www.katewestwood.net
to receive the subscriber exclusive story *'The Gift'* as a welcome gift!

Here is your preview of
Woodston

Early October, 1798

Catherine Moreland, without claim to any particularly remarkable antecedents, herself being the recipient of an adequate but undistinguished education, and boasting tolerably pretty but not exceptional looks, felt herself the most fortunate girl in the whole of England. As she stepped from the carriage and took her new husband's offered arm, she wondered if anyone had ever been so happy as she was at that moment.

Natural modesty had allowed her to concede that she could not, as her mother and father had pointed out numerous times in the last year, do any better considering her own unremarkable station in life. Her father was a clergyman and had the parsonage at Fullerton, Catherine's home. While not exactly poor, Mr Moreland had neither the means nor the consequence to provide his oldest daughter with a large income or that rank which would bring wealthy beaux to her doorstep. He could provide her with merely four hundred pounds a year, and that, for a young lady of modest origins, must be fortune enough. She had been brought up to be humble, and never in expectation of more than she deserved. But in catching the eye of a tolerably set-up young man such as Henry Tilney, the youngest son of General Tilney of Northanger and heir to a comfortable stipend sometime in the future, Catherine had managed to elevate herself to a station neither she nor her parents had expected.

Expected or not, however, this new situation in life she was willing to embrace with all the natural eagerness and optimism which love could furnish her with. Now, as she stood on the semi-circled sweep of a gravelled driveway, eyeing the pretty stone house which was to be her home, love, or whatever it was which passed for love with young and inexperienced females of eighteen years, would allow her to admit no fault with the vision before her. Woodston parsonage was not only handsome and agreeable, it was utterly charming, simply because it was Henry's home and therefore her own.

Although it was not the oldest building in the area, the large, white-stoned house formed the central focus of the bustling village of Woodston, being at the end of the village and thus commanding the view from almost every street as the eye was led to its pleasing, distant form. It was tolerably disengaged from the rest of the village which gave it an air of distinction, without its being at all superior. It had been built only thirty years ago, having succeeded a much older and rougher building which Henry's father, General Tilney, had insisted be torn down, despite its history. And despite the building's comparative newness, the parsonage had been already refurbished ten years ago at the Generals insistence, for the General had a passionate regard for modernisation, whether that be in his gardens, his furnishings, his carriages or in the buildings which populated his estate.

To a new-married woman, entering her own home for the first time, nothing could appear more auspicious than the pretty picture made by the elegant stone house before Catherine. To be sure, Woodston was not as grand as Northanger, nor did it command the solemn respect which the other house did; Northanger Abbey boasted as much ancient history and gothic appearance as Woodston did not. But her new home was larger and much prettier than the old parsonage Catherine had grown up in and left behind her. It boasted no small number of rooms, its large windows were plenty in number, its outlook pleasant from most sides of the house, and it was surrounded by some exceedingly pretty parklands. Due to the season, these were now fully decked in a splendour of golds and reds and made as pretty a picture as Catherine had ever graced to witness. Woodston, she thought complacently, was a most charming home, and she and Henry the most charming and fortunate couple in the world!

"*Woodston parsonage was not only handsome and agreeable, it was utterly charming.*"

She turned her face up to her husband's in eager delight. 'Oh Henry! Is this not the most perfectly happy moment? To be standing here, finally, after everything that has happened! I cannot believe we are truly married!' She squeezed his arm. 'Now all the delay seems merely nothing at all! I am so happy I can hardly blink in case it should all be a dream!'

The young people had been forced to wait a year before being sanctioned to marry by General Tilney. A year earlier, Catherine had been invited by the General to stay at Northanger Abbey. Supposing Catherine to be the future recipient of a large endowment upon the demise of the Allens, a wealthy and childless couple who were on intimate terms with the family, the scheming General had been bitterly disappointed. As soon as it became known that no such endowment upon Catherine had ever been contemplated by Mr Allen, the General had angrily stood in the way of his son's union, accusing Catherine of posing as an heiress to lure Henry in. He had verily sent her away in disgrace, cast his son off almost as immediately, and refused to give his consent to a marriage. Perhaps any other two people might have flaunted parental authority and run away to be married, but Henry and Catherine, having strong characters but even stronger moral principles, had been resolved to part and wait until such time as the General would soften, or to discover if providence was their friend.

It had taken a full year and much patience, devotion, and surreptitious letter writing on the part of the young people to endure the separation, but on the sudden marriage of Eleanor Tilney, Henry's older sister, to a young man of considerable fortune, the General was thrown into a temporary fit of good humour, and in due course they received his begrudging consent to marry. And so, after a year of delay, Henry and Catherine had married at Fullerton, and in order to cause Henry no delay in returning to his duties, they had spurned the new fashion of taking an extensive bridal tour and set off immediately after the wedding breakfast for Woodston.

Her husband being sincerely attached to his new wife, and allowing *almost* anything she exclaimed to be exactly so, now smiled his agreement down at her. 'After all the delays occasioned by my father, I can only agree wholeheartedly with you that there has been no material harm to our future felicity; and even if I cannot own to being the dreamer that you are, Cathy, I submit that if *you* consider we are come to Woodston to be happy forever after, then I shall consider it my husbandly duty to comply.' He smiled down at her and took her hand. 'And we will indeed be so, if you will only come inside rather than keep me standing outside my own house in the cold!'

Catherine had the grace to blush a little and laugh at herself. 'Sorry, my love. Shall we go inside then? Oh, here the servants are come out to greet us! I do hope they will still like me now that I am to give them their orders!'

Before Henry could protest that of course they all did like her already, very much indeed, the large door had given way to a half dozen servants, who had made haste to greet the new mistress of the parsonage. Two young males, and four females, two of whom were older than Catherine, and all of whom had varying degrees of welcome on their countenances, lined up obediently to greet the new-made Mrs and Mr Tilney.

Catherine's heart fluttered. But on the arm of her husband, she felt brave enough to advance with him and be made to hear their various civilities. When Henry stopped at the top of the line, in front of an older woman, he said, 'Of course, you have met Mrs Poulter, my housekeeper. She will be a great help to you, I am sure,' he added kindly.

Mrs Poulter was middle-aged woman of hostile aspect. Her long devotion to Henry's interests and to Woodston had caused her to be filled with suspicion at the prospect of anyone taking her place in the ranks of the Woodston empire. She had not warmed to Catherine, not even after two official visits to Woodston as Henry's betrothed.

But Catherine was gratified when the woman curtsied and said stiffly, 'Mrs Tilney. Welcome back to Woodston parsonage, Ma'am. May I offer my congratulations to you both?'

As Catherine contemplated in astonishment the novelty of being addressed as "Ma'am", Henry smiled. 'You may and we thank you, Mrs Poulter.'

The woman's chilly eyes barely warmed as they alighted on Catherine. 'I hope you will be very happy here, Mrs Tilney. The fire is lit in the drawing room, if you would please to go straight in, or if you wish I can have you shown to your apartments.'

Catherine, much surprised to hear she would have her own apartments and wondering why she had not seen them before or knew such a thing existed at Woodston, exclaimed, 'Oh, how delightful Mrs Poulter! I did not expect to have apartments. Indeed, the house is large enough, I imagine, only I did not notice a suite of rooms upstairs before when I have come to visit...' she trailed off, as there was silence from the housekeeper.

Henry took her arm again. 'I think Mrs Poulter meant only a bedroom, Cathy, which we shall both share of course, plus a small dressing room for my own use which you have not seen, and a little sitting parlour adjoining it which I never use and I thought might delight you to sit in as it looks out over the orchard and woods.'

Catherine's face suffused with pink, both at her own *faux pas*, and in sudden modesty at Henry's mentioning of the bedroom they would share. 'Of course, how silly it was of me to think there was an entire suite of rooms, after I have seen over the whole house. It all sounds perfectly delightful, I am sure!'

She had not realised that Henry's own chamber had such a thing as a small dressing room and an adjoining sitting room, but then, she had only dared to peep inside Henry's bedroom once, the last time she had been invited to visit, with her sister Sarah for chaperone.

Then she remembered too, the few moments on that same visit, when she had been left alone downstairs to amuse herself. She had been enticed by her own curiosity to try a door, hidden in the dim hallway, which had a mysterious look about it. The door had not budged, being quite locked, and she had been forced to conclude her exploration with a guilty start when Mrs Poulter had come up suddenly behind her and sharply enquired if there 'was anything she could help the young miss with?' Catherine had at once dissembled and retreated hastily into the garden, but the incident had incited her interest in the mysterious door.

Perhaps this was the door to the rooms Henry had mentioned? But no, that door had been on the ground floor and Henry's rooms on the second floor. But she would soon make sense of the house, she was sure. Catherine now clasped Henry's arm more firmly and ventured, 'I *am* a little tired—perhaps I should go to our room, my love—I should not wish to trouble Mrs Poulter.' Mrs Poulter, noted Catherine, made a remarkable effort not to smirk. Her heart sank further.

'It is no trouble, Mrs Tilney, and beside that the master has immediate parish business to attend.' The older woman turned to Henry. 'Your curate Mr. Stevens is here, Sir, and awaits you in the study.'

Henry turned to Catherine. 'I am sorry, my darling. Can you forgive my absence just for a little while and Mrs Poulter will take you to our room and to a good fire. You look chilled. And not a little fatigued.' He dropped a kiss on her forehead. 'Rest and I will come to you very soon, I promise!'

Before Catherine had had time to give her assent or reject the proposal, Henry had turned on his heel and gone away, leaving Catherine to the mercy of the eyes of Mrs Poulter. She withered a little beneath them.

'If you'll follow me, Ma'am.'

Catherine was grateful to be left alone in Henry's great master bedroom a few minutes later, where a fire blazed cheerfully. She watched the disappearing back of Mrs Poulter with great relief. Goodness! She had only been "Mrs Tilney" for less than a day and already she was feeling as if she might have entered Woodston unprepared for the taxing of her every nerve! But she had Henry and she would soon find her place and feel less intimidated by the good Mrs Poulter, she thought. Putting off her bonnet, gloves and spencer, she threw them down haphazardly over a large cushiony chair which fronted the fireplace. It was not as if she had never entered the house before, she thought, and she was familiar enough with the rooms and their placements. It was not Northanger, with its maze of staircases, back passages and hidden doors! No, this was Woodston, cosy and cheerful and welcoming, and if Henry was beside her, she thought she might enjoy no greater felicity than to live in a simple style, in a home which could house no secrets, and harbour no misery such as Northanger had!

She went to the window, and gazed down momentarily upon the garden, but as quickly turned away and went to the door to see if her bags were being brought up. Ascertaining that no footsteps were heard as yet, she turned back to the room and this time, being unable to avoid the point any longer, forced herself to look at the huge, white-dressed bed which dominated the chamber. It was not as if she was a child, she thought, but even with that thought her colour rose and she found herself nervously contemplating the image in her mind of herself and Henry, sleeping there together, talking, and doing things she understood to require no conversation at all!

These thoughts brought a pink to her cheeks, and a quiver to her insides. Mama had told her all that she had seen fit regarding the producing of offspring, and if that good woman had left anything out, Catherine had been an avid student of romantic novels long enough to understand the details. She longed for Henry to take her in his arms, just as the novels described, there to find the mysterious bliss of which they spoke, but she could hardly help being just a little nervous, all the same!

Henry's room was as it had ever been on the last occasion of her chance viewing. It was pleasant, warm and cheerful, with large comfortable chairs before a fire, and two high chests full of drawers. An end wall gave way to lovely ornate cupboard roomy enough for more gowns than she had ever owned, and there were some modest, pretty landscapes hung on three of the four walls. Another table sported a large pitcher and basin, where Henry must carry out his ablutions of a morning. Her heart skipped strangely as she imagined her new husband, half dressed, stripped to the waist, soaping himself liberally, and she tried to imagine herself doing the same next to him. How did a married couple share the pitcher and basin? How would she cover herself, and what if she wished to bathe? At home she always bathed in a tub before her own fire!

Although her mama had given her the advice and admonitions which every young girl receives upon her marriage if they have mothers that care for them, the answers to these lesser mysteries had not been explained to her. Nor had these finer details, even with all her reading, been gleaned from any of the modest novels she had poured over all her life. But she had long ago given up the childish imaginings which such reading had aroused in her; she would never forget the lessons learned at Northanger last summer. Then she had been a child; now, she thought to herself, she was a woman, a wife, and more grown-up than she had ever felt in her life. Sharing a bed chamber, and all that this entailed, she welcomed, and if Mrs Poulter's slight unwelcoming attitude had unsettled her at all, she would by-and-by have Henry to cheer her up again! She went to sit upon the end of the bed to await her trunks and when Henry did finally find himself free to come upstairs to attend his new bride, it was to find her curled fast asleep at the end of the big bed, the lemon and rose sarcenet gown she had been married in that morning a foil for the glossy dark hair which was fetchingly spread out upon the crisp white counterpane.

Four weeks of marriage supplied Catherine with all the delights and comforts that she felt were necessary for perfect domestic felicity. Each day was spent in the company of her husband, whose doting smiles and singular attentions supplied her with all the proof she had ever wanted of his devotion to her happiness. One day he would surprise her with a picnic in the grounds, the next with a visit to a nearby pleasure spot, where he would explain to her what constituted a perfect landscape, or how a watermill was able to thresh wheat which made up the bread she was eating. She drank in his every word, an eager student, and just as eager for the improvement of her own understanding as he was for her entertainment. They rode together daily, Henry having purchased for her a lovely grey mare of just the right height and temperament to suit its rider.

Catherine had been in raptures. 'I shall call her Cleo, after Queen Cleopatra, you see, for she is just as pretty as I imagine Cleopatra to have been!' she exclaimed as she stroked the animal's velvety forehead.

Henry had laughed and given her no argument since she had been making an effort to read more widely, and it had been he himself who had given her *A History of Ancient Egypt,* at her wide-eyed insistence that she would 'indeed read every word; it was not as though she were still a young girl with no interest in serious, adult subjects!'

It had only been a year since she had professed a dislike of history and dismissed it as being a tedious duty to read, but since she had become engaged to Henry she had tuned over a new leaf and determined upon a course of self-improvement by reading more widely. Her parents had by no means been frugal with the education of their children; rather, Catherine had been a very poor student indeed, and had been hard pressed to study when all she had wanted was to frolic and run with her brothers or bury her head in a novel when she ought to have been reading her French grammar.

She had also determined to be at her piano again, having long since abandoned that barbaric instrument of torture for the pleasure of novels. And she wished very much to become competent in drawing and painting, to tackle history with a new zest, to improve her French and she hoped, study a little botany or philosophy, whichever was easier to understand, she thought. Armed with mental images of her own dedication and studiousness and anticipating the pleasant compliments her efforts were sure to evoke from Henry, she was vastly pleased with her scheme. She was full ready to embark upon it, too, for of all the things in the world she wished most for Henry to be proud of her as his wife.

In this regard she had Eleanor to emulate, for Henry's sister was all Catherine herself aspired to be: accomplished in many disciplines, generally clever, elegant and modest, while at the same time mature, and carrying herself with a quiet, self-assured confidence.

Catherine had therefore made a beginning by begging Henry to choose for her a list of books by which she would improve her knowledge, and she had even purchased for herself a painting easel and some brushes and paints, and a new grammar in French which, with its little amusing drawings of objects, — '*un pomme, un cheval* '— did not look too grim and serious.

A month's advancement had also taught Catherine more about married life than she had ever read about in novels. She had been given entry through that doorway into which only married ladies are invited to pass. She had come to accept the non-verbal proofs of Henry's devotion; they had shared a bed, she had bathed in a long tub before the fire, in full view of his appreciative glances, and subjected herself to his ministrations when he insisted on washing her hair. He had kissed her and taken his delight in her, until she, laughing and crying at the same time, had begged for a little rest. She had barely blushed after the first night, so comfortable and happy she was in the warmth of Henry's affections, and when her clear blue eyes opened to meet his own hazel ones in the mornings, she had only smiles and delight in finding herself still living a dream from which she never wished to awaken.

The only shadow which occasionally disturbed this scene of domestic contentment was her nervousness around Mrs Poulter, and her inexperience as mistress of her own establishment. Mrs Poulter had been patient with the new Mrs Tilney, explaining every aspect of the household's running in more detail than Catherine could hope to take in and the older woman made much show about deferring to Catherine's judgement and taste when the day's menu or the question of how many flower arrangements were to adorn the parlour was to tax Catherine's sad housekeeping skills. Even so, Catherine could not help the nervous little skip of her heartbeat when she rounded a corner and found the woman standing silhouetted in one of the windows as if she had been standing there, as still as a statue, for some time, as if waiting on purpose to frighten her, or when the woman came up suddenly behind Catherine without a sound and made her start.

The housekeeper was polite, always, and yet there was still something of disapproval in her light grey eyes, and although Catherine tried to converse, she gave up after few stammered sentences. She began the habit of deferring to Mrs Poulter the decisions for which she herself had been solicited to give.

'I don't know what it is,' she had explained to Henry one evening as they sat up together in the large white bed, 'I cannot but feel so—so inadequate around her. I feel that she thinks I must be a very silly young bride who knows nothing at all about keeping a house! And it is true!' she added sadly.

Henry had kissed her lingeringly then lifted a curl of stray hair away from Catherine's forehead.

'My darling Kitty, as a clergyman it is my duty to live modestly, and it is true that I cannot be seen to have a greater number of servants than any other family in the village, but we are not as hard up as to make it necessary for my wife to undertake those tasks which perhaps your own mother needed to do herself. You need not try to take on everything at once, you know.'

'True, but I should like to know as much as possible about the running of the house so as not to appear ridiculous! Mrs Poulter thinks me a child, I am sure!'

Henry consoled her with a kiss. 'Then allow Mrs Poulter to show you how everything is done and learn from her. It takes courage and patience to learn something new, especially if it is something which does not come naturally.'

'Cannot *you* show me?'

Henry smiled kindly. 'I cannot be here all the time, Cathy. I have naturally taken a small leave from some of my duties to ensure you are settled in at Woodston. Next month, however, I shall have to be more and more from home to attend to parish matters. Mrs P will have to be your guide in these things. She is long used to running the house for me, and now she must give way to your authority; I daresay it must not be easy for one who is so used to running everything. Perhaps she is taking a little longer to adapt, but she has been very kind to you, and I am sure you will come to rely upon her advice in every domestic matter. You need not be shy of her, you know, she is as harmless a creature as your own dear mama!'

Catherine made a little moue. 'I know you are right, for you are always right, only I do want her to like me. Oh, my heavens! Henry!'

Henry had already begun to silence her with his lips and for a while the topic was abandoned in favour of pleasanter matters.

Catherine, for all her faults, was humble enough to acknowledge them, and in seeking her own self-improvement she truly felt that she would be forming herself into a better wife for Henry. She observed the servants as much as she could, and asked many questions, until Mrs Poulter chanced to find her in conversation with Jane one morning and chastised the poor girl for indolence and shirking her work. After this, Catherine was careful not to prevent the servants from carrying out their work and only observed and tried to glean some idea of the workings of the house from a distance.

She did not neglect her mind, and dutifully picked up *A History of Ancient Egypt*, or *Kings and Queens of England*, almost every day, reading at least a few pages until she could not absorb any more. Then she would take her paints and pencils outside and try to make sketches of the house and grounds. Painting and drawing she found less tedious than reading history, so she had more success with her art than she did with recalling which queen was beheaded in which year and which king responsible. She recalled Henry's tutoring of her a year ago, when they had been at Beecham Cliff in Bath, when they had discussed what made a scene picturesque. Now she laboured to add in the right amount of foreground and background, and to ensure her focal point was clear, although she was seldom sure she had gotten it right.

Henry, noting her efforts and being very much flattered by this desire to please, promised her a tutor. 'If you really mean to become more accomplished at drawing, then I shall get you Longstaff, Eleanor's old master; he is living only two miles from here, and I am sure he would come once a week to look over what you have done. But Catherine, you know you don't need to be able to draw and paint, or speak French to make me happy? My parishioners hardly expect you to hold a conversation in French with them! If you are so good as to sometimes deliver them some game from the estate or butter from our dairy, I think you will be as successful a clergyman's wife as any other!'

'I know,' she replied plaintively, 'but I so want to make up for my laziness as a girl, to be a good wife — one of whom you can be proud! I may not,' she added seriously, 'be very good at housekeeping, but I can at least be as accomplished as Eleanor — it would be shocking thing indeed if your parishioners were to discover I cannot even pick up a needle and darn your socks, or play something simple on the pianoforte, or paint a scene tolerably well! They would think me a great oaf, indeed!'

Henry laughed. 'Dearest creature, I hardly think being able to play one of Mozart's sonatas on the piano will further my career as a sermonizer, but by all means shape yourself into as accomplished a young lady as you like — I am quite excessively love with you already, and your not speaking French or understanding the difference between the sublime and the picturesque will not make me love you any the less, you know!'

Nevertheless, at Catherine's insistence the painting master was summoned in due course, and Catherine spent a not unpleasant two or three hours each week improving her painting skills under the watchful eye of Mr Longstaff, with the hopes that, in time, she might manage one or two little watercolours to give Henry.

Read the rest of
Woodston

Get it at

https://www.amazon.com/dp/B09JL89P4T/

Go to
www.katewestwood.net
and sign up to Kate's newsletter for release notices and more!

Other Books by Kate Westwood

A Scandal at Delford
Beauty and the Beast of Thornleigh
A Bath Affair
The Value of an Anne Elliot
Woodston